RESTLESS GRAVES

An Irish Family History Exhumed

S J MONEY

authorHOUSE

AuthorHouse™
1663 Liberty Drive
Bloomington, IN 47403
www.authorhouse.com
Phone: 833-262-8899

Published by AuthorHouse 01/19/2024

ISBN: 979-8-8230-1598-1 (sc)
ISBN: 979-8-8230-1599-8 (e)

Library of Congress Control Number: 2024900823

Print information available on the last page.

CONTENTS

PROLOGUE

A mixture of hair balm and sweat seeped from under the hat band of the fedora that hung sloppily over his bloodshot eyes. The motion of the car rocked him nauseously as he fought the effects of his drunken binge. Sweat puddled around his thick neck, soaking his shirt. The city seemed unusually warm under the weight of heavy clothing worn to camouflage his identity and the deadly weapon he cradled. Every puking episode drained the concentration of his vengeful bottle of confidence. Each bump in the road caused the Thompson, uncomfortably wedged under his arm, to land with a jolting crack on his knee. Head and knee throbbed; it had to be done before he sobered up and lost courage.

The dark Chevrolet shined in the orange glow of the streetlamp, surrounded by the buzz of the neighborhood.

An unexplained knot in Michael's throat begged for attention, and his stomach swirled as the young family settled in the back seat. Uneasiness was shoved aside as his legs strained the fabric of his suit pants. His chest heaved as he took a deep breath and squeezed his tall frame into the driver's seat. Black curly hair fell onto his forehead as he leaned in. Commotion from the back seat drew his attention.

Conrad yelped, "Noinin, your mamma told you to use the pot."

The gray wool-upholstered seat glistened darkly under the glow of the orange street light that encircled the car. Noinin's tears flowed uncontrollably. Her angelic cheeks flushed red with embarrassment. Noinin had wet herself.

Shrinking back from the deluge, lips pressed tight with annoyance, Conrad passed the wet toddler to her ma.

Eveleen's violet-beaded dress and headpiece clattered as she received her soaked child. A strand of red hair peeked from beneath the beads that covered her head. Her green eyes flickered with annoyance, but she wasn't angry. She understood the child's excitement and impatience.

Noinin's starched mint green party dress, and its layers of stiff white ruffles, crunched, and her mop of red curls bounced in rhythm.

The beads on Eveleen's violet headpiece and those that covered her matching dress continued to clatter like wind chimes in a strong breeze. She leaned over to place the child on the floorboard between herself and Conrad.

Noinin's crying swelled; loud gasps escaped between the swells. Her green eyes were magnified by her tears, she whispered, "Da, I love you."

"I love you too, *mo stór*" (my treasure). His tightened lips relaxed into a smile. This child and Eveleen were his life. It was impossible to be angry with this treasure. Tonight was the night they would celebrate a new beginning, an exciting new chapter of their lives.

The commotion in the back seat was interrupted by explosions from repetitive bursts of brutal gunfire. The impact of a red-hot round in Michael's shoulder spun him, slamming him fiercely into the steering wheel of the bullet-torn Chevrolet. A stifled groan hissed through his clenched teeth. His right hand moved instinctively under his bloodied overcoat to the revolver tucked into his dinner jacket, but it was too late.

The assassins escaped the bloody chaos they had created.

The car door was jammed tightly by the barrage. He banged his shoulder into it. A sudden razor slice of pain shot down his side as it lurched open. He untangled himself from his overcoat, tossed it on the hood of the car, and surveyed the bloody carnage. Conrad and Eveleen lay splayed over the back seat. Their bullet-mangled bodies were drenched in blood. Noinin was motionless on the floorboard, her limp body entangled with her mother's lifeless legs.

CHAPTER 1

In harmony, the old chair creaked as Nora's elbow cracked when it reached for the coffee mug on the table. The old fingers were deliberately bent before they slowly reached out to the mug. Dark clouds blanketed the room in a gray dreariness. A corner lamp shone in a small blue circular glow.

"We must stay active, both body and mind, or we become rigid and weak," the doctor had said.

"*We*, my ass." She snarled into the half-full coffee mug. Dr. Moore was no older than thirty-five, nearly half Nora's age.

Over the years, night courses, an earned degree, and raising a family had kept her mind engaged. Every day had become a constant struggle. Heavy fog rolled in, clouded memories, choked thoughts, and snatched names. Memories were melted, burnt film clips projected onto a darkened screen, and a word was trapped on the tip of her tongue, never spoken, dissolved before it was captured. The confident, self-assured, fiery redhead with the deep green eyes had evaporated over the past few years. Aging was an unforgiving thief, and constant second-guessing tore at Nora.

The front door opened. A familiar voice bounced off the ceramic tiles and echoed off the walls. Green eyes blinked to attention, chair creaked, and the room glowed yellow. The fog lifted. The voice was light. A bright light switched on.

Corazon was a welcomed connection to reality with a similar past. A Filipina in her forties, she was five feet tall and slender, with clear onyx-black eyes and flawless golden-brown skin. Thick, silken shoulder-length black hair swayed with each body movement.

Corazon's father had been part of the Philippine Commonwealth Army during World War II; he was called into active service for the United States Army during the Japanese invasion of the Pacific Islands. Subsequently, he was transferred to an Army post stateside. Corazon was born on one of those US army bases.

Nora and her late husband, Samuel, lived at a desert military outpost for several years after the war.

Samuel's mammoth personality and contagious laugh were magnetic; his gray eyes blazed with excitement when he spoke, drawing the listener in. Superior mechanical skills brought him to the desert to repair and make combat vehicles ready for action. His first passion was the law, which was placed on hold during his enlistment. His search for adventure controlled the first few years of the couple's marriage. He was used to army life and the base environment. Acceptance of a job at what appeared to be the end of the world seemed natural to him. Her husband was home—whole, safe, and sound—after the long, bitter war. Her absolute love drove the young woman to follow him to the end of the world.

The desert outpost was on a dusty two-lane road, thirty

miles from what was considered town. Town didn't have housing available for the influx of civilian personnel who were employed at the newly opened desert camp. The military was ill prepared for the wives and families that accompanied the employees who would maintain the base for the army.

The farther the car plunged into the desolate desert, the tighter Nora's jaw clenched, lips pressed white and ready to snap. Hot wind slapped her face through the open window. With each slap, her sand-coated red curls whipped at her cheeks. Each breath choked sand into her throat and lungs. The petite young woman from Manhattan had landed in a barren, Mars-like, desert outpost. Love overshadowed doubt.

Dust that caked the young woman's face, like thick facial powder, cracked and then rose in a slight puff from under her green eyes as she attempted to smile when the car slid to a stop in front of their new home. Army housing was constructed of OD green wooden frames and unfinished drywall. The frame sat on a horizontal wooden slat foundation about two feet off the ground. Heat was provided by a large freestanding gas furnace in the corner of the kitchen area. An open oven door often accompanied the corner furnace to combat the chill of the hastily built housing. Summer saw the constant hum of a swamp cooler as it desperately tried to banish the unyielding desert heat. Amid the summer hum of the cooler, the city transplant became captivated by Samuel's law books. With her red curls pulled tight in a pony tail Nora would sit with a large ice-filled glass of sun tea on the floor under the flow of cool air from the swamp cooler, gobbling up every word. The ravenous reader was unable to get her fill. His passion was soon hers.

Filipino neighbors dried fish, caught during group fishing trips to the Gulf of Mexico, in the searing summer heat on the black asphalt roofs. This was followed by huge parties in the small, shared grass courtyards. All the neighbors were invited to join in the celebration. The army comradery preordained everyone as family without consideration of military status or rank—with the exception of officers. Officers lived in a different sector of the base, away from the enlisted and civilian families. The celebrations consisted of a trail of tables that zigzagged through small dark houses with only one way in and one way out. Filipino food covered the tables that trailed onto the sidewalk area. The aroma filled the houses and danced slowly from each table packed with fish, rice, and other items. The couple's stay at the desert base was short, but the memories of it and the friends made attracted Nora to Corazon when they met at the community center potluck.

"Hello, good morning. What's on the calendar for today?" Corazon's voice sang down the hallway. "How about breakfast on the patio?"

Her shoulders straightened, and the earlier fog dissipated with the conversation. Their heels clapped on the polished tile, like maracas, as the two headed to the kitchen.

"Breakfast on the patio sounds terrific," Nora announced loudly, which flung the fog to the corners of her mind. Clarity had become increasingly difficult. Fending off the fog was exhausting. Nerves tingled, eye squinted, and her head ached at the strain of word searches. She was still aware enough to know her time was limited. The headache was reduced to a dull throb on the patio. The warm, yellow glow of the morning sun eased muscle aches and lifted old spirits. Conversation constrained the fog. Recent events were swallowed by gray fog, like headlights that faded, slowly surrounded, and then engulfed. At times, the distant past was more vivid than the present.

A pen and pad held in a front pocket recorded any fragment that might be otherwise lost. Accompanied by the foggy sludge was arthritis, which painfully attacked her writing ability. The painful swelling and stiffening of her joints was an added insult.

What a savage fate to have one's very soul drained, as through a sieve. All that you loved, learned, the whole of what you were, replaced by a swell of thick, blinding gray fog and sludge.

Silence shrouded the patio after the two ate. The thick fog swept back in. Corazon finished the dishes, unaware of the storm that had overtaken her friend.

She was abandoned in a desolate abyss, slothfully sucked under the gulping sand and dust, it overtook her mind and body. Desert sand encased her age-ravaged frame, a last gasp for air. There was no escape, no rescue for a soul lost.

"Hello, I have the mail," the young voice sang out as she entered the patio. She slowly realized her mother was unaware of her presence. "Momma?" Elizabeth whispered. Tears blurred the young woman's vision, and salty beads stung her cheeks. A knot lodged itself at the back of her throat as she gently reached for her mother's back, rubbing it slowly and yearning for acknowledgment.

"Elizabeth," the elder choked. Dust cleared from her throat and mind.

Her daughter was well aware of the monster attempting to consume her. She held the frail frame tightly until the trembling subsided. The child was the comforter of the parent.

"Not a victim." Dry words forced the imaginary dust from her throat. She refused to give up all that she was without a fight.

The day's mail was crushed against the now calm frame. The two women clutched each other in the warmth of the sun that encircled the patio.

Mail and documents had become more urgent as the fog became more frequent.

Among the normal bills and junk mail was an envelope from a New York law firm. The firm apparently represented the estate of Maureen Donahue, a deceased elderly relative. The enclosed letter listed everyone in order of their relationship to the dead woman. The immediate family was listed by columns with their children underneath each member. Nora was listed under different parents than her siblings. Eveleen Quinn and her husband, Conrad, their only child. According to family gossip, the couple met a violent death during Prohibition. Nora's siblings were listed as her cousins by marriage.

Tears welled up. Nora's hands shook. Her lungs tightened as she tried to absorb all she had read. Old eyes read the letter several times before she broke the silence that engulfed the room, crushing the paperwork. "This horrendous disease stole who I became, and with the stroke of a pen, I am to lose who I was. This is wrong. My entire family history obliterated. What am I left with? I have no idea who these people even are."

Tears gushed. There was no consoling her as she dropped to the floor in a pile. The papers were wadded and tossed. "Elizabeth, I can't," she choked out between surges of tears.

"I can't do this. I don't have the strength to fight this battle. Instantly, I have no idea who I am or who my family was. Why now? Why wait until I'm near death to stir this pot? There is no one left to answer the questions. This is wrong." Tears drowned out any remaining words.

Elizabeth hung onto her mother, pulled her close as if she was falling from an invisible cliff. "We'll deal with this together, Momma. You are not alone. We know exactly who your family is. We are your family. Together, we'll get this sorted out. That's a promise."

A clerical error, her older brother insisted during a phone call from his assisted-living facility. Although older and frailer than his sister, his determination had not been weakened. The declaration in the letter meant that Nora was entitled to a larger share of an inheritance than her siblings; more importantly, her siblings appeared as cousins by marriage rather than blood. The family she loved and grieved over with each passing was not hers to love or lose. Ida Doyle was Nora's ma—till her death—and the only mother she ever knew. Thomas Doyle was her one and only pa. According to the documents, Thomas's sister-in-law was the younger sister of Martin Donahue, Maureen's husband. The letter contended Maureen was the only sister of Nora's birth mother, Eveleen Quinn.

CHAPTER 2

During a lengthy phone call with the attorney handling the matter, he assured Elizabeth every avenue of research had been exhausted. A search by Maureen Donahue's name was done to find heirs. A backwards search using Nora's name resulted in the same conclusion. None of the surviving older family members chose to argue Nora's status in the family, so the attorney completed the documents in the manner that was presented to the family. When her brothers questioned her birth certificate, the attorney stated, almost gleefully, "There are two birth certificates on file with similar names and matching birthdates. The one that matches my research of the deceased's family history is considered the certificate of record and identifies Nora Eveleen as the child of Conrad and Eveleen Quinn."

The brothers' only concern was that their sister remain their baby sister. Their lives were at an end. The inheritance was of no consequence. They insisted, "We were all told that child died with her parents. How could all these years pass—and no one was ever alerted to this?"

The inheritance meant nothing compared to the heart-wrenching pain of the document that destroyed everything they had all understood about their family.

"The legal document is what I have presented. That is what I was hired to do. Your family can handle the results in whatever manner you choose."

The phone calls between the exasperated family members, attempting to sort out what they believed was a clerical error, and the attorney who concluded he had done what he was hired to do dragged on for a couple of weeks. He had completed the task set before him and wanted to collect his fee.

Since none of the children had been born in hospitals, there were no medical records. Nora's parents had temporarily left the older children—brothers Bradley and Robert, and her sister Hannah—in Ireland with family and immigrated to New York with their youngest child, a toddler, Keira. Nora was born after they arrived. The Doyle's planned to send for their older children once they were settled in the city. The other children arrived when Nora was about three.

Although Bradley and Robert were still in Ireland when Eveleen and Conrad were murdered, over the years, the brothers became familiar with the neighborhood gossip about the young family that was brutally murdered in front of their home. Bradley, the eldest, would not even discuss it. There was no explanation why there were two certificates of birth, citing different parents. He contended that the birth certificates were of two separate births and insisted the dead toddler was actually the heir, not his sister. He refused to lose his sister in such a coldhearted manner. A clerical error on the attorney's part? Elizabeth wondered, if the attorney was correct, what was so important that this knowledge went to the grave with an entire generation of a family?

This mystery was a heavy blanket that weighed down

their family. Nora found new strength in her anger and curiosity. The fog had a new opponent: anger. Nora sank deep into silence, but not with the horrid fog. She forced herself to remember her childhood. It was as though she was forcing cold catsup from a bottle, spreading the goo thinly on a plate, and smearing through it for memories that could produce a clue about how she had landed in a stranger's family. Memories coaxed from a clouded brain became notes, to be sorted later, which covered her once neat desk. It was exhausting. Time was running out. The urgency increased daily, and every nerve pulsated. The task had to be done before the fog formed its final storm.

The notes were jotted down as they slowly churned through her mind. How was she to identify a true memory from a dream? *Write it down. Figure it out later. The papers hold the answer.*

A toddler in a beautiful frilly dress, a stunning red-haired woman in a lavender evening dress, a comforting scent, a fresh flower aroma, a car, a loud popping noise, a rainbow. Sadness, overwhelming sadness. The unforgiving fog made it painfully difficult to sort a memory from an idea that floated through her mind.

Keep writing. Papers hold the answer. Papers began this chaos; papers will solve it.

She concentrated on her memories. Had her brothers known?

"What would it accomplish for your brothers to lie to you? They are as upset as you are. Your birth certificate lists the parents you know. That is your family." Elizabeth tried to console her mother as the desert wind sent the garden wind chimes behind them twisting in song.

"Sweet child, who ordered the birth certificates from our parish when Keira and I were sent to Tarrytown? Any name could have been noted as my parents."

There's no time to waste. Why did it take a woman's last wishes to finally bring this to light?

"I remember Maureen, a warm kind memory. She took Hannah in after our mother's death. Memories are smeared together, like a finger painting. Maureen visited Tarrytown with Hannah and my brothers. Keira and I spent time with her in the city."

As the last glow of sun fell behind the trees, the two sat in its remaining warm glow that reflected into the kitchen.

Elizabeth grasped at any idea to ease her mother's mind. "Maybe it was an error. It could be a mix-up. Maybe Hannah should have been listed instead of you. We will get this sorted out together, Momma. I promise you."

There was no time to dwell on why this happened. There was no time for self-pity. There was a new goal: find the truth. A road through the fog had to be cleared, and memories had to be uncovered before it was too late. The warmth of the setting desert sun gave the old frame and mind renewed strength.

CHAPTER 3

Perched on the window seat in Aunt Maureen's apartment, the anxious child waited to see the familiar car rumble down the street. Her starched party dress crunched, and her curly red hair bounced with each movement. The child was in constant motion.

"Nora, my little gem, be patient now. Your papa and momma will be here before long." Aunt Maureen squeezed the excess water from the stockings she washed in the sink. Maureen and her husband, Martin, spent many happy hours with their niece. The child kept the woman busy and feeling youthful. This child was a godsend after the tragic death of Eveleen's infant son.

The child pulled at her ruffled mint green dress, then at the ribbon that held the curly carrottop in place, then finally she stretched to lean through the curtains and gaze out the window. Constant motion.

Most of the street below was visible from the window. The neighborhood boys were clustered like moths under the streetlamp's orange glow. Lights from adjacent apartment buildings began their nightly dance. They blushed in a rhythmic pulse as the neighborhood transformed from day to night. Activity on the window seat intensified; feet kicked at the seat, ruffles pulled, and ribbons yanked. The ball of energy was a precious gift that brought immeasurable joy to the entire family. Her constant motion was like a hummingbird with a fiery glow that matched her red mop. The toddler's temperament echoed the constant fire of Eveleen.

Maureen smiled as she hung freshly washed stockings and moved to smooth ruffles and hair. Maureen relished living within Eveleen's fiery glow. There was always excitement and fireworks. An electricity pulsated in Eveleen's presence. Maureen lived quietly within her younger sister's pulse, observing the fireworks without any danger of being burned.

Maureen's dark hair hugged slight shoulders, and innocent, large brown fawn-like eyes looked for the good around her with quiet serenity. The siblings were opposite ends of the world: Eveleen a simmering volcano, and Maureen a quiet beach.

The neighborhood was alive, music echoed from the apartments above the street. Nora tapped on the window as the older boys played under the glow of the streetlamp. The child jumped to attention, palms slapped the glass, as the car stopped at the stoop. Her eyes shined with excitement as she balanced herself on the seat.

Michael exited the driver's door. His black eyes gave a quick look and a knowing smile in the direction of the window. Wide dimples traveled down his face, pushing their way deep into his cheeks, and his straight white teeth glowed as his smile widened. Calm, kind, and thoughtful, his smile warmed the child.

He paused slightly and looked from one end of the

street to the other. He slowly walked toward the car's back door, eyes still focused on the street. The sight of a man's tall, full frame and black hair exiting the back seat sent the child running to the apartment door and then back to the seat with a shriek.

Conrad wasn't as tall as Michael, but his slender build made him seem taller. Nora's excitement overflowed. Her feet tapped loudly on the window seat, and her eyes danced at the door and down to the street. Tonight, the entire family was celebrating. Nora didn't know or care what was being celebrated; she was just excited to be included. She loved going out with them; it rarely happened, which made tonight very special.

On those rare occasions, there were trips to the club with Momma to meet Papa. Dancing while the band rehearsed before an evening event was a given on those trips.

The child watched as Conrad's lean frame exited the car in a black suit, a crisp white shirt, and a black tie. White and black shoes polished to a glass shine glowed under the streetlamp. A large shiny rainbow flashed from the center of his chest. He tossed his overcoat onto the seat, almost skipped to the other side of the car, and reached through the open door to grasp a gloved hand.

Eveleen smiled lovingly, pulled herself close to Conrad, inhaled, and caught his breath in hers. Her eyes held his constant gaze. A beaded headpiece of violet and silver beads covered her curly red hair. Her bejeweled wig sparkled and clattered with the slightest movement. A silken, beaded violet and silver dress danced in rhythm with the headpiece, and her shoes matched the violet of the dress. The beads clapped happily as she pulled herself into Conrad's embrace.

Even in heels, the embrace left her snuggled tightly at the bottom of her husband's rib cage.

Whenever she spoke, intense green eyes dove deeply into the listener's soul. With a quiet, demure exterior, a ceramic doll with ivory skin, and curly red hair, she was beautiful, fragile, and always a lady. However, if she or any family member was injured, the culprit was set ablaze with a tongue that scorched like a hot poker.

Michael waited on the stoop while the couple climbed the six floors to Maureen's apartment to collect their child. A red-haired blur bounced from the window seat, and her feet barely touched the floor as she charged toward the door.

"Nora, go use the pot before we leave." The beads on her dress and headpiece danced as Eveleen guided the ruffles in the direction of the water closet in the hall. She continued excitedly, "Maureen, I'm sorry we took so long. We dropped by the club. Conrad wanted to be sure everything was in place while we are out this evening." This was a special celebration, although what they were celebrating remained a mystery.

Aunt Maureen gently nudged Nora toward the chamber pot in the corner. The chamber pot was much more convenient for the child than the hall. There was too much excitement to waste time on either.

"Don't have to go." Nora snorted and folded her arms on the fullness of her dress.

After one last unsuccessful push toward the pot, Eveleen gently tucked all the ruffles and lace into a spring coat. Music of dancing beads and rustling ruffles filled the hallway as the family made its final stop in the building.

An auburn-haired woman opened the door without a

knock. Tara, Michael's wife, chirped, "Give me a minute. Go ahead … go ahead on down." She gathered her lush, long hair and with a quick twist, it was secured in a clip. She kissed the top of the child's carrot curls and then disappeared to the back of the apartment.

Where Eveleen was fair and bubbly, Tara was dark and sultry. Tara's dark auburn hair and brown eyes contrasted with her friend's curly red hair and green eyes.

These two young lives had intersected at a vital turning point for Eveleen and her sister Maureen.

CHAPTER 4

After losing both parents, Eveleen and Maureen moved to the city. Their two older brothers remained behind to work the family farm. Their parents passed away within a year of each other. Both sisters agreed their father died of a broken heart. Without their parents, the farm was cold and bleak. Staying on the farm without them was unimaginable for Eveleen. She thought about her future for several weeks. She gathered up all her strength, and informed her brothers she was moving to the city. Both brothers balked loudly at the idea of her traveling to the city alone. Maureen jumped at a chance for adventure and volunteered to accompany her younger sibling.

Eveleen had craved adventure beyond the farm for as long as she could remember. As a young child, during summer evenings, she would lay on her back in the thick cool grass, inhaling the evening bouquet and listening as frogs croaked their love songs and crickets chirped in harmony. She contemplated the stars, wondering what wondrous places they shone upon. She dreamed of exploring exciting places and meeting mysterious people.

Mama taught both girls to read, write, and sew. Sewing came easy to Eveleen. Women in town clamored for the young woman's clothing. Chores around the farm occupied the long days; evenings were spent sewing dresses for women in town.

Maureen, although the older of the two, was in awe of her younger sibling. She embraced her zest for life and adventure. Their shared sewing skills meant little to the elder; a duty tasked to them by their mother became a direct thread to Eveleen's escape. Her younger sister's adventurous spirit was exhilarating. As long as they were together, no harm could ever come to them.

Eveleen always stood out, and her red curls and vibrant personality drew suitors. She was a wild rose in a barren field. Settling down on a farm was out of the question. There was so much life to live; the farm and small town had been her entire world and were not enough.

The brothers reluctantly agreed to the move since Maureen's mature presence would bring stability to the younger of the two.

Eveleen rationalized her own fears, thinking, *We'll be fine. If we can't make it in the city the farm will always be there.* Although the thought comforted her, it was swept away, only to be considered in a dire emergency. She had to take a shot at her dreams; failure wasn't an option. They agreed to live with family and work in a neighborhood shop with an aunt. Ashley was their mother's sister, and the brothers felt less apprehension with the arrangement.

The day the siblings boarded the train, Eveleen's emotions pulled her in all directions. Anxiety clung to both young women like wet wool coats. The sisters summoned their composure and said goodbye to their brothers and the only home they had ever known. Restlessness and excitement surged like an electric current that encircled the two. Eveleen's heart pounded in her chest. She was sure those seated around her could hear it, but she made a determined effort to concentrate on life in the city to calm her mind and body. Maureen took longer to settle. With muscles locked, her breathing became loud and shallow. With her eyes closed tight, she held her brothers' faces for a few more seconds. Her knuckles clenched the wooden armrest until they were white. As the train jerked forward, Maureen gave out a gasp. Eveleen pulled her cold, shaking hand into her lap with a pat of reassurance.

The train's wooden interior creaked and swayed in a side-to-side rhythm as it picked up speed. Farmland rolled past their railcar, and as it gave way to the city, the two young women held hands. Their bodies jerked as the train chugged toward their future.

Eveleen struggled with the emotions that whipped through her mind. She feared Maureen could see her face as it contorted with each thought. She took a deep breath, her heart pounded with anxiety, and her temples throbbed in unison. She closed her eyes and thought, *I control my body, my mind, and my future.* She took another deep breath, and the pounding in her chest slowed.

I control my body, my mind, and my future. The throbbing stopped, and she dozed off as the train rocked.

CHAPTER 5

Working at the tailor's shop was a dream come true for Eveleen. The fabrics were luxurious and plentiful, and she was making wonderful clothing that was fit for royalty. Their home life was drastically different. Ashley's husband took charge of both sisters' money. He claimed their brothers would expect as much. He was a hateful drunk. The two would hide out of his sight, huddled in a corner of the small apartment, shaking in fear until he passed out. He degraded his wife and the sisters and their family, calling them ungrateful whores. The abuse came to a head when he tossed all their belongings out the window and into the gutter after a daylong drunk. No explanation or apology was ever offered.

Eveleen racked her brain daily for a way to escape his vile grasp. Deep in thought, she admired an especially beautiful bolt of material. "You would look lovely in that color. Buy it. Mr. Riley would agree it's your color." An auburn-haired woman uttered.

"I can't pay for it." Eveleen never lifted her eyes from the material.

Auburn hair bounced as the woman swung her head and glared at Ashley. "Please, there is no reason you can't buy the entire damn bolt. Next to me, you are the best seamstress in this shop. I'm Tara."

"My uncle handles my affairs." Eveleen choked on the words as they clawed their way out of her throat.

Ashley's shame encircled her like heavy smoke, and she glanced around the shop to be sure no one overheard. Slowly and softly, her words pierced the smoke. "He would beat me if he heard me. His abuse is mine to bear. You don't deserve his hatred and rage. Your brothers' anger would have no bounds if they knew how my husband treated you. Escape while you can. If he tries to stop you, mention your brothers. I can handle him alone. He'll pop off to the wrong person someday ..."

"With your skills, after an extra dress or two, you'll be set. I'll square it with Mr. Riley. It's our secret." With a flip of her hair, Tara was gone.

Within a few months, the sisters had saved enough to finally be on their own in the city. However, the two farm girls still had a lot to learn about city life.

Tara's family had lived in the city her entire life. Her farmer friends' naivety was entertaining. As the horrible first few months faded, self-reliance was regained. The two young women built a lifelong friendship. Tara's dark eyes danced when she teased Eveleen.

Green eyes squinted and curly red hair snapped as Eveleen turned away from Tara's teasing. As the fiery redhead recovered her spark, Tara cautioned, "Eveleen, You aren't on the farm anymore. People in the city don't give a damn about you. Always be on guard."

Eveleen made quick decisions, trusted easily, and acted with no thought of consequences. Tara was centered, similar to Maureen, yet she had no qualms about rebuking her friend when they didn't agree. Tara appeared more reserved than Eveleen. She had the same desire for adventure, but she chose not to verbalize it. Her dark eyes analyzed words and actions before the speaker was aware of it. Friendship wasn't given quickly or taken for granted.

Maureen loved the city, the noise, the different languages, and watching people. Church was a wonderful place to watch people. That was where she met Martin. They were matched bookends, each quiet and caring. Martin was a few years older than Maureen, and his eyes were clear as blue glass, encircled by wire glasses and thick graying hair. After more than a year, with the consent of her brothers, a quiet wedding joined the two.

During the same year, Tara and Eveleen became inseparable. The two moved into an apartment together, not far from Maureen and Martin.

The apartment was small and barren, but it was theirs. It wasn't much different than the apartment Eveleen had shared with Maureen, but it seemed more like her own. For the first time in her life, she wasn't living with family. To make it homier, the young women made curtains and tablecloths from remnants brought home from the shop. Walls were dark wood with faded flowered wallpaper. What claimed to be a kitchen was merely an icebox, a small stove, and a sink, which also served as a laundry. A claw-footed tub doubled as a table when covered with a piece of wood and a tablecloth. One window, above the sink, overlooked the street.

From the fourth-floor apartment, they saw and smelled all that went on in the neighborhood. The water closet was a short walk down the hallway. The two young women shared an overstuffed bed that sat, like a chubby, hibernating bear, in one corner of the apartment. Smells from every other apartment wafted through the walls and window. During the warm summer months, smells mixed and became impossible to identify. At times, the mixture grew nauseating.

CHAPTER 6

Trips to the tailor shop were never a chore. A short distance from the apartment, it was a quick walk. The small shop was bright and pleasant, and the morning sun shone through the windows with a warm glow onto the cutting tables and sewing machines. Eveleen's red curls eagerly bounced from cutting table to sewing machine as each product progressed.

A great deal of the young women's time was spent at Riley's tailor shop. One afternoon, Mr. Riley was in a tizzy. Some custom suits had to be delivered to Dan Malone, but his wife was very ill and needed to be tended to. He paced the shop and pulled at his curly gray hair. *How to get them delivered on time?*

Eveleen stopped him, placed her hands on his shoulders, and looked right into his stressed eyes. "Where are these suits? Give me the address. Do they need to be signed for or paid for?"

Riley breathed heavily, and small beads of sweat bubbled on his forehead. He took a deep breath, pointed to the suits, and handed her a card with the address.

She patted his shoulders. "Go home. Take care of your wife. The suits will get delivered."

Tara volunteered to accompany her, and the two of

them headed to Dan Malone's club. It was a quick trolley ride. The two gossiped about the club, which sent chills up Eveleen's spine. It was a chance to see inside a speakeasy, to see the inside of Dan Malone's club. Excitement vibrated up and down her spine as they approached the club.

The suit under her arm quivered along with the excitement as the redhead sprinted to the door. Tara lagged behind, clutching the other suit. Shadowy figures stood in the darkness just inside the door. They came into view as Eveleen approached. Tall young men, maybe brothers, with dark hair and dark eyes.

Eveleen's red hair recoiled as she came to a dead stop, straightened her back as her heart quickened. With a pleading glance, she sought the support of her friend, who had stopped at the entry way. With a tongue that was inexplicably tied, a deep breath was taken and exhaled in an attempt to untangle an uncooperative tongue. "We have a delivery for Mr. Malone from Thomas Riley." Eveleen tried to muster a genuine businesslike voice.

Tara walked slowly toward the bold young woman. Her eyes adjusted to the darkness, as she took in the room with a deep lingering breath. The blue and silver velvet wallpaper danced with reflected jewels as a huge crystal chandelier swayed and chattered with the breeze from the opening of the door. The combined smell of polished wood and smoke tickled the young woman's nostrils. One entire wall of the room was rich mahogany shelving, and glassware of all styles adorned the thick shelves.

One of the young men quipped, as he looked in the direction of his friend, "I may need to change tailors.

Does your Mr. Riley always send two lovelies to make his deliveries? What do you think, Conrad?"

"We are doing him a favor; it's not our job." Tara prayed her voice wouldn't crack.

"Michael, ease up on the ladies. I say this is the best thing to happen here in a long while. Excuse my friend. He is just joking. I am Conrad, and this is my *cara maith* (good friend) Michael. May we be so bold as to ask your names?"

Conrad was slightly shorter than Michael, with the face of a film star: square jaw, high cheekbones, onyx-black eyes, and hair so black it looked blue. His curly mop was slicked straight back. A sliver of a mustache rested below his nose. He was the silent thinker of the two.

Michael's frame was stockier than Conrad's. He had the look of a young pugilist. Large arms swelled beneath the sleeves of his jacket, and his knuckles bulged, like mountains and valleys in the back of his hands. His volatile temper could take a 180-degree mood spin in an instant. It wasn't always easy to figure out his mood as he was usually quiet until the explosions began. Michael and Conrad's personalities matched their appearances. Conrad was the planner, and Michael was the doer.

"I am Eveleen, and Tara is my associate. Our business is with Mr. Malone if you don't mind."

Tara nudged Eveleen and threw her a swift scowl after the "associate" remark.

Conrad said, "Of course, Miss Eveleen. Right away. If we were to come to the tailor, Thomas Riley's, would we be able to take you for tea?"

"It would depend on when you arrived and where you planned on having tea," Tara said before Eveleen could reply.

With Dan Malone's suits safely delivered, the young women made their way back to Thomas Riley's shop. On the trolley, the two laughed at the awkward meeting and decided Tara was suited for Michael and Eveleen was suited for Conrad. The two young seamstresses never expected to see the dapper men again.

A week later, both women had their heads buried in bolts of material when the bell on the shop door chimed. Voices were muffled at first, and then Mr. Riley loudly introduced himself. After a short conversation about his business, he called out to the women.

Eveleen pulled the lint from her hair and tried to control the exhilaration she felt as she saw Conrad and Michael in the center of the shop.

Conrad smiled. "We've come for tea."

Eveleen continued to pull at the lint in her hair. Excitement shot up and down her body like ice tossed down her blouse, as she unsuccessfully tried to form a coherent sentence. "Lint from cutting." That was all that her tongue could form.

"Please, you look perfect."

Michael looked through the bolts of material until he saw Tara. The city girl had more composure than her redheaded friend. She slowly walked toward Michael and tried her best to show no interest.

"Good day. Are you up for tea?" Dimples dug a deep hole in his cheeks as he bowed.

How could such a gallant invitation be refused?

Thomas Riley accepted two orders for suits and shuffled his trusted workers off for tea.

CHAPTER 7

Many afternoons were spent getting to know one another. Eveleen was attracted to Conrad from the moment he first spoke. Never had a man sent such anticipation through her body, and she thought of adventures together: Conrad and herself skating through life, two explorers who together would discover new places and people. There were long walks in the park, dinner spent in quiet restaurants, dancing at Dan Malone's club, and even Mass on Sundays. Conrad was quiet and thought things through before making decisions. Eveleen, on the other hand, had always jumped into life. She no longer jumped as quickly as she did as a small-town farm girl. She listened to his side and then presented her thoughts. A mutual decision was usually the final result.

Michael and Tara complemented each other. It could probably be better described as Tara, much like Conrad, had a calming effect on Michael. Conrad was always the peacekeeper, the thinker, and the planner. His presence kept Michael in check most of the time. If he couldn't tame Michael, he stood beside him, shoulder to shoulder, during whatever punch-up he managed to get into. Tara understood his fire, and it was one of the many things she loved about him. The four were constant companions.

Once the couples decided it was time to get married, it was celebrated within a few weeks of one another in small ceremonies at the church where Maureen and Martin were married. Eveleen's brothers made it to both sister's weddings. They were more pleased with Maureen's choice of husband than Eveleen's. They thought Conrad was a very good man, but his grand ideas and plans were too much for the farmers to understand.

Tara became pregnant first. It was a difficult time for Tara and Michael; she was very ill and couldn't do much. Eveleen was with her daily. Although Eveleen wanted to start a family, she was thankful that she was able to take care of her friend. William's delivery took a great deal out of Tara. It took countless hours for her son to enter the world. The young woman never totally recovered, and as a result, the couple had no more children. William never lacked for attention; between his mother, Eveleen, and Maureen, there was always someone fussing over him. Maureen and Martin never had any children. Maureen didn't discuss it, other than saying it just wasn't meant to be. Eveleen prayed to start a family and give Conrad a son.

Three years after William's birth, Eveleen finally became pregnant. She and Conrad were beyond thrilled. Her pregnancy was much easier than Tara's, and the delivery of her son was, compared to Tara's ordeal, normal. Conrad and Eveleen delighted in their new son, Conrad Jr. (Connie). Their son was small in comparison to William. Eveleen tried not to notice that he seemed less active than William.

When Connie was about five months old, he came down with a fever along with a cough. The doctor's only advice was to get the fever down and the cough would go away. The family did everything they could to get the fever down, and they took turns comforting the small child.

At one point, Connie was too weak to even cough. His body would wretch, but nothing came out. Breathing became short gasps, until he slowly drifted into death. Conrad and Eveleen were devastated by the loss of their young son. The young mother's heart was ripped from her chest with the death of her infant. Conrad tried to mask his pain and buried himself in his work. The couple found comfort in one another and tried to fill the void the child's death left. Eveleen went to Dan's club to visit with Conrad during the afternoon, or they went out in the evening. Although Eveleen's heart ached, she enjoyed the distraction, the excitement of the club, and all the people she saw. She loved seeing all the different evening clothes. She continued sewing to stay busy during the day. Tara and Michael came out at least one evening a week. Maureen was thrilled to have William to herself for an evening. The four of them became accustomed to this family dynamic. They truly were one family.

After working years for Dan Malone, Michael and Conrad bought their own club. Dan helped the two men find a place and complete the deal. Dan knew a lot of people in the city. He knew who to trust and who to avoid. Conrad and Michael didn't want to involve bankers. Dan agreed bankers were bottom-feeders. Dan Malone treated Michael and Conrad like his children. He took pride in their hard work and honesty.

They finally had their own club, *Cara Dílis* (Faithful Friend). Conrad and Eveleen concentrated on each other, the new club, and Eveleen's sewing business.

Eveleen slowed down and became ill. Afternoons were spent sleeping rather than going to the club. Tara and Maureen had the same idea, but they never mentioned it to Eveleen. They suspected she was pregnant. Tara took Eveleen to the doctor.

Eveleen was in complete shock when she was told she was pregnant. She didn't want to get her hopes up, and she didn't want to tell Conrad. She didn't want him hurt again. Deep down, the thought lingered. *Had she done something wrong to cause Connie's death?* Her joy got the best of her, and she told Conrad the minute he got home.

The two cautiously awaited the arrival of their second child. They were overjoyed to welcome their healthy baby girl, Nora Eveleen.

CHAPTER 8

Corazon's hair was wet with sweat as she returned the last box to the garage. The morning was spent plowing through old papers and looking for anything that was connected to Nora's past.

Nora's old hands and legs groaned with pain when she headed down the hallway. A tall jewelry box sat on the corner of a long dresser. Her stiff, cracking fingers reached into the box, as her mind flashed at the familiar items. A diamond engagement ring, a huge square solitaire, was forced over her deformed knuckle with a dull groan and then spun around her thin, twisted ring finger. A simple Black Hills gold wedding band, with a split, never repaired, sat in a red velvet box in the center of the jewelry.

Exasperation had grown as the process stretched from breakfast to lunch. Nora clenched her eyes tight and slammed her aching, swollen fists on the dresser. Her life was a fog-filled sandstorm; trying to remember a past that didn't belong to her was intolerable. After a moment, her eyes opened. She shot like a bullet to the antique vanity; its tall, oblong mirror had been the only constant that was evident.

When did it enter her life? How?

Unanswered questions skulked through aging sludge. She never bothered to look at it. Each of the cherrywood drawers was intricately carved. The drawer pulls were carved wooden roses. Six small drawers, three on either side of the mirror, bookended a wider drawer that sat under the mirror. It was pristine.

Tears welled up in the timeworn eyes with the acknowledgment that she wasn't able to pull the information from the sludge. She stood in front of it straining for a scrap of familiarity, but nothing came to the surface. The old vanity was pressed too close to the wall, and a quick wiggle had to be applied, one side at a time. Her aching hands forced it forward. A loud popping sound came from the mirror as it wobbled. A gaping crack appeared halfway down the mirror reaching from one side to the other.

Corazon and Elizabeth rushed to the room.

"Why do I have this? Shit … I don't remember." Misshapen fingers wiped over the vanity's finish, and her mind weighed through the heavy sludge. Anxiety overtook her old frame, nausea lurched from her as she rushed to make a path to the toilet. The younger women were pushed aside.

Elizabeth stood at the door.

"Leave me be." The words echoed from the bathroom. Tears flowed, and an overwhelming sadness gripped the room. Elizabeth pushed into the room, as her mother sat on the floor. Her words cracked between sobs, and crushing sadness surrounded her. "I'm so sad. I don't understand."

"We'll get everything straightened out. I'm sure it's just a clerical error. Don't worry." Elizabeth believed the paperwork had to be an error.

"No, it's that damn piece of furniture. It reeks of sadness. Don't you feel it?" Her frail frame shuddered between sobs.

Elizabeth pulled her mother to her feet. The two walked to face the sadness.

Corazon and Elizabeth removed the broken mirror's sharp edges, which hung precariously from the polished frame. Carefully folded newspapers, yellow with age, fell from behind the jagged pieces. Glass was removed, and the newspapers were neatly piled in the closet.

An investigation of the vanity began. Bent fingers swept across the vanity's finish, jolted by hiccups between continued sobs. Empty drawers were lined with yellowed newspaper, all in perfect condition, but nothing else. The pages had apparently been untouched since they were carefully placed there during the 1920s. The final drawer was jammed, but after several gentle tries and a fierce effort, the two old hands pulled it open. The façade of the vanity broke free sending the old body back onto the carpet. A document drawer had been camouflaged as a façade. A sob hiccup followed by a belly laugh from the old woman relieved the two younger women, as they jumped to gather her and the drawer off the floor.

Glue sealed the drawer's edges, but years in the desert had loosened the old glue. Small tacks had been hammered into the drawer before it was glued. What landed on the old lap was a flat document drawer reminiscent of those used during the Civil War to protect important family documents and money from marauders.

A thin piece of wood covered the drawer. It slid off with ease, and it was also lined with folded 1920 newspapers.

Sobbing controlled, Nora shaped her hands to reach

the only item tucked in the corner of the drawer. It was cushioned by more folded newspaper and a bag tightly wrapped in yellowed tissue paper. The tissue paper caressed a small purple velvet bag monogrammed with "CQ" embroidered in gold stitching. CQ meant nothing to Nora. Old fingers struggled and snapped. The room went silent as the contents of the jewelry bag shook out onto the bed. A matched set of simple gold wedding bands rolled out first. After some coaxing, an elegant piece plopped onto the bed. It was a diamond stickpin with a stone larger than Nora's own engagement ring. At least a carat, pear-shaped diamond sat in what appeared to be a golden claw with talons. Swollen digits clenched to hold the pin up to the light, the facets created a rainbow that danced around the room. After a choking gasp, Nora spat out a hoarse cry. The rainbow made her stomach tingle with excitement, but the sadness still engulfed her.

"Oh my God … I know this. I know this … why?" Her tired eyes watched the rainbow dance across the room.

Corazon twisted the velvet bag in her palm, placed it back on the bed, and whispered, "CQ … Conrad Quinn?"

The weary old woman sat on the bed and shook her head in disgust. She couldn't grasp what she knew about the pin. "There's no time to waste. I don't have a single moment to spare. My future is a dark cave, and my past is being erased." Her shoulders slouched in despair. Time was her unseen enemy.

"Momma, there's definitely more to this than a clerk's typo. No matter what, you are who you are. Your family is your family, that has never changed. What do we know?

Maureen died thinking you were her niece. Who hid the jewelry?"

"A message was sent to me from the grave, and I can't ignore it. I need to pack."

Yearning to uncover Maureen's mystery revitalized her worn soul. New medications cleared the sludge, and her concentration improved.

Nora's sister Keira called to say plans for Maureen's memorial had been completed.

Elizabeth's husband Brendan would accompany the three women on their quest to New York. As always, Corazon would be Nora's companion. She was part of the family.

CHAPTER 9

A doorman approached Nora and her family before the bags were unloaded from the taxi. He wore a long green morning jacket with epaulets, a black top hat adorned his head. Crisp white gloves signaled a bellman who stacked the bags on a golden luggage cart. They followed him into the hotel like a row of curious ducklings. All were stunned by the elaborate beauty of the building. Green carpet stretched from the curb to the huge gold-framed revolving doors. A green awning was embossed with large gold script: The Didean. The hotel's exterior façade of light brown brick had detailed crescent shapes carved into the bricks framing the tops of the windows on each floor.

Chandler, the doorman, tipped his hat as he introduced himself.

Brendan couldn't hide his smile. "This is my mother-in-law, Nora O'Hara, and we are the Connelly family." He waved his hand to include Corazon as she stood silently in awe of the hotel.

Chandler was a handsome young man of medium height with a slender build. He appeared to be in his twenties. His sharp gray eyes jumped to attention, and he became more formal after the family introduction, "Welcome to the city," he said with a slow, deliberate bow. "We have been expecting you. Would you like anything to drink or eat while you check in? It will only be a moment."

Brendan thanked the young man as he shook his hand while trying to slip a tip into it.

Chandler declined, "No, sir, Mr. Connelly. I can't take that."

Brendan was embarrassed and thought it extremely odd. Chandler had gone out of his way to be of assistance and welcoming, but refused a tip. He smiled as the group, along with their luggage, followed him through the lobby.

The elegant lobby was a combination of bright white and gold. The white marble floor featured light green carpet. The furniture was upholstered with moss green brocade, and the elevators and revolving doors were polished brass. The elegant lobby was encircled by columns that met each other in the shape of arches as they reached toward the ceiling. The ceiling was a masterpiece of blue skies, white clouds, and an orange and pink sunset. Not quite in the center of the lobby was a white marble registration desk. Behind the registration desk, stood a pair of wide staircases that were accessible from either side of the lobby. Both were covered with the same light green carpet with brass carpet stair rods. Each staircase made a sweeping turn until they met in the center of the landing of the next level of the building.

Chandler signaled to a young man at the front desk. He smiled as the front desk person jogged over to meet them. "This is Nora O'Hara and her family."

The clerk introduced himself as Fredrick. He was younger and taller than Chandler, with dark hair and eyes.

"Hello, we are pleased to have your family visit us here at the Didean." Fredrick smiled.

Chandler clicked his heels and clapped his gloved hands together. "Well, O'Hara family, enjoy your stay—and let me know if you need anything."

Brendan smiled at his mother-in-law. "Your hospitality is aboveboard." He attributed it to being in the city. With another smile, he thanked Chandler again.

Fredrick announced that the rooms were ready. A bellman would take the luggage up. Fredrick gave Brendan the keys. He offered the hospitality of the lounge to relax while the luggage made its way up to the rooms.

Nora felt the sludge beginning to take over, and she nudged her daughter gently. "Fredrick, please let Mr. Ryan know how much we appreciate his hospitality. You all have been so kind."

"Oh, Mrs. Connelly, Mr. Ryan didn't arrange for your rooms. Mr. Byrne did. He let us know that you were VIPs and very special to his family," Fredrick replied with a quick smile.

Uneasiness crept into the pit of Elizabeth's stomach. She had no idea who Mr. Byrne was or why her cousin Ashley told them her nephew, the director of the hotel, had arranged the rooms. She kept telling herself it had to be a misunderstanding. The assumption was the rooms were a family member's perk. After seeing the hotel's elegance and the royal treatment, the unknown benefactor set off alarms. Was Ashley deliberately vague—or was she in the dark as well?

"Who the hell is Mr. Byrne? And why did he arrange our rooms?" Elizabeth mumbled under her breath.

"It will sort itself out. I am sure it's just a misunderstanding." Nora leaned on her daughter for support.

Corazon helped the older woman balance herself and whispered, "I have a weird feeling. I can't put my finger on it, but the men downstairs added to that feeling."

Elizabeth responded, "It was awkward. I'm sure it's because Ashley told them her aunt was checking in. Her nephew is one of the directors."

It was a quick elevator trip. The hallway looked like a French chateau; mirrors and beautiful artwork decorated the walls, and huge vases of lightly scented fresh flowers sat on French provincial tables. The walls were lightly colored delicate wallpaper with gold-trimmed white wainscoting. A short walk ended at a huge set of white double doors trimmed with gold. The doorknobs were golden eagles with their wings extended; curved talons became door handles. The slot for the key card was just above one of the eagles' heads.

Brendan looked around and laughed loudly. "Baby, I don't know who this Mr. Byrne is, but we need to make friends with him."

Lights turned on automatically as the door opened. The room was like something from a James Bond movie. The only word to describe it was *regal*. The enormous suite had a living room and a dining area, all French provincial. Their bags had been taken into the vast bedrooms, all three had king-sized canopy beds. The four-post beds in each room reached to the ceiling. White taffeta canopies swept from the head of each bed, along the top of the post railings, and down the sides of the post at the foot of the bed. The canopy was tied to the bedpost with green satin ropes at the center of each post. All the rooms connected to its own bathroom.

While the family explored the vastness of the suite, Brendan answered a knock on the door.

A small man with messy white hair, wearing a gray suit and gloves, carrying a darker gray hat stood in front of him. The man's hair looked like the uncontrollable fuzzy feathers of a white duckling. His piercing eyes were foggy gray like soapy marbles. He seemed out of place, but there was nothing that could be pinned down. He was just an odd little man, somewhat overdressed, who smelled like he bathed in cheap cologne. The man seemed surprised that Brendan answered the door. "Uh, I am Charles. I, uh, want to show you the details of your suite. I'm sorry I didn't meet you at the elevator. Please forgive my rudeness I thought you had gone to the bar. I would have seen you to the room myself." He swept past Brendan and let himself into the suite.

Elizabeth and Brendan watched as the small man slid around the room. His cologne filled each room as he darted through the suite, like an aging rat scurrying to find his treasure. His beady eyes took in everything. He opened the French doors that led to a balcony overlooking the city, then he directed the couple to the fully stocked wet bar that was in a glass cabinet and then to a walk-in closet with a wall safe. "I would recommend you place anything you value in the safe … any money or important documents. You can't be too cautious."

Charles slowly walked around the room, his arms waved as he disclosed all the necessary features of the room. With one last look at the room, he said, "What would you folks like for breakfast? And what time do you want it?"

The four looked at one another for a moment.

Nora spoke first, "Oh, Charles, thank you for asking. We have a full morning. We'll just call for something light when we get up."

"As you wish." With one last glance over his narrow shoulder, he was gone.

Elizabeth whispered, "I am uneasy about all of this. There's more going on here than any of us know. The stickpin looks very much like the doorknobs of this place—and who is Mr. Byrne?"

Brendan said, "Sweet Jesus, Lizzy. Is that what you are basing your theory on … a couple of doorknobs? Come on. You need to get some rest. We'll get things cleared up in the morning. Mr. Byrne may be an uncle or some other family member you've never met. You don't know all of your mom's side of the family. That would explain why Keira didn't say anything. She may have thought you knew Mr. Byrne. Baby, I don't want to pile more on you and Mom. With all that is going on, perhaps it wouldn't hurt if we were more aware of our surroundings."

Brendan said, "We let that old man—who didn't seem threatening—into our suite with no questions asked. He had no identification. He just told us he worked here, and we bought it."

Elizabeth quipped, "Why would he lie? You aren't making me feel any better, Brendan."

"Lizzy, he wore his gloves the entire time he was in our room, and he had a hat in his hand. Who in the name of God carries their hat around while they work? He seemed really surprised that we were in the room. I'm not saying he was casing the place, but he was definitely an odd duck. We all need to be more cautious."

CHAPTER 10

Morning brought the group together for breakfast in the large dining area of the suite and a discussion of the day's plans. At the top of the list was Aunt Maureen's service. They had scheduled a meeting with Father Bryan. Cousin Angela had chosen him as the officiant.

The church was cool and dark. The smell of polished wood and burning candles filled the air. It took a few minutes to adjust to the darkness. The church's interior was old, but it was not in disrepair. The architecture gave away its age. Tall gray columns were intricately carved and arched at the ceiling. The arches appeared to be support beams that encircled the pews dark polished wood and red velvet seats like a protective fence. The concave ceiling's, light blue sky, clouds, and saints looked down upon the altar. Intricate stained-glass windows let in light every few feet with a mosaic of delicate color. The alcoves were filled with the warm glow of red glass candles. Statues of every saint imaginable sat silently in the cool darkness. The heat from the candles reached out to those who passed. The stained-glass and the candles were the only light in the church.

Father Bryan met the group at one of the alcoves; after introductions, he led them to the rectory. A small man in

43

his eighties, he had only a wisp of white hair. Plump, rosy cheeks pushed against his lower eye lids, making his blue-gray eyes look dreadfully small. He was round, and his black cassock fit him snugly, making a swishing sound with every step he took. He had an unidentifiable accent.

After some small talk, his cassock crunched as he directed his attention to the old woman. "Noinin." His body language reflected his alarm. He had misspoken. He looked away as he searched for a suitable reply. He gazed at the stained-glass window: Jesus sitting on a bench in a glowing white robe, with a child at his feet, surrounded by a bed of colorful flowers. It seemed like an eternity before he finally answered. "I meant to say *Nora*. Noinin is an Irish pet name. It means Daisy." He pointed to the prayer cards in Nora's hand. "I meant Saint Teresa, the Little Flower, a mere child. We are all seen as children of Jesus."

Nora held the prayer cards she had chosen for Maureen. Although she only had a vague memory of the woman, she felt compelled to show her some respect. She looked at the picture of the child in a brown and black habit surrounded by pink peonies and white daisies. Saint Teresa held a special meaning for her. She had placed her prayer card in the pews of her church every Sunday for many years, but she had no recollection of how the saint became her favorite.

Nothing added up: the unique and expensive stickpin, the stranger who had arranged the hotel, the feather-headed old man, and the backtracking priest. This was just the first day of a very strange trip.

The family sat in the first couple of pews of the church.

We need name tags with who our parents were, Elizabeth thought as she glanced around the church.

Nora and her family didn't have a lot of contact with relatives in the East. She knew names and who belonged to whom on a family tree. Over the years, she had added new family members and updated it when someone died. Recently, Elizabeth had taken over. There were no pictures to connect the names to faces. Cousins were names on annual Christmas cards.

Angela gave the West Coast group a wave of acknowledgment when she arrived. She hugged Nora and Elizabeth while reintroducing herself. Elizabeth wouldn't have recognized her. The two hadn't seen each other since they were teens. It was assumed she was with her family: a large group with similar features and dark hair and eyes.

Nora glanced around the church; the number of families coincided with the family tree, but without a list, she was unable to put a name to a face. The church service was brief, a simple Mass, but there wasn't a graveside service as Maureen was placed with her husband Martin. After the service, family became more animated and talked to one another. The families laughed about the need for name tags.

A man at the back of the church who sat with an older man caught Nora's attention. The younger man was clean-shaven with thick, dark hair. The older man was at least ten years her senior, seemed familiar. Did she know him? How?

This damn fog won't get the best of me.

The two men looked to be father and son. The older of the two was slightly slumped in a wheelchair. He caught Nora's glance and smiled. Her old eyes squinted so tight her cheek twitched; she hoped a better view could clear the fog.

The old man's face was weathered, a large scar ran from above one ear through his eye ending near the middle of his cheek. From the way he turned his head, it appeared he was blind in that eye. Nora smiled back, as one did in church to show fellowship. The younger man pushed the wheelchair toward the front doors of the church. A bright flash of a rainbow pierced her strained eyes. The same rainbow of color had danced through her bedroom when the elaborate stickpin was pulled from its pouch.

The wheelchair stopped at the doors of the church in front of the round priest.

Every part of the old woman's body was focused on who these two were. While the families were engrossed in getting reacquainted and making plans for a good old-fashioned Irish wake, she walked slowly to the front of the church, as though sneaking up on a bird, afraid it would take flight. Before she reached the front of the church, the two men passed through the huge wooden doors.

A crunching cassock rustled behind her, and Father Bryan tapped her shoulder. A wave of anger and determination came over her, but it was diverted by the priest. He pressed a note into her stiffened hands:

> It wasn't my father, William's, intent to interrupt today's service. There's something important he needs to discuss with you. We will join the family for the wake. We can talk then. Regards, Luke Byrne

A wave of horror and excitement flowed over her, like a fever from head to toe. The note shook in her aged hands. Her blood pumped into her bent fingertips. The hair on the nape of her neck rose with a chill that caused her to shake from head to toe. The two faces matched the mystery name from the Didean. The past few days had included a lost past, the discovery a wonderful treasure, and a stranger with the same elegant treasure who wanted to meet.

Corazon saw the distress that overtook her travel companion. With a soft touch and voice, she calmed Nora, and the two rejoined the group. The family planned to meet at a pub near where Angela lived.

Nora's head throbbed as questions swirled within the fog.

Angela's voice swept away the fog, "It is in the old neighborhood. There will be plenty of food and drink."

A sense of excitement and dread engulfed her old frame. Her head felt like a swollen, soaked sponge after the events of the past few days. The sponge had to be squeezed to release the information before it vanished in the fog and was lost forever.

"He has a pin … that old man in the wheelchair … he has a pin just like the one we found in the vanity. The priest gave me a note from the younger one. Luke Byrne is his name. Byrne … his name is Byrne." The words scratched out of her throat.

CHAPTER 11

The cab ride from the church was quiet. Elizabeth held a twisted hand softly, as Nora reached for Corazon, pulling both the younger women's hands to her heart. "I think we're in for a ride."

The cab arrived at the pub just behind Angela and the rest of the East Coast family. Angela and her siblings lived in the same neighborhood of Hell's Kitchen, where Keira and Nora began their lives. The old seven-story walk-ups had been replaced by modern apartment buildings. The old pub was on the corner of a renovated business district. The front of the pub revealed its age. The building was red brick with oval windows, framed with the same red brick. The pavement in front of the pub was cobblestone. The edges of the cobblestones were smooth and rounded with age. A green awning displayed the street number, 790, like a welcoming hand that reached out to passersby. The two oval windows reached from a few feet above the pavement to the height of the awning. Both were etched with the name, "Cara Dílis," (faithful friend). The pub had been refurbished, but its history had been preserved.

Angela wanted to show the group around the pub and introduce them all to more extended family.

Elizabeth whispered as she held her husband's hand tightly, "Brendan, we are meeting the old man from the church."

Without skipping a beat, he replied, "You don't even have to ask. I wouldn't leave you ladies alone."

Angela handed them both a beer and swept them off to meet more family.

As they walked through the pub, it was as though they had walked through a doorway into the past. There were modern fixtures, but the pub had the feel of a bygone time; the bar was dark polished wood with a tall mirror behind it. The frame of the mirror swept from one end of the bar to the other in a stretched half-moon shape. A huge mantel with a floral etched border hovered over the mirror. The bar's lighting was mounted on the walls which gave the impression of early electric lighting. It gave out very little light. The walls' wainscoting matched the dark wood of the bar, green floral wallpaper reached from the edge of the wainscoting to the ceiling. The dark hardwood floors didn't help light up the bar. There were pictures on one of the walls that dated back to the 1920s. They were pictures of neighborhood policemen and firemen standing outside of Cara Dílis. In the center of the wall there was a larger picture of two well-dressed young men.

Angela hurried the group past the photos. Nora's old eyes only had a glancing look at the two men. Her eyes were suddenly drawn to the men's ties. They wore identical stickpins in their ties—the very same pin found in the vanity and worn by Mr. Byrne.

Elizabeth gasped and turned to her mother.

Brendan touched Elizabeth's shoulder knowingly. He had seen the picture as well.

At that moment, the young man from the church entered the pub. The patrons of the pub and the New York family acknowledged his presence in a respectful manner, but they didn't approach him. He walked toward the back of the pub stopping in front of Nora. "My name is Luke. My father, William, is in the back of the pub. He came in from the alleyway. It's easier to maneuver the wheelchair back there, and he doesn't like to draw attention to himself."

Nora was surprised by her own confidence. "I understand, Luke. We didn't anticipate so much New York family. I would like my family to join us if you don't mind."

"Noinin, we aren't here to frighten you. My father has carried a huge burden for many years. He had a recent health scare and shared this burden with me. I urged him to free himself of it. I only regret we have to do it after your Aunt Maureen's death. She loved you dearly. I'm sorry. Obviously, I've never met you. I am not sure how to refer to you. My father refers to you as *Noinin*."

Thoughts of Father Bryan shot to the front of Nora's mind. Luke used the same pet name as Father Bryan, *Noinin*. A sick feeling rolled in the pit of her stomach. As much as she wanted to know the secret William wanted to share, she was fighting a battle to salvage her own memories. Was his secret something her old soul could stand?

They followed Luke through the door and into what can only be described as a speakeasy. They were transported, yet again, to a time long ago. Where the pub was quaint and original, this room was elegant. It had an enormous bar which was encased with a massive mirror surrounded by an intricately carved bar-back that reached to the ceiling. Two immense chandeliers covered the ceiling of pressed copper tiles. The room had a soft reddish glow from the chandeliers reflecting off the copper tiles. The polished dark wood wainscot walls met green velvet wallpaper mid-wall. It was similar to the pub, but more elegant. The ceiling had no sharp corners. It made soft curves as it met the tall walls.

The room had a mild lingering smell of aged wood, cigar smoke, and alcohol. Poker tables sat on one side of the room. Small lounging couches, upholstered in light green brocade, sat gracefully near the walls. White marble-topped cocktail tables with dark wooden legs rested in front of each couch. Larger tables, more suitable for dining, sat at the opposite end of the room. The lounge area and dining area were separated by a set of five wide stairs that swept along the far end of the lounge. The stairs were covered with pale green carpet that was held in place by polished brass stair rods. The dining tables all had white linen tablecloths with short crystal candlesticks in the center. There was a stage at the far end of the room, past the dining area and beyond a polished dance floor.

Luke smiled, and his dark eyes gleamed. "This room has that effect on everyone the first time they see it. Since the renovation, it has become somewhat of a novelty. Tourists are interested in dining in an old-time speakeasy, and Cara Dílis is happy to oblige. This is one of only a few surviving places of its kind. The poker tables are original fixtures, but now are merely for show. They are used as additional dining tables when Cara Dílis is really busy."

William sat at one of the dining tables. His face flickered in the candlelight. He didn't look frail seated at the table.

Luke guided his guests to meet William. Crystal glasses and a plate of soda bread sat on the table.

Nora reached for the soda bread as she sat down. She looked into William's eyes and whispered, "Where is the piano? There should be a piano."

William merely smiled and directed her to sit on his right so he could see her when he spoke. He was blind in his left eye. She passed the plate of bread around the table.

Luke fetched a bottle of Jameson's and tall frosted glasses of beer from behind the bar. He returned to the table, but he didn't sit. He started to walk away.

William stopped him saying, "Son, this is your story as well. You all have to know the truth and share it with your families … so this secret no longer hovers over all of us like a banshee. I just wish I could have found the answers my da searched for most of his adult life. I must ask you first to forgive me and to please understand that I was following orders."

His voice scratched out the words as he directed his attention to Nora. "I thought I was protecting you and your family. Bradley, Robert, and Hannah had no knowledge of your history. They were in Ireland and thought you were born in their absence. Keira was too young to ever know the difference. Please eat something. I have more food coming. We may be here for a while."

Shit, what is this old guy saying? Elizabeth's stomached rolled, and her neck hair stood on end which sent a chill down her spine.

Brendan perched himself between mother and daughter, placing a hand on each knee.

Nora leaned in closer as William continued.

"A few weeks ago, as I rested in a hospital bed, comfortable with the idea it was my time to go. I had seen my son and daughters grow to be fine adults. I had made my peace, and I was ready to move on to the better place everyone talks about. As I closed my eyes, a voice shattered my serenity. 'You can't go. You aren't finished.' The voice was shouting at me. I knew the voice well; it was my da, Michael. I also recognized his tone; it was the tone he used the night I was shot. He shouted nearly those same words at me as I laid bleeding in the street." William slid his hand over his jagged scar. "The voice continued, 'Our past must not die with you. You must share our past, for the future of our family.' I chose not to include my son, Luke, in my life of uncertainty. Throughout my entire life, I looked over my shoulder as I waited for the next attack, which never came. You remained safe, and the family thrived, but what was my da trying to tell me? Obviously, I didn't die. I shared my dream with Luke and explained our family's secret. He was angry that I hadn't entrusted him with our family history. I tried to explain it had nothing to do with trust; it was my burden to carry. There was no point in upsetting so many families with this bizarre story. Luke is why we are all here today. I will share as much as I remember. I hope I can shed some light on our family's past."

William poured a large glass of whiskey. He drank it down, then took a deep breath. It was as though it was the first breath he was able to breathe freely in a very long time. William knew Nora when she was a child. His father, Michael Byrne, and her father, Conrad Quinn, were close friends and business associates.

Nora thought, *CQ?*

William remembered quite vividly the last time he saw her with her family. He was a teen, playing in the street with the boys from the neighborhood. Conrad, with his daughter in his arms, and his wife, Eveleen, came out of the apartment building where both families lived.

"We were all going out to dinner. It had to be a special occasion as they were all dressed up. My da made me wear my church slacks and shirt. Nora accompanied her parents on occasion, but not when all four of them went out. My da stood near the car at the edge of the stoop and waited for them to reach the bottom."

Nora tried to grasp what he was saying. Her mind raced. *Eveleen, my mother, and Conrad? I have never heard these names. Concentrate … you have to listen.*

"Da called upstairs to my ma, Tara, to hurry. She called back that she'd be down in a minute. Da opened the door when Conrad and Eveleen reached the car. He looked around, and then got into the driver's seat. Ma was at the top of the stoop when there was a commotion in the car. Nora was crying and being handed to Eveleen, who put her on the floorboard.

"As I walked toward the car to open the door for Ma, a car rolled slowly into the neighborhood. I was more interested in my friends razzing me about my clothing than the car. The car slowly drove toward Da's car, and then I heard shots and screams. I felt a hot streaking lightning bolt of pain, then warm moisture began flowing down my face. I collapsed to the ground. I could hear my own voice crying out in pain—and then everything went black and cold."

The old man poured another whiskey as a waiter knocked at the door. Luke opened it and let him in. The information that poured out of William was dizzying, and food was a welcome sight.

Elizabeth was taking notes, desperately trying to keep all the names straight.

Nora was in awe of what William had just divulged.

Brendan remained calm, calming his wife with a touch of his hand on her knee.

Nora wished she had her tape recorder. It was way too much information for her mind to capture. Between her daughter's note-taking and Corazon's memory, Nora hoped nothing was lost.

William continued, "So many times I have wished I had paid more attention to the shooter's car. Things might have been very different. My da, Michael, was in a family business with your da, Conrad Quinn."

The second mention of the name brought goose bumps, the hair on Nora's arms stood on end. *Holy crap! CQ? The initials on the purple velvet bag.*

"The two childhood friends from Ireland came to this country as young men. Your da was the dreamer, the planner, and the peacekeeper. He was a diplomat and great with people. My da was the action guy. Don't get me wrong … he was also good with people, making sure all of Conrad's plans went off without a hitch. But as a young man, my da was dynamite with a short fuse. Conrad balanced my da. It was the perfect relationship. Both of them wanted to own and operate the largest and best club in New York; Conrad also dreamed of owning hotels. Prohibition was poison, it almost killed the dream. Out of desperation, they agreed that drastic times required drastic actions. Lines were blurred regarding what was lawful. Selling bootleg booze and running some games kept the club afloat. They were young men trying to survive, not gangsters. Those times saw scum who wanted what you had, and it didn't matter if you were just trying to survive. You could get sucked into a dangerous situation before you even knew it. They remained forthcoming, helpful businessmen, and they shared their wealth with others who were struggling. Our entire neighborhood loved and protected them. They knew Conrad and Michael would protect and take care of all of them.

"Having survived the domino effect of the potato famine, it disgusted them how the British ignored the starving farmers and their families in Ireland. Their disgust bore a sworn vow to never forget where they began. It was the Irish way. The family prospered, helped their neighbors, and grew stronger. There wasn't the same desire for absolute power like the Italians, who used threats and violence to gain control of as much of the city as possible. A gentlemen's agreement with the Italians meant our neighborhood was off-limits as long as my da and Conrad remained neighborhood businessmen. They would never make any power grabs outside of Hell's Kitchen. They were happy just to survive. The agreement was easy since the friends had no interest in a war with the Italians. The Italians considered them small-timers who were not worth their trouble. The two had no stomach for the killing the Italians were into. The Italians even fought among themselves for control of their organization. My da and Conrad stayed low-key and didn't spend their money on expensive houses or cars. There were only a few extravagant gifts ... one being the stickpins."

William looked down at the pin on his chest. Even in

the darkened room, it flashed a rainbow dance. When he touched it, a kaleidoscope of colors bounced across the white linen tablecloth.

"It represented their friendship, all that they had overcome, their combined strength, success, and the partnership they created. I am telling you this, so you have an idea of what they dealt with. Conrad your da, and Eveleen your ma were gunned down in cold blood the same night I got this beauty mark." William slid his index finger and thumb across the jagged scar on his face. His voice trailed off as he reached for Nora's twisted hand.

Blood seeped from Nora's head. Her arm hair stood on end, and her ears were poker hot. Her mind strained to grasped whisps of memory. *So much time lost.*

William inhaled deeply, "The family protected you from an unknown fiend by never revealing your identity. For that, I am truly sorry, especially since my da never solved why our family was attacked or who bankrolled the shooting. All the families, not just the Irish, searched for the killers. None of them condoned butchering innocent women and children. It was beyond anyone's comprehension. There was an attempted retaliation, but before my da found them, the bastards were wiped out, mutilated leaving no trace of who they were or who slaughtered them. My father took over the family business, never knowing with whom or where Conrad had invested a large part of their savings. Conrad's accounting records showed he had withdrawn a large sum of money from the safe several days before his murder, but his posting was cryptic and showed Conrad's feelings about the withdrawal. In the 'Pay to' column of his journal, according to my da, it was written, 'Our Bright New Future.' There was no hint of who he gave the money to or for what. After Conrad's murder, my da ran everything with a stern hand to be sure there wasn't another attempt to destroy the family. Part of my da died with his best friend. He realized Conrad's plan of making everything legit with the end of Prohibition. I was sent upstate with my ma after the shooting. My da was never able to determine whether the shooter had one specific target or was trying to eliminate our entire family. Ma was only a few feet from the car, and by the grace of God, she avoided being shot. Da had his doubts that my being shot was accidental. None of the other boys were hit."

William stopped talking for a few moments and ate some of the food on his plate. He was very pensive as though he was deciding what he should reveal next.

Nora was mesmerized by him. Knowing she must eat—and determined not to miss a single word—she ate when he did.

William said, "Da never doubted that Conrad had something big in the works. The day he was murdered, he told my da he was working on something that would make them rich and take them out of the city to paradise. It was something so new and exciting that no one else realized how big it could become. They would be in on the ground floor. Da said Conrad was really excited about the meeting, but he never had a chance to tell him about it. The big deal that Conrad had closed was what they were going out to celebrate. Da had no clue what the deal was, and no one ever approached him.

"I'm sorry, I'm going on like you're aware of our family bond. When Da felt especially melancholy, he would say he wished he had pressed Conrad to tell him what the hell was going on. Conrad was thrilled with his deal, and he wanted to announce it with a big celebration. He always believed Conrad's deal and the slaughter of his friends were connected. Da felt Conrad's death was meant to muzzle the deal. That was the one and only time the two of them didn't finalize a deal together. It haunted my da for the rest of his life.

"What I am about to share with you is totally coincidental. I only mention it to prove how closely we are all connected—whether we realize it or not. While I was recovering from my gunshot wound, Ma and I stayed in a cottage near the shore. It was only a few yards from the beach and a pier. All I was able to do was sit on the porch swing. I wished I could fish, swim, or run—anything a normal thirteen-year-old could do. A doctor visited once a week for several months. After his last visit, my ma was very melancholy and quiet. She had kept herself busy taking care of me, reassuring me I would be fine in no time.

"One afternoon, a car rolled up to the cottage. I could barely see the driver. Only a tuft of red hair was visible in the window. A slight woman in a white dress and gray sweater bounced out of the vehicle. She pulled a black bag out of the back seat and headed toward the front door. She was extremely petite, but she walked with great confidence. As she approached the porch, she chirped, 'Why aren't you doing something fun on such a lovely summer afternoon?' This fireball with flame-red hair took me by surprise. I was very depressed. I felt as though I would never be normal again. I hadn't spoken to anyone except the doctor and Ma for months."

CHAPTER 12

Maggie O'Hara had been a traveling nurse to young and old for decades. After her brother lost a leg in a farming accident, she started aiding an overworked doctor in Erie County near Buffalo, New York, where she was born. Maggie was compelled to help others, and she had a keen sense of how people dealt with illnesses and injuries. She wasn't any taller than five feet, but she made up for her size with a huge heart and a determined mind. Her gray eyes flashed whenever anyone questioned her capabilities. She refused to allow anyone she tended to wallow in self-pity. Her philosophy was that there is always someone worse off than you. Maggie was as loyal as they came, but if you wronged her, you were out of her life forever—no questions asked. There were no excuses or second chances. Although she was petite, she could lift and tend to an injured man. She traveled Erie County in a horse-drawn buggy, attending to the injured and ill and delivering babies.

She met and fell in love with a railroad worker, Philip. Philip was medium height and stocky with a thick head of brown hair and dark eyes. He was smitten with Maggie's free spirit. Although he wasn't ready to settle down, afraid he would lose her, he asked Maggie to marry him. The two moved to Kansas. Philip was gone for weeks at a time, building rail lines out West.

Maggie tended to the ill near Shawnee, Kansas, traveling to a makeshift trading post called the Big Tree, where people would come from all around to trade food and goods and seek medical help. Osage Indians brought pelts to trade. Maggie attended to some of the injured Osage tribal members. The settlers and the Indians were able to live peacefully, sharing their land and goods. There was enough trust between them that the settlers didn't lock their doors. It wasn't uncommon for settlers to occasionally wake up to find a tribal member had borrowed some food, leaving pelts in exchange.

Maggie and Philip managed to start a family even though his work kept him on the road most of the time. After the birth of Maggie's first child, she stopped traveling. Before long, she had three young sons, which coincided with Phillip's visits. She helped the doctor in town and raised her sons. Philip's trips home became less frequent. Then a telegram arrived; Her husband had quit the railroad and was no longer coming back to Kansas. He was moving on. He said he would send for her when he found a job, but he gave her no idea how long it would be or where she could find him. Although heartbroken, she knew she didn't need Philip to survive. She wasn't waiting around for him to decide to be a father and husband.

Living alone with three lively boys in the desolation of Kansas didn't suit Maggie. She packed up the boys and took the train East. She got as far as New York City. The city captivated her. Having saved enough money to get an apartment, she found work at Bellevue Hospital. Maggie buried herself in her work and taking care of her boys. The city was so busy and alive that she was able to bury Philip as well. She took home nursing jobs to make extra money, so her boys could go to camp in the summer and get out of the city.

Chapter 13

William took a swig of whiskey and a deep breath. "Maggie barreled up the steps, stood right in front of me, and asked, 'Where's your Ma? I'm Maggie O'Hara. The doctor sent me to check on you. The only thing I see wrong with you is you have nothing to keep you busy.'

"Maggie smiled when she spoke, and her gray eyes sparkled, like crystals, with each word. She cinched her red hair back at the bottom of her neck. Her energy swirled in the air. It surrounded me. Ma heard the voices and came to the door. Maggie took one look at Ma and announced, 'You two need to realize how fortunate you are. Madam, your son is alive and well. Yes, he has a scar and lost an eye, but he still has two arms and two legs and can still see with his remaining eye. Appreciate that and hold onto it. The only limitations he has are those that he puts on himself.'

"She looked Ma up and down. Ma wasn't much taller than Maggie, and Ma's dark auburn hair overwhelmed her pale skin and large brown eyes.

"Maggie put her hands on each side of Ma's face, slid her hair behind her ears, and softly spoke, 'My pet, first, you both are to call me Maggie. Mrs. O'Hara is too formal. Secondly, Mrs. I think you need some care too. You look a bit tired. Taking care of an ill child takes its toll. I have three boys of my own.' Maggie's tone was like a soft hug that embraced us.

"Ma seemed to light up a bit and stood a little straighter. It had been a long haul having her best friend and her entire family murdered, her only child shot and disfigured, then being whisked away from everything she knew. Maggie seemed more concerned with my ma than me. She stayed most of the afternoon, talking to Ma while fixing food for us. She sent me for a walk on the beach. The sun felt amazing on my body; it seemed I had been stuck in the house or on the porch forever. I walked without a care in the world. As the sun started to set, I walked back to the house. Maggie was getting ready to leave, 'Tara, I will be back at the end of the week. Eat what I have prepared for you, take the medicine, and be sure to get lots of rest. I want to come back and see you feeling better. William will be fine; it's his turn to take care of you.' With that, she reached up to tap me on the head and bounced down the steps to her car.

"At the end of the week, as promised, Maggie's car came chugging up the beach. This time, she brought her two young sons, Sean and Samuel, with her. Yes, Maggie O'Hara was our nurse, and your husband, Samuel, visited with me while she tended to my ma. Maggie never said anything about what was wrong with my ma. She spent time with her, gave her medicine, and made sure we had food to eat. She even changed the linens, did the laundry, and tidied up the place while she chatted with my ma. The boys and I played cards, told stories, and—when no one was watching—we shared cigarettes and threw dice. They saw me through a very dark time. As far as I knew, the O'Hara's only knew that I had been shot in a hunting accident. I didn't think they knew my last name or my family.

"Maggie came weekly, and with each visit, Ma was weaker. Maggie sent the doctor on several occasions. He spoke quietly to Ma either in the kitchen or in her room, and she remained silent, merely nodding. I was never included in what was going on. After the doctor's first visit to check on Ma, my da showed up. It was odd. A car came before him, the men in it walked the beach. When Da's car arrived, he didn't get out until the men on the beach gave him a wave. I had been so involved with my own self-pity that I had forgotten, maybe deliberately, the horror Ma and I left behind. Da spoke to Ma in the kitchen. They spoke in whispers, as he caressed Ma's face. I could hear the sadness when he spoke; it swirled throughout the house. I couldn't distinguish his words, but I was drenched in the sadness. They came out of the kitchen, and Da's face was ashen. I don't remember ever seeing him like that. I have no recollection of his reaction the night I was shot, other than his shouting at me. He held my ma's hand and told her very gently with great sadness, '*Leah* (baby), I can't bring you home yet. It's too dangerous. There's too much going on. Believe me, I will come for you as soon as I can. I promise to find a way to come out to see you often. Please, take care of yourself; I don't know what I would do without you. I love you with my life.'

"I heard Maggie tell Da, 'Tara needs to be near you. Forget what the damn doctor said. Take her home with you. She is going to have difficulties; if she stays here, she will surely die. William is fine; he needs to be exposed to others. Yes, he has a bad scar, but in all other aspects, he is healthy. He'll adjust. Mr. Byrne, I'm no fool. I've been around the block. I know there is a dark cloud hanging over your head, and I know you fear for your family. If you must, for his protection, send William away to school, but by God, if you love Tara, take her back to the city. She will not survive in this solitude.'

"My da stayed with us until dark. The men on the beach waited until he was in his car, and then they all drove away. Maggie continued her weekly visits along with the boys for a couple more weeks. She came each Saturday so the boys could keep me busy. Maggie changed my life. I was ready to give up and crawl into a deep well of despair and self-pity. I realized I had a scar, but I could do whatever I set my mind to. It was discussed that I would have a tutor in the fall so I wouldn't drop any further behind in my schooling. On a Saturday at the end of the month, without any notice, Da showed up with two other cars. Men barreled out of two of them, then Da cautiously exited last. He jogged through the sand and skipped up the stairs of the house. 'Get yourselves packed; we are blowing this pop stand.'

"Maggie whispered, 'Praise be to God.'

"Ma smiled from ear to ear. She even got up and had lunch with all of us. Maggie, the woman who pretty much brought me back to life, and her sons drove out of my life that afternoon.

"Da, Ma, and I had a long conversation on the ride back to the city. I told them I understood and had no problem going away to school. I had an inkling of what Da was up against. I knew people were trying to kill our family. I knew Ma was sick, and I knew I could make life somewhat easier for both of them if I went away to school for a while."

William took a long breath.

Elizabeth choked, "Holy Shit." She nearly spat out her food.

Nora was uncertain how she felt. Anger topped the list. She was grappling to keep her life together—only to discover her past was a twisted mess. Her mind was spinning. *How was my Samuel involved? Did Maggie know the connection between the two families?*

Elizabeth's mind was going wild with conspiracies. With a look of total bewilderment Brendan reached for her hand.

William took another long draw from his whiskey glass. His good eye peered over the glass, the other held an empty stare. It was as though he was reaching into the old woman's mind. "I am truly sorry. I realize I should have liberated this tragedy a long time ago, but after such a long time, it seemed like it would cause more damage than anything. As more time passed, more people became connected. Now I'm babbling and getting ahead of myself. As I said, Samuel had no knowledge of who my family was; his family didn't live in our neighborhood or travel in the same circles as mine. Maggie was referred by the hospital. She was a single mom with three children to support who needed the extra money. After that summer, I heard from your da about once a year. Maggie kept in touch with me through letters sent to my school. She knew who we were, but she never mentioned it to me. How could she not know? The last time I saw Samuel was right after he joined the army. I only found out later that you two married. You could say it was a happy coincidence—or the touch of an angel. There was no possible way, even if he knew who I was, that he would know Conrad's family. Knowing you had married into Maggie's family told all of us you were safe. Samuel sent a Christmas card every year. I never forgot Maggie or her kindness. She was a special woman who changed people's lives."

Samuel sent out a Christmas card separate from the rest of the cards Nora sent, and each year, a card arrived from a man in New York. It was always thought to be from an army buddy.

Things got more confusing the more William spoke, like a spider weaving a backward web. Nora let out a loud sigh, and Corazon squeezed her hand.

Luke appeared to be as confused as the rest of the group. Apparently, his dad had not told him the entire story.

William apologized again, "Sweet Jesus, I am screwing this all up. I need to get back to how you ended up living with Thomas and Ida."

OK, those names I recognize. My parents, the ones I remember. Keep fighting the fog.

"I don't have the full story ... only what Da felt he needed to share. After the shooting, he led everyone to believe Noinin was murdered along with Conrad and Eveleen. Mae Moore, Declan's ma and a close family friend, had a business arranging for immigrating families to have jobs and a roof over their heads once they arrived in New York. At that time, you had to have a sponsor before you could come over. Someone had to vouch for you and guarantee you would pay your own way, and if you didn't, the sponsor was responsible. Mae knew a young family, Thomas and Ida Doyle, with a child, Keira, who was very close in age to you." William reached for Nora's hand. "Three older children remained home in Ireland. At my da's request, Mae approached Thomas and Ida. Thomas Doyle was related by marriage to Maureen Donahue, Eveleen's older sister.

Maureen's my aunt, and Eveleen is my mother. Let it sink in. Nora's brain was trying to put everything in its proper place.

William squeezed Nora's hand. "Mae made arrangements for them to take in an orphan child, Nora—Noinin—and raise her as their own. In return, Mae would see that the rest of the family made it to New York. Tom and Ida Doyle were aware that Nora was someone special and had to be protected. They were new to the neighborhood, so the addition of another child wasn't noticed. For everyone's safety, they were sworn to secrecy. When the three older children arrived, Nora was an accepted member of the household. The boys, Bradley and Robert, were given suitable jobs with the family, and Hannah worked in the candy store. Ida was very protective of you; she never let you out of her sight. Ida didn't even allow you to go to school; she was terrified that whoever was after you would find you. She would have never forgiven herself if something happened.

"Children, I realize I've opened Pandora's box. Forgive me. I am exhausted, and you have family to tend to. I promise I will tell you everything I know, but for now, we must end our meeting."

No one wanted to push the poor old man. William had held these secrets for so many years.

Nora's fog-ridden brain felt like mush, and even though she needed to hear all he had to say, she was overpowered by fatigue. Her brain couldn't retain all he had to say, and it needed a chance to rest and absorb it all.

They all agreed to meet in the morning at the pub.

William pulled her crippled hand to his lips and gave it a gentle kiss. "There are many regrets, but the greatest was that you were robbed of your heritage. You deserved to know all the wonderful souls who loved and protected you throughout the years. I will never forgive myself for that."

Nora's voice cracked, "William, you were following your father's wishes. You protected me and my family."

Luke walked the four back to the pub's door, then guided William out through the alley.

They joined the rest of the family in the pub. There was a sense in the room there was something more to this visit than Maureen's funeral. There was a new air of respect. Nora felt numb from all the information William had hurled at her. Her head swirled as she tried to sort out all the names and people William had mentioned. *How had he kept them all straight? This group really needed name tags with a family tree attached to keep them all sorted out.*

All of a sudden, she was ravenous. The four—numb from all that had been poured out to them—ate silently at a table set for the family.

CHAPTER 14

Michael joined Eveleen and Conrad at the stoop, gave Nora a kiss on the top of her red curls, and watched as the family maneuvered themselves into the car. He gave his son, William, a wave of acknowledgment as he stood with his young friends in the glow of the streetlamp. William returned the wave. He was a younger, leaner version of his father. William waited for his mother to exit the apartment building, and then it was time to leave his buddies.

Michael felt his friend had something important to share. He didn't like the idea that he hadn't been included in whatever business Conrad had completed.

The two had been friends long enough for Michael to know when something weighed on his friend's mind. An air of uneasiness surrounded Michael. He and Conrad had been like brothers since they were young boys in Ireland. He could read Conrad. An air of excitement about his business meeting surrounded him, but there was anxiety about it all. The two young men hadn't had a chance to discuss any of it. Michael could see Conrad was anxious, but he was trying to stay calm in front of Eveleen.

Once Conrad, Eveleen, and Nora settled themselves in the car, Michael took one more look at his son in the orange glow. He watched as the youngster moved from under the streetlamp towards his mother who was smoothing her hair at the stoop. Just as he leaned into the driver's seat Conrad let out a high-pitched yelp. "Nora Eveleen, your ma told you to use the pot."

Nora wet herself. The seat between the couple shone dark in the aftermath of the child's accident. Nora was soaked under all her ruffles. Conrad gingerly handed Nora to Eveleen. His arms stretched as far as they reached in an attempt to stay dry as he passed his soggy daughter to his wife. Eveleen's violet-beaded dress and headpiece chattered, and her lightly scented perfume flowed through the air as she attempted to avoid getting soaked. A strand of red hair peeked out from beneath the beads that covered her head. Her green eyes flickered with annoyance, but she wasn't angry. Nora's starched mint green party dress and all its stiff ruffles crunched, and her mop of red curls bounced as Eveleen leaned over and placed Nora on the floorboard between herself and Conrad. Nora started to cry. She looked up at her da, her green eyes magnified by her tears, and whispered, "Da, I love you."

"I love you too, *mo pheata*" (my pet). He couldn't help but smile; Nora and Eveleen were his life. There was no anger for this treasured child. Tonight was the night they would all celebrate a bright new chapter of their lives.

Eveleen whispered as Nora let out a loud sob, "You should have gone potty when you had the chance. It's all right, Noinin. We'll go upstairs and have Aunt Maureen get you clean clothes. I know it was an accident, but next time, please go when I ask you to go."

Eveleen slid to reach for the handle and said, "Give

me just a minute, my—" Without warning, rapid popping sounds silenced her words.

Nora stiffened on the floor, frozen, her eyes fixed on her parents.

Michael knew exactly what the noise was. Before he was able to react, a hot poker slashed into his shoulder. The impact of the red-hot round spun his body. It slammed him fiercely into the steering wheel of the Chevrolet as bullets tore through it. He listened helplessly to the mind-numbing sound of bullets as they ripped into his friends trapped in the back seat. The car jerked and creaked with each deafening rip. All he could do was lean over in the seat. He pressed his aching body away from the door and prayed they would survive the assault. His shoulder throbbed with searing pain, but he was powerless to reach into his jacket to retrieve his gun. He was angry at himself for not being prepared. *What sort of animal attacks a family this way?*

Michael heard a sickening thump and a shallow gasp from the back seat. In less than a minute, it was agonizingly quiet. There was no sound from the back seat. The car finally stopped jerking. Dust from the onslaught and wool fiber from the shredded seats settled on the floorboard. Michael choked as the dust and wool fibers packed his nostrils and burned his eyes. Coughing, he sluggishly tried to drag himself from the car. He was furious that he couldn't pull himself from the car to return fire and put up some type of defense. The windows were shattered, and the door was jammed shut by the barrage. He slammed his throbbing shoulder into the door and stumbled out of the car.

His body ached like he had been digging ditches all day with a hundred-pound shovel, and his stomach rolled as though he was adrift during a storm at sea. An unfamiliar groan came from his throat as he painfully rolled his pulsating frame out of the shattered remnants of the car and fumbled to draw his gun. It was too late. Whoever was responsible for the bloody ambush had escaped.

Maureen was at his side in an instant. She was crying hysterically. "Michael, are Conrad and Eveleen all right? The baby … where's the baby? Are you hurt? Can you see?"

Michael moaned, gave Maureen a wave of his hand, and pulled off his jacket. Using the car to steady himself, he dropped his jacket on the hood. His body ached, his mind moved in slow motion, and his eyes were blurry. Thoughts flew through his mind; his first responsibility was to his best friend and family. As he opened the car door, his heart dropped. His stomach churned like curdling milk.

Conrad was in a bloody, contorted pile, slouched halfway in the seat and hunched over on Eveleen who lay rolled in a ball on the floorboard. Eveleen's beaded headpiece slipped unnoticed into the gutter with a quiet slap. Michael was overcome by emotion, anger, and pain. His shoulder throbbed. He felt his heart in his throat, and his airway was blocked. An attempted deep breath to clear his airway was halted by a faint whimper. He gently moved Conrad, which enabled him to lift Eveleen onto the seat. Nora was entangled in Eveleen's twisted legs, huddled in a blood-soaked pile on the floorboard.

He groaned with pain as he squatted down to check her wounds. She was drenched in her mother's blood, shaking with fear, but physically uninjured. He backed away from the horrendous carnage in an attempt to regain his composure. With no thought of his pain, he gingerly pulled his jacket from the hood of the car, wrapped it around the child, and lifted her from the floorboard. Her body was rigid, frozen with fear. The youngster who was normally in constant motion along with nonstop conversation was eerily silent.

"Dear Mary, mother of God, dear God, what kind of bastard could do such a thing? I swear to you, child, they will pay for what they have done. I will see that you are safe as long as you live, Noinin." Michael whispered to Nora as he pulled her close wrapping her tiny motionless body in his overcoat. Folding it as though it was empty, he placed Nora and the jacket over Maureen's arms. "Take my jacket through the alley to Mae Moore's. Nora died with her parents. Do you understand what I am saying to you? She is dead." Michael's eyes pierced Maureen's tearful gaze. "Tell Mae the child is dead. She will know what to do. Let her know I will be by later."

Michael turned his attention to his dead friends. The storm of bullets had been too much for their bodies to endure. As the suffocating wool and dirt settled, a familiar fresh scent drifted through the air. It was the last scent of Eveleen. The aroma was stifled by the grotesque death scene. The twisted remains appeared almost in an embrace after he moved them to retrieve their child. Michael's emotions swelled in his chest, but he had to remain in control.

His thoughts were interrupted by sharp wailing screams, like the sound of a gravely injured kitten. He realized the cry was from Tara. She was on her knees in the street, hovering over a body. William's bloodied body was sprawled next to her in a small, dark puddle. The street was littered with Tara's shoes along with other belongings tossed during her mad dash to her son's side. The teen had been hit in the face during the barrage.

Michael rushed to his only child. The bullet had ripped through William's cheek, brutally damaging his eye. He tried to hide his terror at the sight of his son's wounds. "Be strong, *mo mhac.* (my son), I know it hurts like hell. I am with you, son. Stay with me. Do you hear me, son? Stay with me!"

The youngster's body went limp. The pain was too much, he lost consciousness. The bullet created a slicing gouge from William's left cheek tearing upward slicing through his eye, taking the top edge of his ear upon exit. An accidental ricochet? Blood ran down from the boy's ear into what remained of his eye socket. The flow continued from the gaping crevice on his face into his open mouth, choking off his air.

Michael rolled his unconscious son onto his side to allow him to breathe. Never leaving his son's side, he turned to the rest of the boys. "I need all of you to pay attention! Stephen, go get Sullivan and Flannery, tell them what has happened. Have them gather the family together and meet me at Cara Dílis. I'll be there once William is taken care of. Conrad, Eveleen, and the baby are all dead. If anyone asks, you saw their bodies—but you didn't see the shooters."

Michael made sure Tara had no injuries. The blood on her clothing belonged to William.

Declan Moore pushed through the crowd. He was not much older than William, but he was mature beyond his years. Mae Moore's son had been at Conrad and Michael's side since he was about ten. He was forced to grow up fast after his father was killed while working on the docks.

The rail-thin kid's deep brown eyes flashed with excitement whenever Michael or Conrad spoke to him. He had a head full of curly brown hair that overwhelmed his face. His brown curls fell into his eyes as he gathered Tara's shoes and other belongings, and then ran to Michael's side. He always appeared when he was needed.

Michael's thoughts shifted to who was responsible for such a cold-blooded massacre. He and Conrad were not part of any of the city's gangs. The North Side gang didn't bother with them since the two weren't considered competition. The Italians were too busy with the North Side to bother with two nobodies who ran their business on the fringes without interfering with anyone else's profits. Conrad and Michael had no grand business ventures or political schemes.

Michael still cradling William pulled at Declan's pant leg. "Run and get Flanagan, the beat cop. I need to talk to him right now. After I leave, stay with the car and do not let anyone but Flanagan near it."

The ambulance arrived, a pillow was placed under William's drooping head.

Declan put his hand under Michael's good shoulder and helped him to his feet.

He acknowledged Michael's request, gave his head a shake to get the hair out of his eyes then rushed down the street to find Flanagan.

He nearly collided with Flanagan as the cop rushed in the direction of the carnage.

Through his pain and grief, Michael continued to organize his thoughts and concentrate on what he had to do. His eyes darted wildly through the crowd as he searched for trustworthy men. "Patrick, make sure everyone is aware of what happened here tonight. We all need to be extremely cautious. Don't let anyone in the neighborhood who doesn't belong."

The street overflowed with people. The entire neighborhood came out of their apartments. Many were in tears, and some were on their knees in prayer. An overwhelming sadness engulfed the neighborhood. The hum of voices and crying filled the night air.

Michael lowered his voice to a whisper, "Flanagan, I need you to take care of something for me. I need you to make sure the coroner understands there is also a dead child in the car. Do you understand?"

"Yes," Flanagan choked in a matching whisper. "It won't be a problem. Let me know what else you need. Anything you need, I am here. You and Conrad have always been there for all of us. Don't worry. Take care of your family. I will take care of Conrad and his family." Flanagan touched Michael's arm.

Michael cringed with pain and pulled away from Flanagan's touch. He ignored his own injuries. "I am going to the hospital with William. I'll be back as soon as I can. We'll meet later at Cara Dílis with the rest of the family."

The shrieking of the ambulance's siren rang in Michael's ears as William was taken away. He grabbed some blankets from one of the neighbors and took them to the bullet-riddled car. Painstakingly he covered Conrad and Eveleen. Silently he made them a solemn vow to protect their treasured child and find the responsible cold-blooded bastards.

Declan gathered more blankets. He and Michael placed them in a small pile under the blankets that covered his friends. Any onlooker would think there was another body beside the couple. Several regulars from the back of Cara Dílis surrounded Michael offering help.

He grabbed Jerry, a tall, solid blond man about his age, who had worked for the two partners since they purchased Cara Dílis. He was known for his persuasive personality and loyalty.

"Jerry, get a hold of Murphy at the funeral home. Let him know all the bodies are going to his mortuary. I will contact him about the arrangements. Don't talk to anyone else until I get back. Shit, man. I don't have a car. I need a car to get back and forth. I can't get into a cab looking like this."

Jerry held Michael by his forearm as he placed a key in Michael's hand. "Take mine. It is in the alley next to Cara Dílis."

"Where is Stephen?" Michael spat as he feverously surveyed the crowd on the street until he found the man.

"Please, my friend, I need you to come with me to the hospital to watch over Tara and William. I will send someone to relieve you later. Right now, I need someone I can trust at my son's side."

Stephen, a middle-aged balding man, nodded in agreement. He gave Michael a slight hug which caused him to contort.

Michael's entire arm—from shoulder to wrist—was soaked with his own blood. He continued to ignore his wounds. On the way to the hospital, he insisted on driving—even though Stephen tried to get in the driver's seat. Michael's mind raced as he drove. *What if they were trying to kill all of us? Was William being hit an accident? If they had killed Noinin, William, Tara, and me, there would be no one left with a direct connection to our business. Was it mere luck that Tara wasn't shot? Who would commit such a vile act? Was it the Italians? We have stood by our arrangement. They can be brutal, but this kind of unwarranted bloodshed is beyond them. It's beyond any sane person.*

He needed to protect his family. He would send them to the shore as soon as William was strong enough to travel. He knew his son would survive and recover. He would not have it any other way. The thought that another family would violently attack them weighed heavily on his mind. He knew Conrad had great plans. Had he stepped on someone's toes in his attempt to see his plan come to light? Had the people he was dealing with decided that his plan was too good for them to pass up? Why hadn't his best friend included him?

Conrad was a diplomat; his personality never left anyone with the impression that he was not totally true to his word. His friend was the most honest, forthcoming person Michael had ever met. This was the only time the two of them hadn't discussed a business agreement. Michael hadn't pressed the issue before the morning meeting as Conrad was wound as tight as a Swiss pocket watch and Michael had to go to Atlantic City to pick up more product. Was he aware he was swimming in dangerous waters?

When Michael arrived at the hospital, Tara was sobbing in the hallway. Her face was buried in her hands, her nails were encrusted with her son's blood, and her auburn hair was sticky with his blood from cradling her head in her hands. William would survive, but his eye was destroyed by the bullet. It took a great many stitches to close the wound on his face. He would have a disfiguring scar. A glass eye would be inserted once the wound healed in the hopes of giving William a more normal look, in other words a less freakish look.

Michael placed his hand on Tara's back and said, "Tara, William and I are both alive. That is more than we can say for Conrad, Eveleen, and the baby."

In her fear and despair, she had forgotten what the rest of them had been through. Tara broke down in loud sobs that echoed in the empty hallway.

Michael's throat closed as he attempted to hold in his own grief. He wanted to ease her anguish and tell her that Noinin was safe, but this was not the time or place. She would have too many questions. He would explain the toddler's situation, but he would wait until they were alone—after she and William were in a safe place.

Tara was so engrossed in her own grief she had not lifted her head until after her husband spoke. When she did she was jolted to see his arm soaked in blood, "Dear God, Mickey. You're bleeding. Sweet Jesus, you've been shot as well."

Michael had ignored the pain in his shoulder, but now that he had a moment to reflect, it throbbed with each beat of his heart. Without a word to Michael or even making eye contact, a young doctor cleaned the gaping wound and stitched it shut.

William's room was cold and dark. A single dim gray light burned above him. His head was wrapped in gauze, and the left side oozed blood. He was motionless in the bed. He looked so small—not the lanky, vibrant soul who had nodded at his da's acknowledgment just an hour earlier.

Tara sat silently in the darkness holding her son's hand.

She had lost her dearest friend along with her entire family in a violent barrage. Her own family barely escaped.

Michael posted Stephen at the door of William's room. Assuring himself they were safe, he headed back to the neighborhood. He had to talk to Tara about going upstate, out of harm's way, on his next visit to the hospital. Noinin had to be moved to a safe place, close by, afterward he would meet the men at Cara Dílis.

He drove in silence back to the neighborhood. As he considered his next steps, he rubbed his shoulder and let out a groan. He was concerned he couldn't trust everyone who gathered in the back room of Cara Dílis. He had to keep a tight circle of those he could trust. Noinin was to remain dead for her safety. Maureen, Declan, Flanagan, the coroner, and the mortician were the only ones aware the toddler had survived. They had no reason to divulge that information. The child had to blend into another family and become anonymous.

Mae Moore, a devoted friend helped immigrating Irish families get settled in the city. She had to place Noinin with a trusted family, new to the neighborhood, fresh off the ship. That way, an additional family member would not be questioned. They were only to be told she was an orphan in need of a family. Michael would make sure they had jobs and that the family stayed in the neighborhood to be certain Noinin remained safe.

It was unfathomable why anyone would butcher his friends. He knew Conrad had met with someone earlier in the day about the family's future. It was a "simple sale," but he didn't want to talk about it. He didn't want too many people to know what he was up to in case it fell through.

That worried Michael. He had no idea what had happened at Conrad's meeting. He knew Conrad was working on purchasing land with railroad access, but it was just a plan until that morning. They never had an opportunity to discuss it. Michael had no idea who his partner met with. Both men knew Prohibition would not last, but while it did, the two would save enough money to invest in their future. Conrad dreamed of a move West. He had heard about a hotel and possible casino that was being developed in a small desert town in Nevada. He had written letters of inquiry about plots of land. The excitement in his voice was contagious: "This place is booming with gambling and drinking—even though it is illegal. They are working on making gambling legal throughout the state. Can you imagine what it will be like if they legalize gambling out there? It will make Atlantic City a ghost town. It is only a matter of time before *Volstead* is overturned. We must hold out and save our money. We will have our own piece of paradise. Paradise, Michael. It will be paradise."

Conrad's words burned in Michael's ears. Not knowing who Conrad had met left a hot, pulsating knot in the pit of Michael's stomach. He had no idea where to begin. He couldn't help but think the meeting and the people involved were responsible for Conrad and Eveleen's murders. Conrad hadn't had a chance to tell Michael anything about what had transpired that day. He assured Michael it would all be clear at dinner.

Michael was anxious about waiting until dinner. They were dining in Brooklyn at Peter Luger's. Michael usually jumped at a chance to have steak at Luger's, but he would have eaten hot spuds off a cart if it meant saving Conrad and Eveleen. Michael had a gut feeling that if he knew what had transpired at the meeting, he could easily track down the scum who had ambushed them. He feared he would never know. He wished he had pressed Conrad for information about the meeting. He couldn't avoid the thought that if he had more information, he would have been more attentive out on the street. Conrad wanted to make a formal announcement at dinner. That was one of the many things Michael enjoyed about Conrad—he made even the smallest event a celebration.

Michael had to make sure the rest of the family didn't fly off the handle and try to seek revenge. It was no secret he would be looking for those responsible, but he wanted them alive. He needed answers.

Michael entered Cara Dílis through the alleyway to find it filled with all the men he had sent for. He chose his words carefully as he looked around the room. The men were all ready for a fight. It was the consensus that the hit was the Italians. Michael was well aware the family would never survive a war with the Italians; they were larger and accustomed to killing rivals. He and Conrad operated a family business. The use of force was a last resort. Michael knew they would be targeted if he didn't show he could take charge, and he wasn't convinced this was a hit by a rival family.

"*Mo chairde* (my friends), we must tread softly. There is no reason for us to be hit by another family. Conrad and I have been very generous with all the families, and we have agreements with the Italians. There is no need for them to do such a gruesome thing. Our anger will be directed at the specific men who pulled the triggers after, and only after, we find out who hired them. When we find out who set this in motion, we will rain hell's fire on all of them with no restraint. I guarantee it. That will take patience along with our full attention. There will be a private funeral for the family—no outsiders in the neighborhood. We are all feeling anger and sadness, but we must continue. In honor of Conrad, we must show everyone our family is solid. We all loved Conrad, but we are not one man. We are a community, and we will go on. Trust me … we'll grieve and then get vengeance on the bastards who did this. Keep your eyes and ears open—and your mouths shut—and listen for any hint of who these bastards are. Spread the word in the neighborhood. Everyone needs to be aware of their surroundings and watch for anything out of the ordinary. I want all of you to travel in teams of two. Jerry, you are with me since I don't have a car. No one is to be out alone until we find out what the hell is going on. That is all I have for the moment. We will meet again once the funeral date is set."

As Michael left Cara Dílis, the men quietly talked among themselves. They were all in shock from the evening's events, but they were willing to follow Michael's lead. Michael headed to Mae Moore's. His thoughts wandered as he walked through the dark alleys. He couldn't remember a time when Conrad wasn't by his side. They had been like brothers since their childhood in Ireland.

CHAPTER 15

Conrad's father, William, had taken Michael in after finding him starving in his family's cottage next to his dead ma.

William never went into detail about the gruesomeness he found at the cottage. He only told the boys that he found Michael in the arms of his dead ma. The potato blight had wiped out William's crop, and left him scavenging for food. He was searching for food for his family when he came across the cottage. The cottage appeared abandoned; the white stone walls were crumbling, and the roof had fallen in on one side. As he approached the cottage, the smell of rotting potatoes hung thick in the air. His horse snorted and came to a jerking stop. "Come along, ole girl."

The horse stood firm, snorting while shaking her huge head. When William tried to press the horse forward, she whipped her head back in reply, smacking William in the face. The motion tossed him backwards off her back. He hit the ground with a hard, breath-taking gasp. As he inhaled deeply, in an attempt to refill his aching lungs, his nostrils filled with the wretched smell of death. Every inch of his body responded to the horrid smell. William pulled himself up, yanked his neck scarf over his face and slowly moved toward the cottage. At the door, he heard a soft wail, like a baby bird abandoned after falling from its nest. He tried to locate the sound. It came from inside the cottage. He wasn't eager to enter. The cottage was silent—with the exception of the occasional wail.

He followed the gasping wail into the darkness and overbearing stench. William found an infant resting in its ma's arms. Cries were merely the movement of air escaping through its dried lips, making the wail that had alerted William. The stench overwhelmed him. He ran to a corner of the cottage to vomit. He composed himself and returned to the child and its very dead ma. As William pulled the infant from its ma's arms, a Bible fell to the floor. He picked up both the child and the Bible and gingerly moved outside.

The smell of the potatoes rotting in the field was pleasant compared to the vile smell inside the cottage. All William had to offer the child was a bit of bread and some water. He wrapped the child and placed it under a tree. He dug a hole with tools he found near the cottage. He carefully wrapped the woman in bed linens and placed her gently in the hole. He buried her, he whispered as he patted the mound, "Godspeed your way to heaven. I'll give your baby the best home I can."

He didn't think the child would survive, but he couldn't leave it to die alone. William called the child *Marthanóir* (survivor). "Well, Marthanóir, it looks like you are riding with me."

William built a small fire with whatever he could find. The stench was too overwhelming to sleep in the cottage. As he sat by the fire, he was haunted by the thought that this poor child would not last the night. He pulled the child close as he picked up the Bible. Inside the front cover of the

Bible was the child's name: Michael Byrne. His ma was Rose. His da, Arthur, had left his wife and child to fend for themselves after falling ill and dying last winter. He read the Bible until he drifted off to sleep.

William awoke in the early morning; the child was silent. He was prepared to bury the child next to his ma. As he lifted the bundle, the child wiggled in his arms. He wasn't strong enough to cry, but he was still alive.

"Marthanóir, Michael, this is for sure." William rode home, checking on the child every few minutes. He had bound Michael close to his chest so he could feel the infant's chest expanding as he breathed.

Conrad had wondered once to his da if Michael's ordeal of being left to starve next to his dead ma had an impact on his emotions and how he viewed life. Conrad couldn't believe—no matter his age—living through being in his ma's arms as she starved to death, and awaiting the same fate, would not have altered his worldview. William believed Conrad was right. Michael saw the world through the eyes of someone who cheated death. Marthanóir tested fate with his temper.

William encouraged the young men to leave Ireland, to make a new life away from farming. The British land policies and the potato famine had impoverished most of the Irish.

Although born near the end of the famine, the two young men were raised under the devastating effects that blanketed the farmlands of Ireland. William believed the British were deliberately destroying Ireland and wouldn't be happy until all the Irish were dead and fertilizing the ground.

CHAPTER 16

Michael was lost in his memory of the warm sunny day the two scruffy young men landed at Ellis Island with nothing but the clothes on their backs. A single duffel between them held all their possessions. Two adventurous young men made their way to New York "in pursuit of their fortune," as Conrad often said. Conrad was the peacekeeper of the two. Michael's poker hot temper was kept in check by Conrad's calm logic. Conrad often broke up the brawls Michael started. Both came out with cuts and bruises, but Conrad usually brought things to a peaceful end.

Michael remembered when they first crossed paths with Dan Malone. Michael's fiery temper started a clash in a pub, which Conrad was unable to gain control of before the two were tossed into the gutter. Michael dropped like a rock at Malone's feet. Malone was forced to leap backward to avoid being hurled to the ground. The battered young man came up swearing and spitting blood.

Dan, without uttering a single word, calmly pulled a crisp white handkerchief from his breast pocket and handed it to the bloodied youth. Although leery of this well-dressed stranger, he took the handkerchief and wiped the blood from his face. Dan Malone was slightly built, his light brown hair was combed to perfection under his gray hat. It remained in place even when he removed his hat. His hat and pinstriped suit were impeccably matched.

Michael took note of the glow of his immaculately shined shoes as he picked himself up from the gutter.

Dan's lips were pressed tightly together as though he was straining to control his temper. He spoke sarcastically, "Are you boys always this eager to leave a pub? Are you simply hooligans looking for trouble or have you any usable skills?"

Conrad recognized the two were in the presence of someone important. The man's stature was slight, but he radiated strength and power. "It was a difference of opinion, sir. Yes, we do have other talents. I am Conrad Quinn. This is my partner, Michael Byrne. We are new to the city and willing to work hard for a day's wage."

Dan took a chance on them even though they were inexperienced, wild, and young. Their energy impressed him. He took in the two live wires and gave them jobs. The conflicting personalities intrigued him; if they could balance Michael's temper with Conrad's diplomacy, there was nothing they couldn't accomplish.

Malone was a leader in the Irish community. He didn't have political aspirations or the political connections of Enoch (Nucky) Johnson, a powerful leader in Atlantic City. He cared about the poor of the neighborhood. He watched out for friends in need. Dan didn't use his influence to sway votes or gain favors from gangsters or politicians. Dan wanted loyalty for the kindness to his friends. If he needed a favor in return, then so be it. He also expected those he cared for to pass the favor on to the less fortunate.

Michael always felt that Dan saw a lot of himself in

the two young men when he took them under his wing. Malone had just started to come into his own when the two stumbled into him. He was not a big man, by any means, but his personality made him a giant. Malone dressed elegantly—even as a very young man—he always wore a suit with a silk tie, spats, a carnation in his lapel, and a derby. His piercing steel gray eyes could reflect kindness or be as sharp as knives.

Michael had to take control of the family and his emotions. Every fiber of his being wanted to explode on someone, but quiet strength had to prevail in order for the family to survive. His white-hot temper had to be suppressed for now. This was the only way to maintain control of the family. He needed strength against those who would use Conrad's death as an opportunity to take over their business. An ugly gut feeling swirled through the grief. Strangers murdered Conrad and Eveleen. Conrad had no enemies. That gut feeling gave him a better understanding of why Dan Malone ran his organization the way he did—and why he taught his apprentices to run their organization in the same manner.

We have no enemies—who would do this? That thought filled every corner of his tortured mind. His head throbbed, and acid burned a huge hole in his stomach. How could one find an enemy that didn't exist? There would be no rest until he had Noinin settled in a safe place.

His pain-ridden arm tapped quietly on Mae's door.

CHAPTER 17

Mae Moore was a petite woman in her early thirties, with a slow to appear sparkling smile, large black eyes, and porcelain white skin. Widow's black matronly styled clothing added years to her appearance. Her long sleeves were usually pulled up above the elbows, and a black mid-calf skirt covered heavy black stockings. Shiny pitch-black hair was pulled back at the nape of her neck in a crisscross bun.

Mae and her husband, James, arrived in New York among the many other desperate Irish families who fled the horrendous conditions that followed the potato famine. Mae was married at fifteen. Declan, her son was born a year later. Mae and James planned on building a glorious new life together with their son. They often spoke of saving enough money to buy a farm. James worked long hours on the docks to save for their farm. That dream was hijacked when he was crushed to death by a load of crates that toppled over. She was widowed at twenty. With no source of income, she was left alone to raise a young son just a few years after arriving in New York.

Mae was determined to take care of her son at all costs. The resolute young widow scrubbed floors to keep food on the table and a roof over their heads. Her hands were red and raw from scrubbing floors. Life in the city was a daily struggle; some days, there was only enough food for her son. The exhausted widow sat with her son while the youngster ate, telling him she had eaten while she cooked his meal. Although lacking a formal education, she was a shrewdly smart young woman who could read and write. After the loss of her beloved James, she was determined to make a good life for her son—no matter how hard the work or how much the personal sacrifice. There was no room for failure. James would be honored by her success. As a widow, she was somewhat better off than a single woman. A single woman was expected to marry and raise a family. A widow had more leeway.

Family members in Ireland wrote to her about traveling to New York. The young widow impressed upon all of them the need for a steady income, especially during hard times. After many letters, the realization materialized that guiding a family member to employment in the city could help them escape British tyranny while it provided she and Declan an income. In the beginning, there was a nagging apprehension that it couldn't be done without a man's involvement. Quietly, she helped family and friends find their way to the city. Newcomers were directed to places where they could find work. She was extremely selective; she couldn't have anyone who would smear her name. That's when her ledger began. It documented those corresponded with, their skills, and her personal thoughts about the individuals. Noted were how many members were in each family, were they honest, could they read and write, did they have any troublesome vices like gambling or heavy drinking, and were they willing to work hard every day? The ledger also tracked their progress once they arrived and found jobs. Mae continued to scrub floors and clean wherever she could find work.

One of the places she cleaned was a club/brothel whose proprietor was a woman named Garnet. Mae doubted that was actually her given name, but she never questioned it. Garnet suited her.

CHAPTER 18

Garnet, a tough, aloof blonde, never let anyone get too close. It was all business around the club. Her given name, Brigid, meant power, vigor, and virtue, which totally suited her personality.

Brigid arrived from Ireland as a nanny for a young family. The husband, Bryan, came from a wealthy family, taught school, and was eager to escape the tyranny of the British. He had yearned for the excitement of a new country and all it had to offer. Brigid took care of the family's two young children. She had full responsibility for the children along with being expected to cook and clean. The young woman didn't mind the work. She was happy to be in a household with plenty of food and a warm bed. There was no second thought when the family offered to bring her to New York.

Brigid was an orphan with nothing that bound her to Ireland. She was endowed with a full figure, which was kept covered with layers of loose-fitting clothing. Long brown hair twisted into a large bun covered the entire back of her head, and her green eyes could melt ice with the warmth that they held.

The first year in the city went well. She worked hard

as though the household was her own. Meals were served, house cleaned, and children were tended to. Each night, she went to bed exhausted but fulfilled. During the holiday season, at the end of the second year, the wife, Erin, required Brigid to plan a holiday dinner for several of the family's friends, including Bryan's boss. The party went off without a hitch; decorations, the meal, and even the music were all planned by Brigid. She entertained the children while the guests were served a delicious meal that Brigid had planned, along with supervising all the preparations. It was all part of her job and nothing more than what her employer had requested. Bryan and Erin paid for everything, and Brigid felt the praise belonged to them.

After all the guests had left and the party cleanup was completed, she took one last peek at the children in their beds and headed to her room. Bryan and Erin's voices echoed through the wall. It was obvious she was angry about something. Their voices were muffled, but as they got louder, Brigid heard her name. After a few more minutes, there was a moment of calm. Brigid heard Bryan call his wife a fool. He snorted that she was cutting off her nose to spite her face. She had no idea what her foolish jealousy was going to cost the entire family. Then there was complete silence. Brigid dozed off, satisfied with a job well done.

In the morning, Brigid dressed and went to the children's room as she did every morning. The children were not in their room. Brigid knew she had fallen into a deep sleep, but how did she not hear the children stirring in their room? She scrambled down the stairs in a panic, she stopped short on the last step. Bryan was at the bottom of the staircase. His face was squeezed into a hard sneer. With his teeth pressed into his bottom lip, he spoke, "Brigid, we have a problem. Erin feels you have too much control over our household and family."

"Sir, I am so sorry. I only mean to please you all. I'll do better." Brigid tried not to break down.

"It isn't you, child. It is my wife. She's a jealous fool who can't see your wonderful accomplishments—only her failures. Last evening was delightful. She knows it was all your doing. Everyone did. She tried to take credit, but our friends called her out, telling her that you were the mistress of the house. She should be grateful to have you. Unable to just agree and be thankful, it was taken as an insult. She wants you out of the house today. I am deeply sorry for you and for my family. I don't know what we will do without you."

Brigid took a deep breath as she grabbed the stair handrail. What would she do? Where would she go? Her biggest concern was the children. "Where are the children? May I at least let them know I will miss them and that I will always love them like my own?"

"Erin took them to the park. She is trying to avoid the misery she has caused all of us. Here is some money to hold you over." Bryan handed Brigid an envelope, but he was unable to look her in the eye. He pointed a shaking finger to a valise by the door. "Please take that bag for your things. Please know how sorry I am. I have no control over my own house."

Brigid packed what little she had and left the house forever.

Bryan hid—like a scared mouse—in his study until she was gone.

Brigid swore an oath from that day forward to never rely on anyone and to trust only herself. Without a reference from the family, she was unable to find another position as a nanny.

Even being very frugal, her money didn't last long enough for her to find a sustaining job. Brigid prayed for a job, but nothing appeared. When the money ran out, she was locked out of her room at the boarding house. The innocent young woman became very cynical. She trusted no one and felt her goodness was being punished. Brigid was at the end of her rope when she first came across Dan Malone. Sickened by desperation and hunger—and oblivious of her surroundings—she stood shivering in front of his club. She fell into him as he entered the door.

CHAPTER 19

Brigid straightened her back and uttered, "I'm so sorry, sir. I meant no disrespect."

Dan looked at the young woman and said, "Would a warm meal make you feel better, kid?"

"Sir, I would be most grateful, but I can't accept." Brigid was holding to her oath to be self-reliant.

"Kid, it's just a warm meal, nothing more. My name is Malone, Dan Malone."

"Mr. Malone, it has been a while since I've had a warm meal. I accept."

There was no argument; she was too weak with hunger.

Dan opened the door for Brigid. "Let's get you to the kitchen and out of the cold."

The warmth of the club surrounded her, her skin began to sting as her body began to adjust. The club was elegant; crystal chandeliers stretched out from the ceiling like ballet dancers gliding through the air, tile floors shone like glass, and the mahogany walls reflected the glow of the chandeliers. Music could be heard, and laughter came from an adjacent room. All this was seen through a fog of hunger and a shivering body.

Dan waved to a man in a red and black jacket. "Teddy,

take this young lady to the kitchen. Get her a meal and warmer coat.

"My name is Brigid. I appreciate your kindness. I won't be any trouble, sir." Brigid coughed.

She was amazed at the number of people working in the kitchen, both cooking and cleaning. The noise of the pans and the crackling and sizzling of food as it cooked echoed in her ears, and marvelous smells filled her nostrils. It had never crossed her mind that she could work in a kitchen. In the back of her mind, she thought it would be wonderful to run such a lovely club. Brigid ate until her stomach wouldn't hold any more. She was ecstatic to have an overcoat. She stuffed the pockets with whatever would fit, for later. Exhausted, she lingered in the back of the kitchen for as long as allowed. There was nowhere to go. One of the kitchen helpers told her about a community church group that offered shelter for those in grim situations.

She needed work; at this point, it could be any kind of work. Pride had to take a back seat to food and a warm bed. She was not too proud to accept a bit of charity from a church group to get herself back together. Her better judgment was outweighed by desperation. What appeared to be a caring church group home that offered a bath, and a warm cot was nothing more than a flophouse used by those with no other options. It was an old house converted into separate sections by blankets hung from the ceiling. It was filled with makeshift mattresses and bedding strewn on the floor, with only one bath. There was barely walking room between the mattresses.

As Brigid regained her strength, reality slapped her. There was no charitable group—only predators who preyed on the destitute and sick. Residents were expected to work off the "charity." The women were prisoners used by men who came to the building for a good time. Bathing was once a week, food was once a day. Most of the young woman's waking hours were spent in the "lounge." It was where the men chose their women. It was more akin to a meat market. The women lined up in their underwear, and men grabbed and poked until they found something they liked.

The shelter was beneath any whorehouse, and it habitually attracted clients that whorehouses refused: the abusers, the sadistic scum of the earth, and the truly sick bastards who entertained themselves by beating women. There were a few who came to the shelter because they couldn't chance being seen in a whorehouse.

Brigid did what she was ordered to do. She became numb to what her days consisted of. The fat, sweaty bodies hovered over her. Their stench and foul breath seeped into her pores. At the end of her day, she was allowed to wash up before she returned to her sleeping area. Any money she earned was given to the shelter to pay for her room and board.

Near her breaking point, she was chosen by Victor. He looked extremely out of place: sober, middle-aged, with neatly combed thick blond hair. His blue eyes didn't make contact with Brigid at first. He was clean-shaven and seemed somewhat shy. She learned he was a pastor. The shelter offered anonymity along with an escape from his dull life. Brigid wasn't sure how she felt about Victor. He used her, which helped those who held her captive. Each time Victor came, he chose Brigid. She didn't mind since he was always clean, didn't smell of booze or cigars, and didn't beat her. He made the shelter somewhat tolerable.

After a few visits, he began talking to Brigid about her life. He questioned her about her future,

"Victor, this is my present and my future. I have no way out of this place. I will die here. I just hope it's soon." Brigid whispered solemnly. She hung her head as her tears welled up.

Victor lifted her face and looked deep into her eyes. "Don't speak that way. Death is not the answer." He put a couple of dollars in her hand and turned his back to her. "I am not a horrible man. I have needs. I am not strong enough to fix your tragic life."

Her clothes had been taken away from her, but she had hidden her overcoat between some floorboards. After she left the lounge, when no one was around, Brigid hid the money in her overcoat. The thought of never seeing Victor again sent a wave of nausea through her.

Alone at night, she listened to the sounds of the building. For hours, she listened to rats scurrying along the rafters and the occasional weak cry from someone attacked by rats. The building's constant dampness crept into her bones. The dank smell of the place percolated its way deep into her nostrils. It was wretched: sweat, urine, and the unidentifiable. She thought the smell would ooze into her brain. At night, Brigid prayed. "Mary, Mother of God, please get me out of this horrid place."

She was lost and felt sadness beyond anything she had ever felt. Had even the Virgin Mary forsaken her to rot in this hellhole?

She was stunned when Victor called out for her the next

week. In her hopelessness, she had misunderstood what he meant. Brigid realized prayer wasn't suddenly going to rescue her; no doubt, prayer had sent her Victor and strength. He couldn't rescue her or be part of her life outside the shelter, but he could give her the resources and confidence to rescue herself. Victor became a weekly visitor. At the end of their time together, he left several dollars for her to keep. They continued this way for many months until the young woman felt she had enough money. The confidence and the money would be used to liberate herself.

She waited for Victor to return for his regular visit. She shared her escape plan. Once she left the shelter it would be impossible to contact one another. After they had tender relations, he held her close. It was insane that in this hellhole, a man of faith—who betrayed that faith—was the answer to her prayers. She listened to his heartbeat on the small bed. "Victor, thank you doesn't seem to be enough. You have saved my life." She gently rubbed her hand up and down his arm.

Victor gave her a weak smile as she kissed him for the final time. How could she feel both happy and sad at the same moment? He left as he had done so many times before. Brigid washed up as usual and went back to her bedding area.

The place was eerily quiet an hour or so before dawn. She had listened for nearly a week to be sure there was no one to stop her. The overcoat was slowly pulled from the floor, money was pushed deep into the pockets. Revitalized, she started toward the door. A few gentle steps at a time, stopping each time the floor creaked, or someone rustled in their bedding. Drunks passed out on the floor were cautiously dodged. She gingerly tiptoed through filthy mattresses. until she reached the doorway. At one point, a young woman awoke and grabbed her leg, then with a frail smile, she let go. Her hands trembled, terrified someone would catch her and return her to hell. Fear had to be kept under control.

Once safely outside the building, she took a deep, energized breath of fresh air. She acknowledged the fact that she would do whatever it took to survive and would never look back. Buttoning the overcoat, she pushed the money deeper into the pockets.

Brigid found a nearby wigmaker. It was apparent the shop got a lot of business from women in similar situations. It was undesirable for women to have short hair, but many socialites kept wigs so they could wear the new modern style yet remain within the social norm. Acutely aware there was no time or place to take proper care of so much hair, the young woman justified selling it. The money it brought was essential. The wigmaker was more than happy to buy her long brown hair. He watched as the long hair fell loose, resting with a gentle swing at her waist. That was one thing the shelter allowed. She had to appear presentable, and shiny, brushed hair was needed. He took one generous handful of hair, pulled it together, and snipped it at the nape of Brigid's neck. The sound of the scissors slicing through her hair and the metal blade touching her skin sent a cold chill down her spine. It was the last connection to who she used to be. After he took the huge wad of hair, Brigid tossed her head and ran her hand through her short locks. He paid Brigid then wrapped the thick rope of hair in a sheet of paper for safekeeping. Brigid was dead, and Garnet was born.

CHAPTER 20

Garnet's attire was in stark contrast to the interior of The Bad Penny and the other women who worked there. The other women merely walked around in their off-white cotton undergarments. She was adorned in red silk and feathers with a gold cigarette holder dangling from her mouth. Her platinum blonde hair framed large green eyes that shone like emeralds and stood out against her hair and white skin. Her full lips were etched with dark red lip rouge.

The club was narrow and dark. It had a low roof with dim lighting. Although very old, there was an air of neglected beauty. Thick, solid, rounded polished dark wooden support beams ran through the center of the building. A gray rock fireplace sat on one of the walls in the center of the club. Booths lined both sides of the fireplace. Red brick floors had become rounded and uneven with age. A mahogany bar ran from one end of the club to the other. It was surrounded by a carved mahogany bar backing that stretched to the ceiling. A huge mirror hung behind the bar, giving the illusion that the club was twice its size. A smooth polished staircase of railroad tie stairs sat at the far end of the bar that led to the private rooms.

At times, the place had an overwhelming stench, a

mixture of smoke, stale beer, and vomit. Mae used the strongest cleaner she could find, in an attempt rid the bar of the vile smell. On one occasion, Garnet stopped Mac and said, "Sweetie there must be a better way for you to make money. You are aging before your time." She spoke as she waved her cigarette around her head.

"I don't plan on doing this forever. I have something in the works. I just have to get it up and running." Mae needed to believe this. Every morning, she promised herself, *I only have to do this for a few more months.* It was the only thing that kept her going. She dreamed of operating a business where she was paid to find work for people new to the city.

Garnet stuck the cigarette in its holder, clenched it between her teeth, and pulled Mae's cracked, red hands into hers. "Oh honey, this is awful. We can't have this."

Mae felt uncomfortable with this unsolicited attention. She suspected that Garnet was trying to hire her to work in the brothel.

Garnet gently dropped Mae's hands. She took a drag from her cigarette, her blonde hair bounced as she turned and silently walked away.

Mae went back to cleaning. Her hands hurt like hell, but there was nothing she could do about it. She had to clean; otherwise, Declan didn't eat. Garnet walked back to Mae with something in her hands. Her empty gold cigarette holder was pressed between her generous breasts for safekeeping. "Sweetie, this is glycerin and rose water. Before you go to bed rub it on your hands and wear these cotton gloves. It may not totally heal your hands, but it will help ease the cracking and pain. I used to put it on my raw hands when I cleaned floors."

Mae was speechless. She tried to visualize Garnet scrubbing floors. "Thank you, Garnet. I really appreciate your kindness."

"Sweetie, tell me your big plan."

Mae was a bit skeptical about sharing her plan, worrying Garnet would try to scoop up the idea. Finally, she revealed her hopes of bringing people from Ireland and finding them employment and housing. Once the business took off, she would help those already in the city, hard workers who didn't have the knowledge to sell their skills.

Garnet nodded with a slight smile, but she never commented. Garnet kept what she did and how she came to the club tucked deep inside. The two women had a mutual respect for one another. Respect didn't come too often to a woman who spent her days on her knees scrubbing other people's filth or one who spent her time in a club pleasing smelly drunks. Mae never judged Garnet; she dreamed of doing something besides scrubbing up vomit, but she certainly could never do what Garnet did.

Nearly a year after she had started helping families, her husband's cousin approached her at the club. John had come to the city at the same time as Mae and James. "Cousin, my employer, Dan Malone, is interested in the people you send to him. How do you come across them? They all seem to be honest and hardworking."

Mae was unsure of his motives. She glanced around the room to be sure she wasn't going to be scolded for talking instead of scrubbing. She was also seeking any sign of encouragement.

Garnet smiled, gave her a nod of approval, took a long drag of her cigarette, then walked away.

"I have family and friends who long to come to this country, this city, wanting a good life for their families. They are eager to prove themselves. I merely point them in the right direction. Once here, they pay their expenses, and when they are established, they supply me with a small fee. They all understand they must find employment and stay employed; otherwise, they are finished, as am I. I can only help one at a time as I have to sponsor them."

John asked, "How would you like to help Mr. Malone find more honest, hardworking people? He will be their sponsor, but it would be on your head to supply him with hardworking, honest Irishmen who are going to be good employees. Mr. Malone is a good one to work for."

Dan Malone controlled most of the businesses in the area. Job seekers were to pay him a set fee, Mae got the rest. It was more than she could earn on her own. Mae had no concern about her ability to supply the people Mr. Malone wanted. She had spent hours creating her ledger with all the information she needed to find the perfect matches for Dan Malone. She would supply Dan with workers and help locate affordable housing for the newcomers. That was the day her life changed. As she finished her last day at the club, she ran into Garnet, "Sweetie, maybe someday you can see your way clear to get me out of this hellhole." Garnet spoke with a sheepish grin. Deep inside the feeling stung. She would probably die working at the club, but comfortable and safe beat hungry desperation.

"Oh, Garnet … it was you. You told Mr. Malone about what I yearned to do. I will never forget that. I promise I will keep you in my heart and on my mind."

"That's what we do, Mae. We give back. A lifetime ago,

Dan Malone did a kindness for me. I'm sure he has no idea that I'm the cold kid he fed and gave a warm overcoat to. Now it is my turn, and soon it will be yours."

Dan let Mae select those she thought would be successful workers. Mae's ledger grew to two ledgers and then three.

Dan Malone introduced Mae to Conrad and Michael when they started their club. Over the years, Mae helped them find loyal, trustworthy employees. She found fitting homes for those who were in need. When required, she helped a few disappear. It didn't happen very often, but on occasion, she had to find a confidential place for those who had gotten on the bad side of the Italians or saw something they shouldn't have seen that could place them in danger. Mae's son, Declan, was like a small shadow of the two partners. He was always at the side of one of them.

Chapter 21

Mae answered the door faster than Michael anticipated, "Dear God, Michael, what in the name of the Holy family is going on? Maureen is crying hysterically and talking in circles." Mae spat without taking a breath. "Michael, what do you need from me?"

"Mae, where is Noinin?" Michael said in a raspy voice as he looked anxiously around the room. He dared not to sit; he paced the kitchen as Mae spoke. His jacket made a crunching noise as he paced, and his blood-soaked clothing was caked to his skin. Mae lowered her voice as she gave him a once over look.

"Both the child and Maureen are napping. I had Declan go down to Eveleen's place and get the baby clean clothes. She doesn't realize what has happened. She hasn't spoken since Maureen brought her up here."

As they spoke, Maureen entered the room. Her eyes were red and swollen. Her voice was hoarse from crying. "Michael, the baby has to come with me. She is my sister's only child."

"Maureen, that's not possible. We don't know why or who is behind this massacre. You must think of Noinin's safety and the safety of all our family. Mae will find a good family from the neighborhood."

Michael caught Mae's glance as she nodded in his direction. "I will make sure they stay in the neighborhood so you can see the baby as often as you like." Mae spoke as she walked across the room to her rolltop desk.

She pulled out a thick black ledger, which held the information of all the families she helped sponsor. She held it with both hands and clutched it to her chest as though she was waiting for it to speak to her. She opened it and began scrolling through the pages. She licked her finger and said, "Wait, I think I have the perfect place for the baby." She was looking for a specific page. She found the page and said, "This is the family, Michael. They will keep her safe. I know it with all my heart." Mae dropped the open ledger on the table. With a sweeping turn, in an attempt to calm the grief-stricken woman, Mae placed both her hands on Maureen's shoulders and stared intently into her eyes. "Thomas and Ida Doyle would be a safe family for the baby. They are related to your husband, Martin. You would be able to have contact with her without drawing suspicion."

"Michael, I don't understand why she has to be farmed out this way." Maureen's voice was nothing more than a harsh whisper from all the tears she had shed.

"Maureen, we were all targets of those guns tonight; they weren't just aimed at Conrad and me. My son was shot and left for dead. Your own sister was butchered. My Tara was lucky to be on the stoop. We have no idea what these bastards want. A tight circle must be kept to protect all of us. Until I know who did this and what their motives were, the baby must stay hidden. No one needs to know she is still alive. It may seem extreme, but I believe whoever is behind this slaughter tried to wipe out anyone directly connected to Conrad and me. We'll have a private family funeral, and that will be the end of it. Mae, how long will it take for you to get Noinin settled with the Doyle family?"

"I will keep the child here for the night. Maureen you are welcome to sleep on the chesterfield. Declan will walk you home in the morning and bring the Doyles here to make the arrangements. The couple has a toddler with them here in the city. They have three older children boarding with family back in Freemount, County Cork, until the Doyles have the funds to send for them. When last I spoke with them, they were unsure how long their family could keep the older children. They were worried the children could be tossed out on their ears. Once I explain they are helping to keep a poor orphaned child safe, I know they will jump at the chance to help. They are good people. Maureen, you know that to be true. With your consent, Michael, I will tell them; in return for their help, I can arrange for the other children to travel here."

Thomas Doyle was a tall, thin man with a full head of black hair, full sideburns, and thick mustache. Ida was slight and quiet, with gray glowing eyes and silky black hair. The Doyles were both hardworking. Thomas tended bar and did odd jobs around the neighborhood. Ida took in laundry so she could be at home with her baby girl. Ida saved every cent she could manage. The couple came to the city hoping for a new beginning. Even though their lives were hard in their new home, it was a step up from the horrible destitution they left behind.

Ida longed for the day that her family would be whole

again—together under one roof. She had persistent feelings of guilt about abandoning her older children. Her only consolation was that it was a temporary situation. Leaving them behind was the only way the family could escape the bleak future that Ireland held for them. She felt fortunate that their family saw fit to board the children until she and Thomas could pay for their passage to their new home. Saving enough to pay for all three was taking longer than expected. With every letter from Ireland, she worried it was telling her the children had been deserted. Ida knew in her soul of souls that their family was boarding her children as a special favor to the couple. She also knew her children were working hard for their room and board. The quicker she could get them out of Ireland, the better.

Michael whispered, "I trust your decision, Mae. See that it is done."

Maureen was crying again. "I can't believe Eveleen is gone, and now Noinin is being torn away from us."

"Maureen, she will be nearby—within walking distance of your apartment. Please do not make this any harder for me than it already is. I have to keep Noinin and William safe—and the rest of the family for that matter—and this is the best way I know how to do it." A large knot was growing in his throat. He had to leave Mae's apartment before he totally broke down. His body ached, and his eyes pulsated in their sockets. He knew he had to keep ahead of the enemy—even though he was clueless about who that enemy was. The family had to survive this horrible heartbreak. After Michael left Mae's apartment, he felt confident that he would be able to keep the child safely out of sight.

Michael's apartment felt colder and darker than ever.

The grief-stricken young man slowly undressed in the silent darkness of the room. He pulled the stick pin from his tie. His bloody clothes made a sick crunching noise as they were removed, and once again when they dropped in a nauseating pile in the hallway. With the stickpin held tightly in his hand, he made his way to the bedroom in his underwear. The small wall light above his dresser turned on with a loud snap. The glare stung his eyes. He poured water into the basin, rinsed his hands and face, then ran his wet hands through his hair. A wave of his hair fell on his forehead, dripping bloodstained water on his face.

He gingerly moved to the kitchen, ran the water fully open in the sink. He kept washing. It felt like it took hours to get all the blood off his body. He rinsed his hands and ran them through his hair again. He cringed at the sharp pain from his gunshot wound. It seared through his shoulder and down his arm. After a long look at his stickpin, he swished it in the water, gave it a soft shake, and dried it off. After another heart-wrenching look, it was returned to its velvet bag and placed gently in a corner of the dresser. His exhausted mind strained to conceive of life without his best friend. A massive knot swelled in his stomach as guilt swirled around the dark room. Why was he only wounded? He shouted into the darkness, "Conrad, the bastards who brought about this horror will be found, and they will beg for mercy—and die in an extremely slow, painful way."

Sleep was impossible. His body and mind were beyond weary, and his thoughts churned with gunfire, cars slowly creeping down bloodied streets, and women sobbing. He tossed and turned as a vignette of Conrad and Eveleen's contorted bodies in the back seat of his bullet-ridden car flashed with each movement of his body.

Morning slipped through the windows. With a loud moan, he slowly pulled his throbbing frame from his bed; the apartment was uncharacteristically cold and painfully silent. It took him some time to get his bearings; after a hot bath, the sickening reality sank in. He dressed in the silence; every movement was strained and excruciating.

The events of the previous evening played over and over in his mind. There was no explanation for who or why someone was so callously violent. In all the years he and Conrad had dealt with other families, they never came across anyone who could carry out such a savagely unprovoked massacre. Granted, there had been bloody gun battles and executions in the streets, but Conrad and Michael and their family always managed to stay outside the chaos. Somehow, this appeared personal. Shooting down an entire family in such a brutal, public manner just didn't add up.

Michael knew staying on the fringes was no longer an option; he had been forced to get involved. There were no qualms about it; there would be bloodshed. He would keep his promise to do everything in his power to punish the bastards who were responsible for this horrendous terror.

After dressing, Michael walked painfully down the stairs. Andrew sat guard in his car in front of the apartment. Michael gave him a nod as he walked around the corner to Conrad and Eveleen's apartment. Every movement sent pain through his body as he made his way to the door of his friends' apartment, which he had done daily for years without a thought. Eveleen usually met him with a cup of hot tea as Noinin chattered in the other room. It seemed like a lifetime ago that he had picked them up for their great night out. He attempted to ignore the pain and focus on what he had to do.

He let himself into the apartment. The silence in the apartment rang in his ears. He walked over to Conrad's desk. He hoped he would find whatever Conrad had been working on out in plain sight. There was nothing out of the ordinary. Perhaps Conrad was leery of those he was dealing with and had hidden any evidence. *Sweet Jesus,* Michael thought. *What the hell would the evidence be? I have no idea what I am looking for.*

Michael called Declan Moore, "I need you to help me clean Conrad's apartment."

"Clean? What do you mean, Michael?"

"I have to empty the apartment. I need someone I can trust to help me get things in order." He was being deliberately vague. The less the young man knew, the safer he would be.

"Michael, Ma and I will be there shortly."

Declan and Mae arrived shortly after Michael's request. They found Michael with his sleeves rolled up already wet with sweat. His wounded shoulder seeped blood onto his sweat-soaked sleeve. Michael moved methodically around the apartment. It was totally out of character. The explosive persona muted. Declan wondered to himself how long his remaining mentor could keep the lid on himself.

Declan moved slowly toward Michael. He pulled a twisted handkerchief from his pocket, and placed it in his hand. "Flanagan gave this to me last night; he was worried they might disappear." Michael knew the handkerchief held the couple's wedding rings as well as Conrad's stickpin. He gave it a squeeze then placed it in his pants pocket.

Michael and Declan searched every closet and drawer. After Michael had searched every pocket and crevice, Mae boxed up Conrad and Eveleen's personal belongings. He left Mae in the living room to continue her packing and went to Conrad's dresser. He pulled out Conrad's velvet jewelry bag, and placed his friends' jewelry in it. They found nothing that would help them uncover who was responsible for the massacre. The more time Michael had to think, the more he was convinced that whatever Conrad was working on had resulted in his murder. Conrad must have left some inkling of what he was working on, but where and what?

Michael was extremely melancholy as he approached Eveleen's recent purchase: a vanity with an oblong mirror. Eveleen's musical voice echoed in his mind: "I have always wanted a vanity dressing table; it will be a family heirloom someday, handed down from mother to daughter for generations to come."

Michael went into the kitchen and found a hammer, glue, and some small nails. His eyes welled with tears as he opened the bottom document drawer. He placed the velvet jeweler's bag with the couple's rings and Conrad's pin in the drawer. In the silence of his friend's room, he glued the edges of the drawer, then gently tapped the nails to seal the drawer tight. It was as though he didn't want to touch the vanity. He didn't want to get too close to the memory. "Mae, see that the vanity goes to the Doyle's apartment. Explain to them that it belongs to Noinin."

His chest tightened, and his throat swelled; in one evening, his friend's entire family and future was destroyed.

He hoped he would find the murderers soon and present Noinin with her true identity as well as her parents' jewelry. He had to move forward to fulfill both his and Conrad's dreams. How could that ever be accomplished without knowing what his partner's big deal was? It seemed like a lifetime ago that Conrad told him they would all be living in paradise soon. Paradise? The word haunted Michael's thoughts. *Damn it, Conrad. How could you leave us like this?* Michael slammed his fist on his friend's desk. His throat strained with anger and pain.

He would not be at peace until he found out who was responsible for this heartbreak.

Declan made sure the vanity made it safely to the Doyle's apartment. He told Michael that the mirror was really loose, and it had nearly fallen from the frame as it was being moved, but he had secured it.

Chapter 22

Not long after Conrad and Eveleen's funeral, Michael got a message about a lead on the shooters. One of the neighborhood longshoremen noticed a strange car and a couple of suspicious men wandering near an abandoned warehouse on the waterfront. There was no reason for anyone to be anywhere near the warehouse. It was too odd not to share at Cara Dílis.

Michael desperately grasped at anything that might answer who murdered his friends. Michael, Declan, and several of the enforcers from the family rode down to the warehouse. With no moon, the dock was as dark as a cave. The city lights reflected off the dock's soggy planks with a dull glimmer. It didn't matter the time of day, the dock was always wet. The only sound was the lonely horn of a ship signaling to another as they slowly swept passed one another in the blackness. The group parked out of sight and earshot of their targets. Shoes slapped with an empty echo in the dank darkness with each step taken on the wooden planks.

Michael's shoulder throbbed as he feared the prey he hunted would escape his vengeance. Anger mounted, his body tightened, and his chest constricted. He inhaled deeply attempting to ease the tightness. He wanted to kill them the minute he saw them. *But answers first.*

The who and the why had to be answered before revenge was taken.

The group searched the warehouse with guns drawn, ready to attack.

At first glance, it appeared that dirt and dripping pipes were all the warehouse held. A dim musty gray light reached out to the men from the far corner of the building. The smell of cheap cigars followed the light's glow. No noise or movement came from the corner.

Michael closed his eyes and breathed deeply to control his urge to run to the corner, and beat the answers he needed out of anyone he found, then empty his gun into the bastards. He took a final deep breath, and one last rub of the cavernous throbbing wound on his shoulder. His emotions managed, he slowly walked closer to the corner where the light shone. Pressure continued to build in his chest; Declan's breath filled his ears as the younger man walked close to him. Michael's body sank like a rock. A huge knot choked off his airway as the bloodbath came into full view. The corner was riddled with bullet holes, spent shells littered the filthy floor. The filth mixed with blood was splattered on the walls. The floor cradled a mass of carnage. A single body had been totally mutilated by gunfire. A peculiar shoe and a bullet riddled wooden limb were all that was recognizable in the bloody mess. The remains were so disfigured that all that could be said was the body belonged to someone with an artificial leg. No way in hell could he guess who the pile of meat used to be. Michael wanted the men dead, but not before he had answers—and he wanted to be the executioner. Where were the rest of the men? One man couldn't be responsible for Conrad and Eveleen's slaughter. Michael kicked at the floor in an attempt to control his temper. He screamed at the top of his lungs to the empty warehouse, "God damn you, whoever you are. I will find you and take great pleasure in killing you slowly and painfully."

Michael felt this might be the closest he would ever get to knowing who murdered his friends and left William for dead in the street. The mutilated body reinforced Michael's belief that the murders were connected to Conrad's business meeting and not an attempt to take over the family. There was quiet gossip that the longshoreman had seen police cars at the warehouse; if that were true, why leave the body unattended? Why wasn't an officer waiting for the coroner?

Whoever ordered the hit had covered their tracks by viciously murdering the person who could possibly lead Michael to them. The carnage appeared to be the act of an amateur who had no control or loyalty to his henchmen.

The vicious attack on Conrad and the horrendous bloodbath had an unexpected result.

Early one evening, not long after the warehouse slaughter, Michael was going over paperwork with Sam in the back of Cara Dílis.

There was a knock on the door.

Mickey, one of the bartenders, appeared in the doorway. He was noticeably shaken.

"What the hell is it, Mickey?" Michael barked.

Just as he finished his sentence, a short, slender man swept passed Mickey.

"Holy shit," Michael whispered.

Sam looked up from the desk as the man walked into the back room. He wasn't tall, but he radiated an attitude of power, confidence, and strength. His face was small and narrow. He looked to be in his fifties, his gray hair was combed straight back from his forehead. He was clean-shaven with the exception of a sliver of a mustache. Even though he smiled, it was as though it was a painful act. Impeccably dressed, he wore a gray suit, a silver tie, with a matching pocket scarf, and he carried a dark gray hat. His shoes shined even in the darkness of the club's back room.

"Mr. Malone, it's a pleasure to see you. What can I do for you?" Michael tried to act as though men like Malone always walked into the club. Michael's height and commanding physical build was in sharp contrast to Malone's slight physique. Out of respect, Michael stood at a distance. He didn't want to look down on such a powerful man.

CHAPTER 23

In the midst of the Irish potato famine, landlords sent poor families out of the country with promises of jobs, money, food, and clothing. Malone's family was packed into one of the overcrowded, dangerous British ships, which came to be known as "coffin ships." The majority of the passengers died on the harrowing trips, many within view of shore, awaiting medical inspections. Those who died near port were tossed overboard into the St. Lawrence River. Those like Malone's family who survived, arrived in Canada, starving and sick, found there was no money, food, or jobs. No one had any idea who the landlords were. Dan Malone's family came to New York by way of Canada. Many Irish immigrants walked across the border into the United States after arriving in desolate Canada with merely the clothes on their backs. Once they realized Canada, like Ireland, was under harsh British rule, they headed south as fast as they could.

In a quiet voice with a slight slur, as though he had too much saliva Dan Malone spoke, "Mr. Byrne, it has been a while since we last talked. The first time our paths crossed, you were green off the boat. You and your *chara is fearr* (best friend) Conrad, were ready to take on the world. Malone paused.

"I am deeply sorry and saddened by the loss of your

friend." His face was ashen, and his steel gray eyes were empty of emotion. When he spoke of Conrad, his face stiffened in anger. His gray eyes had seen a great deal of pain and hardship.

Michael could see he was extremely upset about Conrad's murder.

Dan chose his words carefully and spoke slowly. "I know how long you two were friends. I watched with great joy as you boys grew your business, and took care of your neighbors. Anything—and I mean anything—you or your family needs, I am here for you."

Michael was speechless. Malone was the head of one of the biggest Irish families in New York. When the two young men were at their lowest, Malone took them under his wing, gave them jobs, and showed them how to run a business. He recognized they weren't meant to be hard-core enforcers or petty thieves; they were special. Malone always knew the two would set off on their own one day. Conrad and Michael worked for Malone, did odd jobs, and learned how to properly run a business. When they had enough money and with Malone's blessing they bought Cara Dílis. Malone had no issues with the young men. He admired them, considered them his extended family, and he knew they were trustworthy. Their successes were celebrated like a loving father might celebrate.

Michael blurted out, "Sir, this is a real fuck-up … I'm sorry, forgive me, but it's true."

"Michael, please call me Dan. I agree. Whoever—and I mean whoever—did this is a cold-blooded bastard with no honor or loyalty. I don't give a damn who they are. A hard death is their future. The massacre at the warehouse topped it off. It is as though they were trying to send a message. By the grace of God, I heard them loud and clear. I don't think it was the message they intended. No one—no one—comes into our neighborhood and disrespects our families this way. I'm with you, *mo chara*." (my friend)

Michael was surprised by Malone's anger, but he was comforted by the thought that he wasn't alone in his search for the bastards who had killed Conrad and Eveleen and orphaned Noinin.

"Michael, whatever you need, call me. All of my family is at your disposal. I know you and Conrad are not into the dark side of our business. It will be messy. I offer the services of my family. We'll hunt down these bastards together and make them pay. We will remain strong and get beyond this darkness. That is the Irish way. Let's have a drink. Show me what you have to offer. No strings, my friend. We are family. We are joined by the blood and sweat of our families and friends. I kept track of you and Conrad while you built your business, and I have been proud to watch you grow and see what great men you have become."

Dan Malone was unique. He worked for what he had, and he didn't covet what others had. If he wanted something, he worked for it. He was satisfied with the power he held, and he wasn't hungry for total control. That's what set him apart from the Italians—and even from Nucky Johnson. They would kill their own for the riches and power, destroying anyone in their path.

Sam walked behind the bar and pulled out a bottle and two glasses. Michael and Dan Malone had a drink in Conrad's honor, and then—as quickly as Malone had swept into the room—he was gone.

CHAPTER 24

Nora settled into her new family. It appeared she had no memory of her parent's murder or her previous life. She had wiped that horrible night, including her parents, from her mind. The only way to erase the pain of the murders was to erase her pa and ma. The older Doyle children arrived from Ireland and settled into their new home.

The Doyles took good care of Nora, and Maureen was able to visit often. She visited with all the children, not just Nora. She brought gifts and played with Keira and Nora. The older children didn't think anything of it. The family was never in need; Michael saw to that. Thomas and the older children all had jobs that paid well.

Thomas and Ida had grown up together on adjacent farms. The potato famine had destroyed both their family farms. The years that followed brought catastrophic poverty to families who once thrived. Each year was worse than the previous one. Their future was dismal. Thomas enjoyed farming with his family in Ireland, and he planned to return to it someday. Once the family took in Nora, they lived very comfortably, and the idea was abandoned.

CHAPTER 25

The couple was excited about the evening and all the new year held for them. Thomas was thrilled to start a new position at the club. He had been promoted to manager of Cara Dílis. He reached for the new pocket watch and chain Michael gave him for Christmas. It was a sign that he was now included in the family's inner circle. Michael was extremely satisfied with Thomas' work and the way he managed his family matters. Thomas had an idea that Nora was somehow connected to Michael. He believed if Michael felt he needed to know Nora's background, he would share it with him. Thomas was now a trusted member of the family—and not just Nora's guardian. Thomas took a long look at the shiny gold watch with its long chain and the whistle dangling on the end. He placed the watch in his pocket then clipped the other end to his vest.

Ida asked, "Tommy, what is the whistle at the end of your chain?"

"Well, *mo pheata* (my pet) it is for my protection. Michael gave all of us a whistle, so we can whistle for help if we are in trouble. Since most of the gents are traveling in pairs, it is fairly certain someone will hear the whistle."

"Sweet Jesus, Tommy. That is quite unsettling. Are you

in danger? Who will hear your whistle? You don't have a partner."

"My sweet, I don't know for sure, but I hope I never find out. I am a bartender ... a nobody. I doubt anyone is going to target me. No need to worry. Help is only a whistle away. I am in the club most of the time, surrounded by all the help I might need. No one has had to use the whistles."

Thomas took one last admiring look at himself in the long oblong vanity mirror. He was quite pleased with how he looked, and he was ready to head out to work. He decided to set up the bar early so he and Ida could ring in the New Year with their friends at the club. Thomas was delighted to have control of the everyday operation of the club.

As he walked down the avenue, Thomas' mind was on the celebration plans for the evening. He was extremely proud of his accomplishments. Although he worked hard he felt indebted to Michael. Nora was his little girl. A gift, not a burden. He wanted to prove he deserved the opportunity. He would get the bar ready then return home to pick up Ida.

Twilight gave way to darkness as Thomas made his way through the alley near the club. Andrew and Flynn had driven north to get enough juice to supply the New Year's revelers plus the normal crowd. They had the duty to deliver the juice for the celebration as well as aid him with its safe offloading and storage. A huge crowd was expected for the New Year's Eve celebration. The two were nowhere in sight.

As he got closer to the back door, Thomas saw a pile of clothing on the basement stairs. The unmanned delivery truck sat in the alley. The strict rule was to unload the supplies into the basement storage as quickly as possible then remove the truck from the alley to avoid suspicion. Once safely unloaded, the liquor was moved from the basement to the club, as needed, without any fanfare. On a night like tonight, a raid would be an absolute disaster. Thomas' blood pumped. The stairs to the basement were steep and awkward. It took time to get the crates of bottles into the basement, then more time to arrange it all, for easy access into the club.

"Where the hell is everyone?" Thomas mumbled.

Thomas saw a hat lying in the alley. He picked it up; it was Andrew's favorite. He walked toward the basement. Someone was sprawled out on the stairs. Thomas' first thought was,

"Damn these two. Andrew is already drunk. Shit, biggest night of the year, and these asses decided to start celebrating early. They are going to catch hell if Michael finds out."

He quickened his pace. "Jesus, Andy, starting a bit early, aren't you? Where the hell is Flynn? And why in the name of all that is holy is the truck still sitting in plain sight?"

Andrew didn't move.

As Thomas got closer, it became clear that the man was not drunk. He had been beaten. Andrew's head was laid open bloodied at the bottom of the stairs. His contorted frame was sprawled over the remaining stairs. It looked like Andrew saw something, started to run up the stairs, and was clouted halfway up. Whoever hit him continued to beat Andrew to a gory pulp. Thomas fumbled to pull his whistle from his vest. He frantically blew it in the direction of the avenue, then towards the truck at the end of the alley. He looked down at Andrew's blood-soaked body, then lifted his head to the rooftops and let out a final screeching squeal of his whistle. In mid-squeal he felt and heard a crushing blow to his head. He thought, *I just heard myself die.*

Thoughts of his wife and family flowed through his veins as his life percolated from his body. He heard what was going on around him, but he was paralyzed by his wounds. There was no pain. He was numb. His body refused his request to move. He blinked his eyes in an attempt to get his body to respond, but to no avail. He felt the warmth of his own blood flowing from his body, encircling his frame, then nothing but darkness.

Two silhouettes ran up the stairs, one of them kicked Thomas in the stomach as he raced by. Thomas let out a hollow gasp as the last air that remained in his lungs escaped.

As the two men headed toward the other side of the truck, they yelled to someone at the end of the alley.

CHAPTER 26

Sullivan arrived first, and then Flannery showed up. They heard the whistle and found Flynn at the front of the truck; he had been clubbed to death. Andrew and Flynn were taken by surprise as they unloaded the truck. It looked as though Andrew was beaten first as he opened the basement. Flynn as he came to Andrew's aid. Whoever was responsible was scared off by Thomas' whistle. They didn't have a chance to steal anything.

Michael was taking the short walk from his apartment to the club when he heard the whistle. He arrived just after Sullivan and Flannery. He spoke to them with force and an angry determination, "Sweet Mary, mother of God, who does this? Do we look so weak that a few sewer rats feel they can get away with beating three of our family to death, then rob us? From this point forward, we are no longer on the defense. We will be the aggressor, and we will beat down anyone who confronts us. I am sorry, Sully, but we have to move forward with the plans for tonight. I need the two of you to take care of our friends first, then we must prepare for tonight. Sully, get a couple of guys to unload the truck and get it out of sight. Get Declan down here to set up the bar.

Shit, I'll go to the Doyle's apartment. I believe Flynn lived alone. Flannery, will you check on Andrew's family for me?"

"Damn it, Michael. This is fucked-up bullshit. I am so sorry. Yes, you can count on me." Flannery snorted.

Michael told both men, "I think it would be best, for now, if we told as few people as possible about this. Tomorrow, we will take time to share our grief. These bastards are amateurs; they could have had the entire damn truck, yet walked away with nothing but blood on their hands. They will spill their guts to someone. We will be at their door in no time. I will be back soon. Give me time to spend with Tommy's wife and family. God damn it. I hate this shit."

Sullivan found a couple of guys to unload the truck. Declan arrived just as Michael was walking through the alley. Michael walked to each of the bodies, and took in all the carnage so he would remember every blow. He touched each one as he whispered, "*Trí gach a bhfuil grá agam, geallaim duit go n-íocfaidh siad*" (By all that I love, I promise you that they will pay.) Flynn had a large amount of blood around his partially opened mouth. Even after a brutal blow to his head, the man fought to his death. Michael squatted and as he held Flynn's shoulders, the man's mouth dropped open, something fell out. It landed on his shoulder, then fell near Michael's hand. Michael jumped, almost losing his balance. He slowly pulled his handkerchief from his lapel and picked up the object. He returned the handkerchief to his pocket and quietly said, "Sweet Jesus, Flynn took someone's nose. This bastard shouldn't be hard to find. He is missing his fucking nose."

"Michael, what the hell is going on? I heard the whistles down the block. Who is it?" Declan said as his voice cracked.

"Jesus, Declan! Tommy Doyle, Andrew Rafferty, and Jimmy Flynn were clubbed to death. They never had a chance to defend themselves. They were clubbed by cowardly bastards. Flynn seems to be the only one who wasn't taken totally by surprise. He put up a fight and got slugs in. He bit off the nose of one of the bastards. It ends here and now. I am done being patient. I tried to do things peacefully like Conrad would have wanted. He would never want us to sit back and allow gutter rats to come into our neighborhood to murder and steal. We have reached the breaking point. Now, we do things my way. No longer will we have targets on our backs. We will aggressively protect what is ours. We won't allow what we have all worked for to be taken from us. Our revenge will be forceful and public. Anyone who thinks they can attack us will have no doubt in their minds that we can defend what is ours. No one is to speak of the nose we found; it goes no further than those in this alley. We'll find this piece of shit. He will talk—and then he will pay.

"I'm headed to Tommy's apartment. I will be back as soon as I can. We have to put on a brave face tonight and keep our ears open for anyone who might be talking big. Declan, know that you have become my trusted friend and associate. I appreciate all that you do. We have got to get back on track at any cost, and it must be apparent that we are not easy prey. I'm done with the bullshit. We are going to have to do things we never thought we would do. We are going to have to get into the sewer with these rats and prove we aren't anyone's meal ticket. With that being said, this isn't your fight, son. You don't have to be involved in this.

It won't be the other families that come after us ... that's clear. It will be small-time hoods with no loyalty to anyone, looking for any easy score ... like these assholes."

"Michael, I am with you to the finish. Don't think otherwise. You are my family."

Declan saw the change that this most recent attack brought about in Michael. It was as though a switch had been flipped. Michael had an angry side which was held in check by Conrad's logic. He knew he needed to protect the family and the business they had built. There was no going back. Michael had it in him to be as tough as—or tougher than—anyone he came across. Conrad had controlled the anger that raged deep within Michael.

Michael hated going through the neighborhood alleys. All his recent walks were after horrible occurrences. Michael slowed his pace; he had to sort out what he would say to Ida. This was one of the rare times he came to the apartment. He never wanted to be the one to put Noinin in jeopardy.

Ida met him at the door. "I heard the whistle. It's my Tommy, isn't it? That's the only reason you would come here."

"Yes Ida, it is Thomas. You know I would never put him in a precarious position. He came upon an attempted robbery."

"Where is he? Is he hurt? Take me to him."

Michael tried to control his emotions. A familiar knot grew in the back of his throat. It was impossible to swallow, let alone speak. He shook his head and looked away from her questioning stare.

Ida let out a cry, like an injured rabbit. She quietly

sobbed as she slid down the wall, collapsing in a lump on the floor. Michael sat down beside her and tried to console her.

Maureen was in the other room with Keira and Nora. She came around the corner, saw Michael on the floor, and did an about-face.

It took a conscious effort to force the knot down his throat to gain control of his breathing. "Ida, I will take care of everything, the funeral arrangements, everything. You and your family will want for nothing. You will continue to receive Thomas' pay. I can't tell you how horrible I feel. I am heartbroken and disgusted that Tommy was brought down this way."

"I don't blame you, Michael. Tommy was proud to know you and to work for you. We both appreciate all you have done for our family." Ida said slowly, consoling Michael, through her own tears and grief. Ida pulled her handkerchief from her sleeve, wiped her eyes, and pulled herself up from the floor. She held out a hand to Michael, and he followed her to the kitchen.

Ida poured him a cup of tea as he stood silently in the kitchen. They regained their composure as they drank the tea. Michael leaned against the sink, but he didn't want to get too comfortable. He could see Noinin in the other room sitting on Eveleen's vanity looking at her reflection in the mirror. She sat on the shelf that was on top of the middle drawer, which rested directly under the mirror. Her face was pressed against the mirror.

After a few minutes, Noinin came into the kitchen and asked, "Do you know my pa? When is he coming home?"

Ida tried to hush her, "Child, be good now. Don't bother the nice man."

Michael was impressed by Ida's strength and quiet manner. Ida was now a widow—her children fatherless by the hand of cowardly bastards—Michael felt responsible for tearing the family apart. His only comfort was, he would find those responsible for Thomas' death. They would make a mistake, and he would be ready when it happened. The one who left his nose behind would have to leave town; there was no way he could stay. His bosses would either kill him or ship him off. Michael would reach out to all his contacts to find No Nose.

Conrad's murderers, on the other hand, would take more effort. Michael didn't think the two were connected because these asses weren't even smart enough to take a truckload of juice. This was a different kind of slime—a slime easily found and destroyed with great satisfaction. He felt his blood flowing hot. This was a turning point for Michael; nothing would ever be the same, and he knew it. He wanted to pick up Noinin, hug her, and take her home to what was left of her real family. In a flash of time, Noinin had lost two fathers. By choice—or by the grace of God— she had no memory of her actual father and mother or their horrific death. "My sweet, your pa, Thomas, works for me." *Works?* The sound of the word made Michael's stomach churn. It was too soon to use the past tense to describe someone who had given his all for Michael.

He avoided answering when he would return. He swore to Ida that her family would be taken care of.

Michael finished his tea and said his goodbyes at the door.

Ida reached out for Michael's hand, pulled him close, and whispered, "Michael, make these fucking bastards pay for what they did to my Tommy. Promise me you will do that!"

Michael was shocked that Ida could be so calm on the outside and have the fire of hell burning on the inside. "Ida, I promise you, on my life, they will pay. They will pray for death before I am finished with them."

Michael quietly spread the word about No Nose among his trusted group. They were told not to approach him but to quietly get ahold of Declan or himself. He was determined not to let this cold-blooded bastard, or his pals, escape their well-deserved punishment.

Ida stood strong during Thomas' funeral service and burial, but she never recovered from the loss of her beloved husband. Ida lived her life for her children. She spent all her waking hours taking care of them. She was obsessed with making sure Nora was safe. Without Michael ever saying a word, she knew who the child was. The woman was determined to keep her out of harm's way. Neither Michael nor Ida ever discussed who she was; it was a given, no words were needed.

Michael made sure no one spoke of the gruesome discovery of the nose.

CHAPTER 27

Elsa and Nora scampered down the avenue. Elsa was shorter and stockier than Nora. Her thick brown hair was pulled into two braids and tied together at the top of her head.

Nora gazed in wonderment at the brick buildings that lined the street for as far as she could see. Black fire escapes zigzagged up their sides. Laundry lines stretched across the alleys between the buildings like flags of all nations proudly being displayed floor by floor. Smells from all the different kitchens filled her nostrils.

As the girls walked hand in hand on this great adventure, it occurred to Nora this was the farthest she had traveled in the neighborhood without her ma. A chill came over her for a moment as she realized she would never find her way home without Elsa. She chased that thought from her mind as they walked steadily toward their destination.

Nora felt very grown-up as she walked down the avenue. Her red curls bounced with every step. She was very proud of them. Her mother always made sure they were kept in control. Her sisters, Keira and Hannah, had thick black hair that fought curling. Nora was the exact opposite of her sisters in almost every way. Their mother would put dozens of rags in Keira's hair to force it to curl. Ida only needed a few rags to tame the red corkscrews. Hannah did her own hair and rags were not involved. Keira and Hannah were sturdy with strong jaws. Nora had lean, petite features. Although they were close in age, for as long as Nora could remember, she had been smaller than her sister.

It took only a few minutes for Elsa and Nora to reach their destination. They stopped at a tall wrought iron gate. The gate gave an angry groan as they pushed it open. A snarling lion's face, embedded in the iron, gazed down on them, ready to pounce. It took both of them to get the gate open wide enough to squeeze through. Inside the gate, they were surrounded by a garden of thick grass edged by neatly trimmed shrubs.

Nora froze for a moment as she took in her surroundings. It was as though they had been carried somewhere far away from the noise and smells of the city. In the middle of the garden sat a huge brown brick building. It was separated into sections by tall, white trimmed windows. Concrete stairs led to a set of large white double doors. The stairs were guarded on either side by more snarling lions. Her neck ached as she stretched to see all the way to the roof. Nora was awash with doubts about entering the building. The lions weren't welcoming.

Elsa nudged her companion. The red mop danced. Elsa knew where to go. She pulled at Nora's sleeve. She had been gushing about this wonderful place for weeks while their ma's gossiped on the stoop. They walked up the guarded stairs into the building. Their small feet made clapping sounds as they walked down a long hallway. The dark wooden floors were lit by gleaming light fixtures every several feet. Tall doors, matching the floors, stretched down the hallway in alignment with the light fixtures.

They entered a sunny room where they were met by a slender, soft-spoken woman with a pleasant smile. A neat blue smock covered her white blouse and long black skirt, and her blonde hair was pulled back in an efficient bun. She welcomed Elsa, took Nora's hand and softly said, "Good morning little one. What is your name?"

Nora replied, "I am Nora."

"What is your last name, Nora? I am Miss Fielding." She said with a smile.

"Nora." The child said again.

Miss Fielding asked Nora's age. Nora gave Elsa a cold stare; she hadn't mentioned there would be questions. Elsa said it was a wonderful place with many exciting toys. Nora had no idea how old she was. No one had ever told her. Miss Fielding could see the child was unfamiliar with her name and age. The child saw the woman's concern. Aunt Maureen had the same look whenever the youngster asked too many questions.

Miss Fielding placed them at their own desks with paper and pencils. Each desk had a seat attached. The desks were lined up in even rows throughout the room. On the corner of each of the desks sat a piece of fresh fruit. The two girls drew pictures, played games, and ate snacks. Nora had never been in a room with so many children. Her time was spent with her ma and the ladies of the neighborhood.

When the girls finally left the tall structure that held all this adventure, the sun had dropped behind the buildings. Nora couldn't wait to tell her ma about the day's adventure.

She swelled with excitement at the thought of returning in the morning.

Nora's excitement was cut short when Elsa's mother met them at the gate. She scolded Elsa in a language Nora didn't understand. She was speaking so rapidly that all Nora could grasp was "*dummkopf*" (stupid).

Elsa's mother wore a long black dress, a long sweater, and a kerchief. At the same moment she called Elsa a dummkopf, she gently took Nora by her arms to hold her in place, then she yanked off her long sweater and pulled her kerchief off her head. She quickly wrapped Nora in her sweater and covered the red curls with her kerchief. She scolded Elsa the entire time they scurried down the avenue toward their apartment building. Every once in a while, she gave Elsa a slap on the butt and mumbled, "Dummkopf." The woman's thick hair had been wrapped in a knot and held tight by her kerchief. With each step, the knot loosened until a blonde winding tail dangled down her back to below her waist. It didn't concern her. She kept Nora close to her side and never spoke to her. The child couldn't understand why her dear friend was in trouble.

As they approached their building, Nora's ma was crying on the stoop. She was surrounded by neighbors who were comforting her. When Ida saw the woman leading the two girls, she let out a yelp. She ran toward them, scooped up Nora, and hugged Elsa's mother as if she had saved the child from a burning building.

Nora had no idea what all the fuss was about. She told her mother about the wonderful place.

"Oh, my sweet angel, you are only six. That's too young

141

to be wandering about. Promise me you will not run off again."

Six? Well, now I know how old I am, but what good will it do if I'm not allowed to go back to visit Miss Fielding?

That evening, Ida bathed the girl, called the child her little carrot top, as she dried the curly red hair.

Keira was allowed to take her bath without her mother's help. Ida wrapped the girls' hair in rags before putting them to bed. The older children were out for the evening.

The railroad flat didn't provide room for privacy. The younger girls' bed was near the kitchen for the warmth of the kitchen stove during the winter and the breezes during the summer.

Nora awoke to low and anxious voices. The volume raised and lowered as the conversation progressed. She strained to hear her mother's voice crack, only hearing a few words. "Michael, I don't think anyone saw the child. She was just another child in a roomful of ragamuffins. She is my child as far as anyone is concerned. You shouldn't worry."

The other voices, a man, and a woman, spoke at the same time and were distraught.

The man cleared his throat before he softly spoke, "We can't chance her true identity being discovered. You and Thomas took her in—no questions asked. The child needs to remain invisible."

His voice was anxious, but it sounded familiar to Nora.

He continued, "Ida, as Noinin gets older, she is going to want some freedom. You can't be expected to be with her constantly."

At the same time the woman seated with him expelled a

soft rasping cough. She kept a white lace handkerchief over her mouth the entire time she whispered, "Fortunately, no one has been looking for her. It could be dangerous for her and your family if it were discovered she's alive. You need to be extra careful. I know you have your boys, and Maureen, but if you need another hand—"

"Tara," the man whispered. The woman looked into his sad eyes and stopped short.

Nora heard the anguish in his voice. Her face radiated with heat from ear to ear. The child's small frame felt too heavy to budge. Her tiny ears burned and rang as she tried to understand what was being said.

Michael spoke as he glanced in Tara's direction—and then Ida's—forcing a weak smile of confidence. "I'll protect the child with my life. But we need a clear plan going forward. There needs to be guidance … as well as protection. The German woman, Ana, has been in the neighborhood for years. She's related to the old mortician. She obviously has some idea that Noinin is special. After today, I have no doubt that—whatever she knows—she can be trusted to keep it to herself."

Nora's body stiffened at the sound of the man's voice. Her face was tingling, and her legs were heavy, but she forced her body forward to see what was going on. She knew he was talking about her, but he was using a name she had never heard. Muck drenched her thoughts, like thick oil, as she tried to identify this familiar voice that held both comfort and dread. Slowly, her rigid body moved forward. She did not want to disturb Keira.

Nora saw a couple in formal clothing seated at the dining table with Ida. The man was tall and strong looking with thick curly black hair. He wore a black suit with a wide lapel, and a white shirt with a black tie. Nora couldn't see his face, but when he moved, a rainbow glistened across the room. The rainbow's glow jolted her like a hard smack. Her small body trembled, and tears swelled inside. Nora searched for what created the rainbow; it was a pin stuck in his tie. The kaleidoscope of color bounced around the room. She was hypnotized. Her green eyes followed as her body quaked beyond her control. A lump of what once was her dinner attempted to escape her throat. The child forced the dinner to return to her stomach and concentrated on the woman.

The woman, close to Ida's age, wore a beautiful green dress covered with ivory-embroidered lace. She removed her long white gloves when Nora's mother served tea. Her tiny shoes matched the dress. The heels were adorned with green and white beads. Her dark auburn hair was curled close to her face. She looked like a princess. The child's imagination dashed forward at full speed. *This woman must be a princess, and he is a prince.*

Everything about the couple contrasted sharply with Ida's meager attire and the simple but newly purchased furnishings.

White lace curtains covered the windows over shades that were usually only opened halfway. The icebox and stove were on the same wall. The kitchen's centerpiece was a massive mahogany dinner table. Its claw legs reached out from under the table like a cat reaching for a ball of yarn. The table had a matching hutch which held dishes that were carefully brought from Ireland. Nora watched as her mother served tea to the couple with china from the hutch. *Ma never used the china.*

The mahogany table and the hutch were the first pieces of furniture that Thomas bought after starting his job with Michael. The size of the two pieces overwhelmed the rest of the apartment. Along with the table and hutch, the apartment had a new davenport; the rest of the small apartment was furnished comfortably, but not lavishly. It was Ida and Thomas' first and last home together.

The child longed to see the man's face; the familiarity of the voice caused a storm of emotions to boil up from her stomach, fear, but not of him. An overwhelming sadness engulfed her small frame. Nora tried to escape the sadness. She stepped back toward the cherrywood vanity in Ida's small room. It had always been there, totally out of place, next to her mother's bed. The bed was lumpy with a headboard and footboard of round black iron pipe.

No one ever bothered the child when she sang at the mirror. It was her safe place. She could see what was going on in the kitchen, yet she was safe from their eyes.

As the voices lowered, Nora moved closer.

A third person, a young man, younger than Nora's eldest brother, in a long overcoat stood in the corner. His eyes were fixed out the window to the street below. He was shorter than Bradley with a slender build and dark curls that swung wildly around his head. Only half his face was visible. He never spoke or looked in the direction of the conversation. He had taken off his hat and placed it on the counter next to the sink in the kitchen. Nora noticed him at the same time the radiator hissed its warming cry.

Ida stopped the conversation with a wave of her hand

and moved toward the curious child. She tried to herd Nora back to bed, but the princess in the green dress needed her attention.

"No, my sweet. It is late. Children should be seen and not heard. You have been seen, and now it is time to scoot back to bed."

Without thinking Michael lit a cigar. The smell was very familiar to Nora, but she had no idea why. No one in the family smoked cigars, and the smoke at Uncle Benjamin's candy store smelled awful. It was nothing like this smell. He quickly snuffed it out as Ida pushed the child toward her bed.

Tara commented to Ida, "She's a vision of Eveleen."

Ida gently tapped Tara's arm to stop her from saying more. "That one is like a little sponge. You may think she isn't listening, but she hears and soaks up everything. Nora is full of questions lately."

Tara whispered, "I'm sorry, Ida. That was thoughtless of me. I miss my friend so much."

Ida replied, "It's all right. I understand how difficult it must be for all of you to keep your distance."

Michael saw a strength in Ida he hadn't realized previously. Although she was overseeing five children of various ages and personalities, she still managed to give attention to all of them with a calming and compassionate demeanor.

"Ida, you are doing a fine job with all your children. I am not here to criticize. We just need a plan to ensure we know what the child is doing when she is not with you." Michael couldn't help but notice how thin and sad Ida looked. She was not the same woman who had taken Noinin into her home.

CHAPTER 28

Ida gave Nora more freedom after Michael and Tara's visit, but she still kept a close eye on her. If she wanted to go downstairs without her mother, one of her brothers had to accompany her.

Nora and Keira were much younger than their sister and two brothers. Bradley and Hannah worked in the candy store down the street from their apartment building. Robert did odd jobs around the neighborhood. Nora liked it when Bradley watched her as they went to the candy store. The store stood at the corner. Dark green awnings shaded the windows, a gold sign that read, "Cara Dílis" covered both of the front windows.

The store was dark inside and the walls were lined with wooden shelves. The front counter held large glass jars filled with a rainbow assortment of candies. Cara Dilis appeared much larger from the outside than it did from inside. It was as though the store had been cut in half.

Uncle Benjamin gave the girls free run of the front of the store where Hannah worked. Bradley spent his time alongside Uncle Benny, doing whatever needed to be done. The girls weren't allowed in the back, which was where Benny and his friends could usually be found. Men's voices seeped through the door, talking and laughing. The smoke from their cigars slithered under the door drifting through the store like a snake that slowly danced its way to the front.

The men entered and left through the alley door. When one of them entered the store from the back room, the smoke would burst out like a flood of water gushing from a dam. On those occasions, Nora's eyes burned, her nose filled with smoke, and her stomach turned. *What possible attraction did the smelly cylinders hold?* The wretched explosion was nothing like what lingered in the apartment after the royal couple's visit. That smell was a comforting, familiar smell.

Once while Keira and Nora played in the store, Keira dared Nora to open the door to the back. "Do it, Nora. Are you a big baby?"

Nora hated being called that name. The family always referred to her as "the baby." It was as though she didn't have a name. Nora walked to the door while trying to look like anything but a baby. Her small, confident fingers reached for the doorknob and turned it.

The door opened slowly, and smoke flowed into the store.

Nora's eyes burned as the smoke and its stench escaped the back room. Her burning eyes squinted through her tears, as a young man with dark curls tumbling into his eyes, stood directly in the door way. It seemed like he was waiting for her to open it. She had turned the knob quietly and only opened the door slightly.

He lowered himself to Nora's level and looked her right in the eyes. He had a kind face.

Nora wasn't frightened by the man. She was no baby.

"Sweet child, there is nothing back here that concerns you." His voice was deep, gentle, and soft.

Nora realized he was the man who was with the prince and princess. Still not frightened, she knew she should close the door.

CHAPTER 29

Although cars were not a novelty in the neighborhood, whenever a strange car approached, Nora was sent indoors until it passed, or the occupants were recognized. The child didn't like cars. It couldn't be explained, but she didn't want to get near them. A chill went through her small body—and her stomach churned—whenever a car rumbled by. Being sent inside didn't bother her at all. The other children in the neighborhood would run and jump on the running boards when the cars came chugging down the avenue.

The neighborhood was a big family. Everyone took care of each other. Being immigrants with similar backgrounds created this bond. Many escaped horrible situations and were more than happy to be able to work and celebrate their new home. The Irish loved each other's company, and they shared gossip, conversation, music, jokes, and each other's grief.

Nora was aware her brothers, sisters, and mother all looked as though they came from the same mold. They all had dark hair, dark eyes, and square jaws. It didn't strike her as odd that she was the only one in the family who was petite with a mop of curly red hair. She figured it was because she was the youngest.

Nora started having nightmares shortly after the couple visited the apartment. It was always dark and cold. She would cry out for her ma. She was terrified her ma was hurt, but in the dream, the woman didn't look like her. It was always the same: rapid popping noises, then darkness and cold. Every time she was overwhelmingly sad. Each time she woke up crying, her ma sat at her side and whispered, "You are safe, Nora. You are safe at home." Then she would sing her to sleep with an Irish lullaby, "Too-Ra-Loo-Ra-Loo-Ra".

CHAPTER 30

Garnet grabbed her coat and swung it around herself. With no time to change out of evening wear, the long coat would have to suffice. She slapped her hand on the bar to get the bartender's attention. "Tony, there is an asshole out cold in the red room. Keep an eye on him. If he comes around, make sure he doesn't leave. No need to rough him up too much, but persuade him to stay. I have an errand to run. I'll be back in a jiff. Don't let that slime out of your sight." The urgency in her voice got the bartender's immediate attention.

Tony gave Garnet a quick nod. "Miss Garnet, are you all right?"

"Yes Tony, I'm peachy. Don't let that ass leave this club. I am depending on you."

"You can count on me. He won't leave." Tony replied as he made a saluting gesture.

Grabbing her handbag from behind the bar, she ran out the door of the Bad Penny. Her step quickened once she was out on the avenue, quicker still as Mae's apartment building came into view. Her heels snapped in rapid sequence as she closed in on her destination. She knew where Mae lived as she had given her the address in case she was ever in a spot. This definitely qualified.

Her red chiffon dress rustled with each step, and a tuft of red spilled out from under her long gray coat with each knee lifted. Garnet wasn't quite sure if Mae was who she needed to talk to, but if she wasn't, Mae would be able to get to the person who could take care of the situation. Garnet's blonde curls flopped into her eyes as she picked up her pace. She tried to hold her coat closed and push her hair out of her eyes as she scurried down the street. She only slowed down to pull her coat tight and knot the belt.

Mae had thought of Garnet many times since she had stopped cleaning the club, but she never expected her to appear at her front door. Mae opened the door and greeted her like an old friend, "Garnet? Are you all right? You're flush as a ripe cherry. Please come in." Mae took Garnet's coat.

Garnet was embarrassed. Mae was always such a caring person, "Mae, I would never impose on you unless it was something urgent. Please forgive my intrusion and my attire. I didn't know where to turn. I know you are acquainted with Dan Malone and Michael Byrne. I am aware of the murders that took place on New Year's Eve. Mae, the bastard whose nose was bitten off is in my club. He doesn't give a shit about anyone. He's either oblivious that someone is looking for him—or he has a death wish." She reached for her cigarette holder, glanced at Mae then put it back between her cleavage, "Shit. I'm sorry, honey. This guy has me so upset. Please know I would never come to your home dressed this way. There was no time to change. I had to be sure I got here and told you about this freak."

Mae noticed cuts and bruises up and down Garnet's arms. "Garnet, what happened to your arms? Are you all right?"

"Mae, that bastard came into the club tanked and looking for trouble. I knew exactly who he was the minute I saw him. He has a large bandage over his nose. He started throwing his weight around like we should all kiss his ass. My man, Tony, was ready to throw him out into the gutter. I tried to get close to him. I spent time with him, he got a little rough. I'm a big girl. I have seen a lot, but this asshole is a real bastard. There is no other way to describe him. He is a pissant, not anyone of importance, just a drunken thug. I can't believe he isn't dead already. He's a poor excuse for a human. He drank himself into oblivion. I snuck out when I was sure he was out cold. Tony is keeping an eye on him."

Mae walked to the window to see if there was anyone in sight who could get word to Declan. There was a group of young kids standing on the stoop. Mae could hear them more than she could see them. She called out the window, "Are any of you boys interested in earning some money?"

A lanky kid yelled back as he stepped into the street, "Mrs., I am ready to work."

"It is a simple task, young man. I can't leave my apartment and I need to get word to my son, Declan, that I need help."

Several voices sang out. "I'll help you."

"That's very sweet of all of you, but I need my son's help."

"Where do I find your boy?" the first young man shouted.

"He'll be at Cara Dílis. Go in the front door and tell the

fellow at the counter that Mae needs Declan to come home. I'll pay you when he gets here."

The kid ran toward Cara Dílis.

Mae turned and waved Garnet into the kitchen. She reached into the top cabinet and pulled down a bottle and two teacups. She poured them each a whiskey. As she handed Garnet her cup she said, "Garnet, you must stay here until this is resolved. There's no telling what that crazy bastard will do. I don't want to offend you, my friend, but you look a little cold. Would you like a housedress to wear?"

Garnet took a long swallow from her teacup and smiled. "Sweetie, you could never offend me. Yes, I could use something to cover up with. I will take you up on your offer. I flew out of the club as soon as that bastard passed out. Mae, you know me to be a hardboiled egg, but that freak is beyond words."

"We'll see to it that trash gets taken care of. I'll get you a warmer dress and make us some warm toast while we wait."

Garnet looked around the apartment while Mae looked for a dress and prepared the toast. The apartment was bright and clean, like it had just been painted. The furnishings weren't fancy, but they were in good shape. By the far window, there was a rolltop desk with three large ledgers. Garnet thought,

There are her precious files. She has done well for herself and for those she has helped. She felt a bit of pride that Mae was able to connect with Dan Malone at her club.

Mae never called on Declan for help. He was at his wit's end when he got word his mother needed him at home. Michael ran into Declan flying out the door as he was entering.

155

"What the hell is going on, Declan? Are you good?"

"Something is wrong with Ma. I have to go."

"Hey, I'm with you, Let's go."

It wasn't just Michael and Declan. Since the family was traveling in pairs, each had a partner. The four men tried to look inconspicuous as they scrambled to Mae's apartment. Declan and his partner left first. Once they were out of sight, Michael and Sully headed down the street.

The kid followed Declan up the stairs, and Declan snapped, "Where the hell do you think you're going?"

"Your ma promised to pay me for fetching you."

Declan reached into his pocket and handed the kid a five-dollar bill.

The kid gushed his gratefulness to Declan and was off like a shot.

Michael passed the kid as he sprinted up the stairs to Mae's apartment. Declan was already in the apartment. He was out of breath from running up the stairs. "Jesus, Ma, are you ok?"

"I'm sorry son. I couldn't think of a better way to get you up here. This is an old friend of mine, Garnet. She runs the club near the river."

"Ma, you had me run all this way to meet an old friend?"

"No, there is more … much more. Garnet needs to get in contact with Michael."

"He is on his way up here. We both thought you were sick or hurt."

"Again, Declan, I am sorry, but this was too important to wait."

Michael opened the door and quietly spoke, "Ladies, this looks like it is going to be a good story."

Garnet sat at the table with Michael and Declan, and each of them downed a cup of whiskey. Garnet told Michael in rapid fire about the man at the Bad Penny.

Michael grabbed Declan's shoulder. "You and Sully go back to the club, get a couple more hands to help us. Have them meet us at them rear of Garnet's club. Get back here with a car. I don't want to waste any time. You know what to bring. I don't want to attract anyone's attention. I don't think we will have a problem with this ass, but I don't want to give him a chance to take off."

Michael whispered, "Declan, I want this guy to suffer. Bring me my knucks. He is mine."

He turned his attention to the women. "Garnet, I really appreciate you giving us the heads-up on this pig. I think you should stay with Mae until we return. I'm familiar with your club. Exactly which room is this scum in?"

The hair on the back of Michael's neck was standing straight up. He was eager to get this bastard in his grip. He and Declan drove in silence. Sully was just ahead of them. As they reached the river, Michael could see the rest of the group had arrived. Declan nodded to Michael as he gave him his brass knuckles then the two stationed the men. No Nose had no escape.

Everyone was ready.

Michael walked to the front door of the club. Tony was drying glasses behind the bar.

Michael pinched his nose, and Tony pointed toward the red room. Michael, with Declan following behind him, slowly turned the doorknob. He could hear heavy breathing as the door opened. It almost struck him as funny. *How can you snore without a damn nose?*

157

No Nose was a whale of a man. He covered the entire bed and smelled as bad as he looked. Alcohol reeked from his pores, and his breath was wretched.

Michael gave him a slap, as if to swat a fly, directly on the bandage that covered what was left of his nose.

The man jumped, "What the fuck is wrong with you?"

Michael gave him a quiet look as he slowly spoke, "I've been looking for you. Do you know who I am?"

"Jesus, shit no. I don't know who you are, and I don't care. Are you that bitch's pimp?"

"No, but I may be your executioner. It's up to you whether you leave this room upright or feet first. Either way, you are going to give me answers. We can do this painfully or extremely painfully. Those are your only choices. What the hell is your name? I'm tired of referring to you as No Nose."

"My name is Duke Lansing. You don't scare me, you dumb Mick."

"Well, Duke, you should be scared … terrified, I think. This dumb Mick owns Cara Dílis. You murdered my friends. There is no doubt you did it—I have what you seem to be missing." Michael pulled a rolled up bloodstained handkerchief from his jacket pocket, waved it in front of the bastard. It dropped on the bed.

The man's body stiffened at the sight of the chunk of discolored flesh that was once his nose. He jumped from the bed as though he was going to lunge toward Michael.

Michael swung, Duke's face and neck whipped around with a bone-cracking snap. Declan never saw Michael take the brass knuckles from his pocket, let alone take the swing. Michael grabbed No Nose before he could fall. "You see

Duke, I want to know who was with you at my club on New Year's Eve. What the fuck made you think you could murder my friends and steal from me without any consequences?"

"I'm … I'm afraid I can't help you, asshole. I was bit by a dog in the park." No Nose was still trying to be tough, but he was visibly shaken.

Michael pulled him from the bed and tossed him onto a chair. Another swing struck with a loud crack to the slob's jaw.

No Nose spat out blood along with a couple of teeth.

Michael took off his jacket and rolled up his sleeves. Declan had never seen this side of Michael. His demeanor was quiet, but rage filled the room like steam from fast-boiling potatoes.

"I've got as long as it takes … so you may as well make this easy on yourself." Michael spoke softly as he struck No Nose again. The slob expelled a huge breath as Michael's fist sank deep into his chest. He slumped into the chair as he gasped struggling to refill his lungs.

"A guy at the docks gave me cash. He was hiring daily workers. All I was told was to make sure the liquor didn't make it to the club for New Year's. I was just doing a job; your guys made it hard on themselves. We were trying to get extra for ourselves before we took the truck. Those dumb bastards decided to fight us."

Michael took another swing. "You piece of shit. You beat them to death, hit two from behind. They never had a chance, now you have the balls to say it was just a job?"

No Nose spat back, "Times are hard, and the money was good. I've got no clue who you're looking for. I'm just the delivery boy. I do know whoever is behind this isn't finished with you."

Michael slapped him across the face. "How do you know so much if you were just picked up at the docks?"

The man inhaled deeply and snorted as blood dripped from the vacant cavity. "I know you don't pay that kind of money to just shake down a bunch of saps. I'm dead as soon as they find out you talked to me. My orders were to do the job and leave town permanently if I wanted to stay alive. I wanted one last party before I left. It doesn't matter what I know or tell you. I'm dead either way—so beat me all you want."

"Who hired you? Who paid you? What did he look like? Who was with you? Have you seen them on the docks before?" Michael rattled off questions hoping he would get something out of this puke other than a sore hand.

"Like I said, I don't know who the hell hired me or who the other chumps were. If you're going to kill me, do it. I got nothing more to say. I'm no rat."

Michael took a deep breath as his blood rushed to the top of his head. His ears burned as the realization hit that he had found Tommy's murderer, but he still didn't know who was behind any of it or why. The rage swelled inside of him, and he thought of Conrad. He pulled his sleeves up past his elbows, went to the basin, washed his hands, pulled down the sleeves, buttoned the cuffs, put his jacket back on, and smiled at No Nose. "Duke, you are right. You are dead. I don't have to bloody my hands any more than I already have. I'll watch and wait. They will find you, and hopefully—by the grace of God—I'll be there to watch you suffer the way my friends did. I'll find whoever is responsible for all this bloodshed. You are the bait. Enjoy your blood money for as long as you have. I will make sure I spread the word that we had a long conversation. You sang like a bird to save your skin. Shit. Who the hell am I kidding? You deserve to feel the pain my friends felt."

Michael clenched his fist, and struck No Nose with a jolting crack in the face, first on one side, then on the other.

No Nose fell limp on the floor, blood oozing from both ears and his nasal crevice.

Michael started to leave the asshole bleeding on the floor. Then like a bolt of lightning, he remembered his promise to Ida. He couldn't walk out on his promise. Michael gave Declan a glance and growled, "I made a promise to Tommy's widow, Ida. If you have a problem with that, leave. I will understand."

Declan looked at Michael. "You don't even have to ask. I'm with you no matter what."

The two men pulled No Nose to his feet and dragged him out of the room.

"Tony, we were never here, neither was this pile of shit."

"Not a problem sir," Tony answered.

No Nose left a trail of blood through the bar.

"I'll take care of it," Tony said as Michael glance at the trail.

Michael signaled the rest of the men to go back to the club.

Michael and Declan tossed No Nose into the trunk of Declan's car like a bag of garbage. The two drove in silence toward a deserted part of the riverbank. Michael pulled the bloody mess from the trunk slamming him to the ground.

No Nose was weak and battered as he begged for his life.

Michael took a couple more punches to shut him up then tied his feet and hands together.

Declan found a couple of busted cement blocks near the water.

Michael nodded to Declan, "Get back in the car. I'll finish this."

Declan slowly moved to the car as Michael tied the blocks around No Nose. He pulled him to the water's edge then rolled him in.

No Nose never made a sound as he slowly sank.

Declan started the car, Michael stomped the river mud off his shoes before he climbed back in.

The two men drove silently back to Mae's apartment. Sully was waiting outside the apartment for Michael. Garnet turned toward Michael as he entered. It was the first time he had actually looked at the woman. He usually saw her red feathers and the cigarette hanging from her mouth. She looked fragile sitting at the kitchen table with Mae, not the flamboyant club manager he saw at her place when he had gone in for a quick drink. Michael gave Mae a quick glance then turned his attention to Garnet. "May I give you a ride back to your place? It has been a long evening. We took out the trash. Know your help is appreciated."

Almost embarrassed, Garnet gave Mae a glance.

"Go home, Garnet. You can bring back the dress whenever you want."

Garnet whispered, "Thank you, Mae, for being so helpful."

"That is what friends do, Garnet. We help each other."

The two women hugged. Garnet put on her coat, placed her red gown over her arm, and followed Michael out the door. Garnet felt the tension in the car as they rode back to her place. She was conflicted about how she felt. She was sure Michael was married. She accepted the fact that he was just doing her a favor by giving her a ride. They chatted about the city and the weather. They avoided discussing the events of the evening.

As Garnet got out of the car, Michael grabbed her hand and smiled. "Garnet, thank you for your help tonight. I know how hard it was for you. If you need anything, let me know."

Garnet smiled and said, "That is what friends do. We help each other."

CHAPTER 31

It seemed like an eternity since Michael had been home. He was beyond exhausted, but he wanted to be sure Tara was all right. She had been slipping away for the past few months. He had delayed bringing William home from school. Tara slept in their bed alone. He slept on the davenport. He hated not being within her touch, but he was terrified he would hurt her by rolling over.

As he slipped into the bedroom, he heard her choppy breathing. She strained for each breath. The room seemed clammy and hot, but she felt cold to his touch.

She slowly rolled in his direction and gave him a weak smile. "Oh Mickey, I'm so glad you are here. I was just dreaming about running on the beach. Eveleen and I were laughing and playing in the water." Tara took a strained pause to catch her breath and whispered, "I think it's time to bring William home. I miss him so much."

"Yes, *mo mhilis* (my sweetness). I agree it is time to bring him home. I will set up a ride home for him and make arrangements with the school in the morning."

The words left unspoken hung in the air. His eyes filled with tears as he held Tara in his arms. Michael knew she wouldn't live much longer. She had been his life, his strength, for so long, now he was going to have to let her go.

"Mickey?" Tara turned his face to hers. "Don't lose sight of what you have worked for. I am ready to let go of this life. I'll be with you always in our son and in the memories we share."

Michael's throat tightened as he fought back tears while he gently held Tara's hand. Life would never be the same without his love. She completed him. She had kept him sane in what had become their tragedy-filled life. She was his rock. "Please, Tara, don't talk that way. We will see our dreams come true together and watch our son become a man … together. We'll grow old together."

Sully picked William up at school. He brought him straight home. William was silent for most of the ride. He knew why he had been summoned. He prayed they would make it in time. William ran up the stairs to the apartment. Sully followed at his own pace.

"Ma? Ma, where are you?"

It had been several weeks since he had seen his mother. William was shocked to see how ill and frail she was. She was propped up with pillows on her bed. Michael was seated next to the window.

Tara tried her hardest to look comfortable. She and Michael both knew they didn't have much time.

William reached for his ma and lightly squeezed her hand. He was afraid to touch anywhere else.

The three of them sat in silence until the sun sank behind the buildings. Once the room was dark, Michael turned on the lamp near the door. He got Tara a glass of water and moistened her lips with a damp cloth.

Mae brought some food for them, but Michael and William refused to leave the room. Tara finally convinced them to bring plates into the room. "Bring me a plate as well." The three sat in the yellow glow of the lamp as Mae brought them all plates.

Michael knew she wasn't going to eat, but he went along with her.

William talked nervously about school. How he couldn't wait for summer so he could be home all the time.

Tara interrupted him. She directed her conversation to her son as well as Michael, "Son, you know I don't have much time left. I want you to be strong … know I am ready to move on. I think it's time we considered you going to school closer to home. Your da will need you and I need you to take care of him."

William forced a weak smile. He feared if he spoke he would burst into frantic tears. Once again the young man reached for his ma's hand. Father and son sat with Tara listening to her choppy breathing.

Sometime during the night Michael noticed Tara gave a huge sigh of relief then was gone from them.

Tara didn't want a big funeral or a big fuss. She was quietly laid to rest after a family Mass. Even though it was planned as a small family goodbye, many of the couple's friends came to show their respect. Michael, although grief stricken was acutely aware he had to remain publicly strong. The day was a blur. He had no idea who was at the service. Mae and Declan saw that he and William got home.

Without a word, William went to his room. He had never seen his father broken this way. The young man never saw his father's reaction to the death of his best friend and partner. Grief surrounded them.

Michael sat in the rocker in the corner of the bedroom he had shared with Tara. He was motionless except for his hands. He held Tara's Rosary beads. He slipped the rose-shaped beads through his fingers. He was crushed. He had lost nearly all that he loved. Death enveloped his entire life. It swirled around him like a dreaded whirlpool. He had managed to stay afloat, ahead of the whirlpool, but Tara's death was too much. He had nothing to grab onto. He was unable to reach the shore. The love of his life was gone. Sorrow gripped at his throat and chest, both of them painfully tight. His chest collapsed in on his lungs. His eyes swelled with tears.

Alone in the darkness of the room he had shared with his love, he finally let loose. He feared he'd explode if he didn't release what he felt. He cried in near silence, but the occasional gasp escaped. He had to be strong for William. His son was all that mattered. All the dreams for the future that he shared with Conrad and the future he had looked forward to with Tara —were gone along with the two of them.

CHAPTER 32

Michael felt the warmth of the sun on his face. When he heard pans clanging in the kitchen, for an instant, he thought it had been a horrible nightmare. His heart jumped as he pictured Tara making breakfast. He rose from the chair, the Rosary beads still wound around his fingers. His heart fell at his feet as reality struck. He squeezed the Rosary beads into a ball, gave them a kiss, as he dropped them into his breast pocket. He slowly walked to the kitchen.

Mae was busy at the stove. Declan and William were talking at the table.

"Good morning, Da," William said as he tried to get a feel for his father's state of mind.

"Have some tea and a slice of toast while I finish up breakfast," Mae said in a very matter of fact tone, not allowing Michael to refuse.

Michael picked up a piece of toast and took a bite. He couldn't remember the last time he had eaten. He looked at William and with a hoarse whisper spoke, "We have to see about getting you in school close to home. I want to be able to see you sitting at the table with me on a daily basis. I'm going to need some time to get myself together, but that is on the top of my list." He turned toward Declan. "I really could use your help, Declan. I need someone I can depend on to stand by me right now. I can't appear shaky or weak. There are those who would jump at a chance to take advantage of my grief."

Declan nodded as he placed a hand on Michael's shoulder. Nothing more needed to be said. Declan was by his side.

William was surprised, his da never discussed business in front of him. He pretended he was involved with his tea and toast so his father would not feel awkward with him present. He wanted so much to be close to Michael.

Mae placed the rest of breakfast on the table. "Michael, you see to what you boys must. I will see that we get William settled in school here. I'll have Sully go to the school to get the rest of the boy's belongings along with any paperwork we'll need."

CHAPTER 33

The family made it back to the hotel just past midnight. They planned to meet William and Luke in the morning. William was freeing his mind of this tragic secret. The group quietly went about their nightly routines in a daze.

Elizabeth wandered around the room soaking in its beauty. As she wandered. she picked out clothing for the morning. The huge room fell silent.

Nora tossed and turned; her mind was full of William's story. A father she never knew viciously slaughtered along with a mother she couldn't remember. What sort of life-changing business deal had Conrad made that caused someone to want to destroy everyone connected to him? What would her life have been like if Conrad and Eveleen had raised her? She fought off the fog of her disease and the restlessness of the day. She slept void of any dreams for most of the night.

The room was still dark when Elizabeth awoke; a sliver of light danced through the blinds.

Brendan was up and had called down for breakfast.

Elizabeth jumped up, thinking she was late, but it was shortly after nine.

Brendan pulled her close and said, "We have time for

a nice breakfast. How about a cup of coffee? We don't have to meet William and Luke until eleven. If today is anything like yesterday, we're all going to need a good breakfast and each other's support."

Nora was up with a snap. Corazon doled out her meds, then they joined everyone for breakfast. The conversation started with the elegance of the hotel, avoiding the revelations of the previous day. They ate and talked. Corazon was confused and saddened that Nora had no knowledge of her family. The disclosure certainly explained Nora's dark dreams.

The smell of coffee filled the room.

Nora's disfigured hands seized one of the china mugs. It was embossed with an eagle on one side and "The Didean" on the other side. She filled her plate with eggs and bacon. Her mind needed fuel to survive the day. The coffee went down slowly, every sip savored. It would keep the fog at bay. She watched Brendan as he drank his coffee. He always knew what to do. He smiled as though he could hear her thoughts. She had a new energy, an important purpose.

After breakfast, Elizabeth pulled their suitcase out of the closet. She placed the case on the bench at the foot of the bed and opened it. She had carefully stored the traveler's checks in the suitcase under her clothing. The traveler's checks were on top of the clothing and pulled out of the envelopes.

After yesterday's conversations with William, a chill went through Elizabeth's body. She shouted, "Brendan, I need you in here—now!"

Brendan came running.

"Brendan, someone has gone through our suitcase. Everything is pulled out."

"Lizzy, is anything missing?"

"I can't tell. It looks like they were looking for something specific. All the envelopes are open. Brendan, you watched me sort the traveler's checks by dollar amount, and I filed them under the clothes."

Brendan said, "I'll call hotel security and William to let him know we are going to be late. Lizzy, go through our things and see if anything is missing."

Corazon and Nora went through all their bags and checked the jewelry. Nothing was missing. All the traveler's checks were intact. The extra money and credit cards were all safely tucked in the suitcase.

Elizabeth thought, *How stupid, I should have put them in the safe. It would have been so easy for someone to just take the envelopes with all the funds for our trip along with the credit cards.*

After Brendan called William he came back into the bedroom and closed the door. "William is livid. He thinks he may have unintentionally led someone to us, and they may be searching for something they think you or your mom may have. He still wants to meet. He wants us to file a report with the hotel and the police. He is hoping someone saw who was in the room or that the police involvement will scare them off."

Elizabeth couldn't decide if she wanted to scream at the top of her lungs or just crawl into a corner and cry.

There was no time to decide because the phone rang.

It was Declan Moore, "Mrs. Connelly, we intend on

handling this in house. Don't worry about calling the police."

"Mr. Moore?"

"Please call me Declan."

"Yes, of course, Declan. We already called the hotel security."

"That is not an issue. William owns the hotel, the staff is very efficient. We will go over any security films to see if we can identify who was in your room. I will pick you up myself. Is forty-five minutes OK? We aren't going to the pub; we are going someplace that has always been a safe haven. I will go into detail when I get there."

"William just told us we were going to the pub."

"Yes, I am quite aware of that. William doesn't quite have a grasp on how fast things can go sideways. As I said, I will talk to you in person. I don't want to waste time on the phone. I will be there as soon as I can." Declan spoke anxiously.

"Sideways," wasn't a very comforting phrase. Her stomach knotted up again. The coffee that she had just enjoyed was revolting.

Elizabeth showered, hoping the hot water would clear her mind and calm it as well. Her mother's past intrigued her, but the possibility of having it jump up to attack their family was terrifying. What was so important that someone was still searching for it sixty years later? Had the animals who murdered her mother's parents done so without completing the deal with Conrad? Had Conrad's big deal been so great that the people he was dealing with decided to take it over? They must have had what they wanted as they never came after Michael or his family. How could they think Momma had hidden something all these years? She had no idea about her past. Michael changed Momma's identity after her parents' slaughter; how was she found? She was supposed to be dead. Was there a traitor in William's circle who knew Momma's identity—, but now was their entire family exposed? Had someone gained William's trust and waited for an opportunity to pounce?

Her mind raced as the hot water flowed over her body. William should have left it alone. She wished he never approached them at Maureen's service. Her mother deserved to live her remaining life in peace without having to deal with a new identity. They were all involved in some dark bloody mystery. Overwhelmed by fear and sadness, she broke down as she dried off. *Lizzy, you don't have time for tears. You have to get your shit together and figure this out. These old guys have been searching for a murderer for years without any luck. Momma may hold the key.*

Brendan met Declan at the door in forty-five minutes to the second. His demeanor was strong and quiet. Declan was older, but still had a full head of salt and pepper hair. He seemed to be a quiet man who listened more than he spoke. An enforcer from the old days, not someone who still would be involved in protection. He could be a supervisor, but not an active enforcer.

After sizing Declan up Lizzy's imagination soared, *Sure, he teaches protection classes to all the other enforcers. It's too early for a drink, but I could sure use one.*

Declan said, "I must apologize to all of you for any additional stress. All the drama with William has been a bitch, and then to have this shit piled on top of all that. I don't think I would be as calm as you are. Please forgive my crudeness. This never should have happened. You should have been able to attend Maureen's service and meet family without all this additional drama."

"Declan don't let appearances fool you. I was a blubbering idiot a few minutes ago. Momma, on the other hand, is raring to go."

"Let's get down to it. William is beside himself. He has been more of a figurehead for the family over the years, and he isn't sure how to handle this situation. I, on the other hand, have been in the thick of things all along. William spent time in the country and in private boarding schools. After the death of his ma, he attended schools in the city and then college. Michael was adamant that William should concentrate on his education. I'm sorry. I know I may sound bitter, but I urged William to be more discreet in contacting you. He should not have come to Maureen's service. There was no reason to open old wounds. None of us know why Conrad, Michael, and their families were attacked or who was involved. The search of your room may have been a botched burglary attempt. There is no reason to believe William—or our family—has any connection. It was probably a fluke, but I prefer being cautious."

Elizabeth couldn't shake the feeling that something was going to happen. Daddy had told her she was born to the wrong generation. She had a kinship with the Prohibition era and its flamboyant lifestyle, clothing, and hairstyles. At one point, she had a mad crush on James Cagney, but she wasn't ready to interact with any gangsters, in the flesh.

Brendan put his hand on his wife's shoulder and pulled her close.

Declan smiled and said, "This too will pass. We will

meet William at a little place I know … where we can talk undisturbed. This place has been around for years and has always been somewhere we could go and know we were in a secure location."

Nora reached for her handbag. "I'm ready whenever you are."

They followed Declan to the elevator and into the lobby. He trailed behind as the group passed through the doors. He stopped to shake hands and talk briefly to Chandler. The doorman opened the door to an awaiting town car.

As the car drove through the city, Elizabeth was finally calm enough to see how amazing it was. The buildings swallowed the sky. People covered the sidewalk like ants at a picnic. Traffic jammed the streets.

Nora said, "Elizabeth, do you remember the vacation when you and Angela stayed with my brother Robert and his wife Julia?"

Angela was Keira's eldest child. The two cousins were very close in age. As teenagers, they stayed in the city to see the sights with their aunt and uncle. Aunt Julia had been a nightclub singer in the 1930s. Uncle Robert tended bar in the lounge where she sang. That was how they met. Aunt Julia gave Elizabeth and Angela photos of Uncle Robert and herself as young people. She looked like Jean Harlow. Her wavy, platinum blonde hair flowed down her back. She wore cinder black eyeliner and dark red lipstick. Robert was tall with dark wavy hair. Julia could have been a plethora of family information, She lived to be nearly one hundred, but she was gone now—along with her stories.

"Yes, I remember. Aunt Julia was quite a few years older than Uncle Robert. She remembered Eveleen's murder. It meant nothing to me at the time. I had no idea who she was, and it seemed like another bit of Prohibition folklore."

Nora spat, "How is it she had a story to tell while my own brothers knew nothing?"

Declan spoke in a low voice, "Robert was still in Ireland when Eveleen and Conrad were murdered. Thomas and Ida were aware of the murders, but chose to overlook the possibility of your connection. If they were suspicious, they ignored the connection to protect you and their own family. I'm sure the couple wondered why someone was willing to pay the travel expenses to bring all their children to this country, supply them with jobs, and then continue to support Ida's family after Thomas' murder. All this in return for taking in an orphan?

"You were no ordinary orphan; you were special. They knew, but it was never expressed. I can apologize, but I can't change the past. I understand how upset you must be to have all of this thrown at you at this late date. I am so sorry it took Maureen's death to finally expose the truth. William is trying to make amends before he dies. A heavy burden was thrust upon him by his father. It would have been better if he just let the past remain buried." He looked out the window.

Brendan gave a nod of approval as Nora squeezed her daughter's hand.

The rest of the trip was silent. The car slowed, but didn't stop near an abandoned bar. A man in a dark suit was standing at the curb, smoking a cigar. The car slowed to a crawl, the man at the curb gave a wave and a nod. The town car turned right at the next corner then right again at the next street. This maneuver placed them at the back door of the bar they just passed.

"I'll wait out here, boss. Give me a shout if you need me." The driver told Declan.

"I think we'll be good. Come on in." Declan said quietly.

Nora guessed Declan was about fifteen years older than her. But he looked and spoke like someone much younger.

The group passed through a long, narrow alleyway sandwiched between two old brick buildings. It forced them to walk single file. It was akin to walking through a musty cave. Lights were attached to the walls in several places. It was a bit of an obstacle course, avoiding low-hanging light fixtures while slowly moving through the tight alleyway. Declan led the way. Davey, the driver, brought up the rear. At the end of the alleyway, a set of metal stairs reached up to a rusty metal door. The door made a loud creaking noise as Declan opened it. It was as though it hadn't been opened in decades. Declan held the door open until the entire group had passed through it.

Luke was smoking a cigarette inside the door. He quickly snuffed it out when he saw the group. "Good morning, all. Glad to see you." He seemed uncomfortable.

"Good morning, Luke. How are you this morning? Are you as confused as we are? I'm sure you are as bewildered as my family is with this entire situation." Nora tried to make the conversation light to connect with him somehow.

This poor kid—like herself and her family— just found out his father had been the keeper of a mammoth secret and his grandfather had spent a lifetime searching for unknown butchers.

"I've been better. I didn't get much sleep last night. How about all of you? How did you fare?"

Nora replied, "About the same as you. I was able to get some sleep, but I think I was so exhausted my body just gave out."

Elizabeth shrugged in reply, but she couldn't take her eyes off her mother. She was in awe of her mother's newfound alertness.

As they exchanged pleasantries, Brendan gently reached for his wife and mother-in-law. Corazon held tight to Nora as they entered the bar. The bar was noticeably worn; it was apparent it had been in business for a very long time. It definitely had character. It had been modernized, but the look of a bygone era still lingered. The dark wood walls and huge carved bar back had faded with time but were polished to a high sheen. The mirror, incased by the bar back, also revealed its age. The bar appeared to be a 1930s nightclub, similar to the back room of Cara Dílis, but not as elaborate or updated.

Luke confessed softly. "I am not sure what to think of this morning's get-together. Da has brought together some old friends to meet all of you. He's left Declan in charge of this morning's meeting. I'm not sure what they are trying to accomplish, but I've come to understand that Declan is actually the backbone of this family. My da is a figurehead. There is a lot about my family's past that I don't know or understand."

Nora spoke softly, "Don't worry, Luke. We understand that your father has endured a lot. We don't want to cause him any more pain. I totally understand your feelings about our families' past. We are in the dark right alongside you."

Nora was in tune with everything that was going on. For the moment, the fog that tortured her was gone. She was trying her hardest not to explode. Her blood began to surge at her temples, her face heated up. Her life was drenched with nightmares and unanswered questions. While she was in the fight of her life against an unyielding demon who was stealing the only life she had known, along came the possibility of a different identity. This old man wanted the weight of this dark secret off his chest. In her heart of hearts, she knew the old guy had just kept a secret his father had entrusted to him. Why share his burden at the end of her life? The evil it took to slaughter an entire family in cold blood was unfathomable. Why not let the ghosts from the past rest?

An older man was visible seated at a large round table along with William. Nora squinted to try to get a good look at the old guy without staring, but her aged eyes couldn't make out his face. A large silver tea service sat on a white linen tablecloth in the center of the table.

William walked toward the group when they entered the room. The other man remained in his chair.

"William, there's no need to be so formal. We can come to you." Elizabeth squeaked trying not to sound condescending. Her mother hated to be treated fraily.

Nora gave a quick smile, then looked passed him to the man seated at the table.

"No problem," William said with a smile. It was the first time he had smiled since they met. William had huge dimples that made wide crevices in his cheeks when he smiled, which lifted his scar upward stretching it in an awkward manner, making his glass eye nearly disappear.

"I see you found Danny J. Do you think he can be helpful?" Declan asked in an almost disgusted tone.

William began to speak, ignoring Declan's tone. "I have someone I would like you to meet. I must tell you that we would not be here if it weren't for an experience I had—and for my son, Luke."

Declan interrupted William, "There is someone who isn't here. He was very close to your da and me when things were really tough. Since we have opened this box, I hope we can shed some fresh light on this mystery. Go ahead and explain what happened. When he arrives, we will move forward."

William began, "Recently while I was hospitalized. My father came to me in a dream and ordered me not to let our family secret die with me. I realized I must let those who are left behind know as much as I do about our families. I will share as much as I remember. I hope the people in this room can also shed some light on both our families' past."

William slowly swung his arm around in the direction of the table and said, "This is an old friend, Danny J. Malone. His father was a close friend of my father, Michael, and your father, Conrad. Dan Malone took my da and Conrad under his wing when they were fresh off the boat from Ireland. Along with Declan, Dan Malone stood by my da after Conrad and Eveleen were murdered. Danny J.'s da was a lifelong friend.

"Declan may have the most knowledge of our group. Although he was merely a kid, he was very close to my da after Conrad's murder. He was Da's right-hand, his confidant, and dearest longtime friend. Declan has been a brother to me. I felt since I was sharing what little I know with you, that perhaps if we got together as a group with different points of view, we might discover some information that was overlooked. Something that could shed some light on why someone wanted our families' dead."

Danny J. was a few years older than Declan. His large belly was camouflaged with a thick tie and loose clothing. His thin white hair was combed over a large bald spot. His gray eyes jumped as he glared at everyone in the room. He had a thick white mustache and white eyebrows. His right eyebrow was much thinner than the left one.

Nora's first impression of this man was disgust and fear. An aura of arrogance seeped from Danny J.'s pores. She still wasn't used to Conrad being called her father. She got the impression William's dream left him unsure about whether this nightmare was over. Was his father reaching out from the grave to protect him? Was there still a reason to be concerned for their safety? It was as though William was making one final effort, before he died to solve the murders that hung over the family for years like a black toxic cloud. Nora tensed up, but her daughter lent a comforting hand.

It was a strange feeling to sit alongside these old men. Elizabeth was anxious about what they might say. She managed a slight smile as she wondered if she was sitting with a group of gangsters. Apparently, they knew what their fathers were involved in, but there was a sense that prior to this gathering none of them had verbalized what they knew.

After an awkward silence, the bar door swung open. Two Black men came through the door. They both looked like New York businessmen, or Wall Street bankers.

The man who came through the door first walked

toward the table, "Gentlemen, it has been a long time since we all got together in one room."

Declan stood up and walked quickly toward the men, "Tallman, I am so glad you could make it."

Declan looked toward William at his place at the table, "This is Tallman Fletcher. He and his family worked closely with Michael and me after Conrad's murder. It was a time when trustworthy associates were hard to come by. During those times, Irish and Blacks didn't mingle. They were in constant competition for jobs—anything that put food on the table—but we saw the benefit of sticking together and protecting each other."

Tallman looked at Declan, then at the table where Danny J. sat. Declan quickly continued speaking, "William invited Danny J. to join us. His da gave Conrad and Michael their start and he remained a loyal friend and adviser."

Tallman took Declan's lead. It was obvious neither of them liked or trusted Danny J.—and that William was totally oblivious of their impression.

The hair on Nora's arms stood on end as she realized her first impression of Danny J. had merit.

"This is my grandson, Marcus. I brought him along so he could get a look at how we got to this point in our lives." Tallman said as his grandson walked up next to him.

Luke pulled a couple of chairs up to the table, Tallman and Marcus sat down.

It was no mystery how Tallman got his name. Tallman Fletcher was a tall black man, well over six foot five, whose age was difficult to determine. His skin was dark and tight with only a small number of wrinkles. His onyx eyes were sharp and clear. Unlike the other men seated at the table whose eyes, with age, had lost their crisp clear shine. At first glance, the only clue to his age was his white hair. Tallman's thick white curls framed his face. He stood tall and straight without the slump of age. A closer look gave a hint to his age, his hands were those of an elderly man, they were wrinkled and deformed by arthritis.

Declan offered the two men coffee and whiskey as he introduced them to everyone in the room. Marcus sat silently at the table making no eye contact. He wasn't as tall as his grandfather, but he was still over six feet. His skin was not as dark as Tallman's, but he had the same sparkling onyx eyes. It was obvious he had no clue why the two of them were there with a bunch of old Irishmen. He took a cup of coffee and a shot of whiskey, poured the whiskey into the coffee, then took a large gulp.

Tallman stirred the coffee and placed the whiskey beside his coffee cup. He slowly tapped his spoon on the edge of his cup, took a sip, and cleared his throat before he spoke. "I knew both your fathers." He looked at Nora and William. "William, I remember the night you were shot. I was nothing but a very young buck, still wet behind the ears. None of us had any idea what could possibly provoke such a horrific slaughter. Everyone believed the baby had been butchered along with her parents." Tallman paused then drank the shot of whiskey.

Marcus appeared surprised with his grandfather's description of himself.

Tallman continued, "I don't know what you all have shared about your memories, but I think Declan and I—as young men coming up—probably have the most firsthand information. Times were hard, and we did whatever it took to stay alive. Lord knows we weren't saints. We did many things we were not proud of just to survive. But the gruesome slaughter of Conrad and his family was beyond the worst of what any of us would ever dream of doing. Only a sick animal was capable of such a sadistic massacre."

Danny J. began to speak, as he shot a restless look at Luke, "Luke, bring over that pot of coffee and the bottle of Jameson."

It was obvious Luke was embarrassed by a stranger barking orders at him. He excused himself from the table and walked to the bar and came back with the steaming coffee and the whiskey.

The table was silent until he returned.

Danny J. added a large helping of whiskey to his coffee.

William spoke slowly, "Children, we are a family. All of us in this room have been brought together by the blood of our friends, fathers, and grandfathers. We all loved them." He looked in Nora's direction. "I was always curious about the past, but I never came right out and asked about what went on during those dark years before the end of Prohibition. My da wasn't open about his business. I hope we each have some personal experiences from our past that might enlighten all of us. I can only hope what I have been holding all these years will open doors to our past."

William took Nora's hand and looked at his son. "What we are going to share with you are our memories and those relayed to us. We have not shared these memories with one another, so it may take some time and patience. After the murders, my father was so worried about who was trying to destroy the family that my ma and I were shuttled away to a safe place while I recovered from my injuries. You were placed with a new family—for your safety—and the rest of the family tried to move forward as best they could."

Michael had only shared the fact that Nora was still alive with Declan and his mother, Mae Moore. Not even Dan Malone was aware of it. The elder Malone had kept track of William and his mother while they were at the shore.

After a long sip of coffee, Danny J. said, "My da kept his business separate from his family. I don't have a lot to offer as far as what he might have known. He was always on guard when I was with him, and when I reached school age, I was sent away to school. There were certain things Da did that make more sense now. He never trusted anyone outside his circle of friends and close business associates. I'm sorry, but I don't think I have any information that would be of interest. I came into my da's business long after the end of Prohibition. I knew he was powerful. We still maintain control of a large organization, but we are a legitimate group. One thing does stand out. It may be nothing, but when I was coming up—before Da gave me control—he took me to dinner at a quiet restaurant on the Lower East Side and told me, 'Look around, son. These are the people who made our business—not the banks or the real estate brokers. The sweat and blood of hardworking men made us who we are. Don't fall into the trap of thinking you are better than any of these hardworking people or so big that you need a banker to help manage our business. Bankers are the biggest crooks in the city.'

"I took him at his word. I don't know what made him make that point. It seemed sinister to me … as though he was trying to tell me something without going into detail.

There was a judge who disappeared while working on a fraud case—Crater was his name—he disappeared after eating at Billy Haas's Chophouse. He left the restaurant and was gone. Da used him as an example of someone well-off who trusted bankers, got involved with them and their cronies, and thought he could make a load of easy money. He paid for it in the end. He never reappeared." Danny J.'s eyes glazed over like he was remembering something or someone, but he was silent.

The silence was broken as Tallman began to cough after taking a drink of his coffee.

"I'm sorry. The coffee is hotter than I expected. I wasn't aware you had control of your da's business."

Danny J. gave him a sneer over the rim of his coffee cup.

Nora knew that people of that time didn't trust bankers, especially after the stock market crash. She hoped the others in the room had something more substantial to contribute.

Tallman cleared his throat, gave Declan a quick glance as he sipped his coffee.

William had been sheltered by his da after he was shot.

Declan sat quietly while Danny J. spoke. He was the youngest of the group, but he actually had knowledge of the people and events being discussed. Michael and Conrad recognized that Declan had no father figure in his life. They were not much older than Declan when they landed in the city and Dan Malone took them in. It was only right that they take care of the youngster; any honorable Irishman would do the same.

Declan was no slouch; he worked hard at whatever they threw at him. He was taller than Danny J. and William. Although he was only slightly younger than the two, he seemed much more vibrant. Declan looked at Danny J. like he had something to say but directed his attention to William. His eyes glistened as he began to speak, emotion filled his voice. He spoke slowly in what appeared to be an attempt to keep his emotions in check,

"Michael and Conrad took me under their wing … much like Mr. Malone had done for them. In the beginning, I was mostly a gofer for them. I was too young to be involved in the real business. I remember the morning Conrad was murdered. I was in the street when Conrad came down the stairs; he was dressed in a suit, as always. He said good day to me, but he seemed preoccupied. I asked if he needed anything. He told me he had an appointment downtown and when he came back, we would talk about what he needed me to do. He gave me a broad smile, patted me on the shoulder, then headed to the corner to catch a cab. When I saw him later that day, he was very excited. He headed straight up to his apartment." Declan's large eyes sharpened when he spoke of Conrad.

"I was just inside the door of the candy store when I heard the gunshots and shouting coming from the street. I ran to Tara and Michael's side. Their pain and sadness hung thick in the air. I ran as fast as I could to get the beat cop, Flanagan. He nearly ran over me as he ran toward the shooting. He was out of breath and cursed all the way down the street.

"I agree with Danny J. about bankers and their types. The bankers and politicians talk a lot of bullshit about honor and honesty, but they are the biggest crooks around. It's not just bankers. There are some jealous, mean-spirited bastards who can't stand to see anyone else succeed. They are the vilest, with absolutely no sense of honor, honesty, or loyalty. They are only loyal to themselves."

Declan was looking right at Danny J. the entire time he spoke.

"I tried my hardest to do all that Michael needed done. It was incredibly hard to know Nora was still alive, right under everyone's nose, knowing I had to guard that secret with my life. Michael was never the same after that day. He was always looking over his shoulder. His sadness and anger clung to him like a wet wool coat. The day we emptied Conrad and Eveleen's apartment was one of the worst days I spent with Michael. Only Tara's death and the massacre of his friends were worse.

"Michael's shoulder oozed blood, and every time he made a sudden move, he cringed and mumbled in pain. His shoulder never healed properly. That day in the apartment, I really felt the impact and pain everyone was going through. Michael meticulously went through every drawer and closet, every pocket and purse. He even checked the shoes for anything that might lead him to Conrad's secret deal and his killer. After he searched an area, I was instructed to box up what he had gone through.

"When he approached Eveleen's vanity, he took a step back and dropped to the floor. I thought he had passed out. I ran to him. He was wiping his eyes, but he didn't want me to see. I pretended I didn't know he was crying. My ma took a pile of Nora's clothes to the Doyle's apartment. Michael asked me to take the vanity at the same time. The mirror was loose when I lifted it. I tightened it so it wouldn't break during the move. It was all that remained of Nora's family." Declan's voice was getting hoarse. His eyes were red and watered. He stopped talking, poured a glass of Jameson, took a deep breath, and threw down the whiskey.

Nora thought, *Maybe bringing these old guys together was a good idea. Declan had information he didn't even realize he had. Of the four old men, Declan and maybe Tallman seem to have the most firsthand information.* She squeezed her daughter's hand as Declan continued.

"Conrad's murder brought sadness and a silent control to Michael. When Tommy Doyle and the others were so savagely massacred, a different Michael appeared. The sadness was still there, but a dark side emerged—one I had never seen. It was as though he had gone back to being that starving kid in Ireland who would survive at all costs. He was determined to avenge the murders. Over the years, he had lost too many friends. He was never able to recover."

Luke had remained silent during this entire time. He cleared his voice and spoke, "Where do we go from here? Do you think Nora and her family could be in danger?"

William snapped, "There is nothing we can do. They are all gone. There are no answers. I don't know if there ever were any answers."

"William, the choice to do something was made for us before any of us were dry behind the ears." Danny J. leaned back in his chair and twisted his eyebrow hair as he continued, "Our fathers came to this country to make a better life for all of us, and they did that. We reap what they sowed, but we are also responsible for their legacy. We can't allow this to go unsolved. There are forces that you aren't aware of that may be involved in these murders, and those forces will surface once they know we are discussing things together."

Declan snapped, "Jesus, Danny J. Why the hell are you being so cryptic?"

"I am going to tell you something my da shared with me. I promised I would never discuss it. Da felt it was his greatest failure, but since we are sharing our past, this may qualify as being important. As a kid, my da took me to the shore and showed me an empty shoreline on a dirt road. He told me, 'Someday, this will be a busy highway filled with restaurants and hotels, and people will escape the city to spend time here. The road will be paved smooth, and the train will have a special stop to let passengers off.'

"I thought about how wonderful that would be. To Da, it wasn't just a nice dream; he had plans and had invested money. About a week later, a balding man in a fancy business suit wearing round black-rimmed glasses came through the front door of my da's club like he was a king. My da didn't answer to anyone. He was in complete control of everything he owned. This well-dressed businessman and his associates took Da into the back of the club. They were back there for a few minutes. I heard the voices raised and lowered, then silence. When they came out of the back, my da couldn't look at me. After they left, Da said, 'JP is a rich and powerful bastard who sold his soul to the devil. If JP finds out about anyone who has a lucrative venture, he uses his money and power to place himself right in the middle of that venture. He and his associates pay them a visit then afterwards, the bastards go to Mass.' I never saw my da shaken like that."

Brendan began to speak, "Are you fucking telling me that Joseph P. Ken—?"

Danny J. waved his chubby hand. "Brendan, I didn't speak a name. I won't ever speak a name. You have to understand that there are things that have to be taken at face value and then buried. These people were powerful beyond belief. This is the caliber of who we are dealing with."

Declan and Tallman shook their heads at Danny J.'s revelation.

The tension in the room was thick as syrup as the severity of his disclosure encircled them.

Poor Brendan was in shock as were the others at what Danny J. had implied. Nora didn't trust this guy. How much was the truth—and how much was bullshit? Her stomach felt like a heavy sausage link rolled into a pretzel. She was sick at what she was hearing.

Elizabeth closed her eyes tightly as she leaned over the table folding her arms in front of her. So much information was being tossed around the room, but there was nothing to be done with it. A heavy sinking feeling gripped Elizabeth as she realized her family may be in grave danger with no clue as to why or where they would be assaulted. She took a deep breath before she spoke, "I would like to believe this is a story from the past—and we aren't involved—but what about the strange little man who wandered into our hotel room and who searched our luggage? We are involved up to our eyeballs."

Declan had a scowl on his face as he glared at Danny J. as he slowly responded, "We are old men, but we are a strong family. We dredged up the past, and there is someone out there who is still interested in this family. The fact that someone was bold enough to search your room is proof enough for me. We can't simply wipe our hands of this and imagine it's over. There is safety in numbers. The fact that we are all here together gives us safety. Anyone involved in this nightmare must know it's no longer a secret. They will be hard-pressed to hurt any of us. They don't know what we have discovered. As long as we keep what we know between us, we will be safe. I still believe there is proof of who is behind all of this. We just have to put our heads together and find it. It must be something valuable and really unique for there still to be interest. I believe whoever is involved will show themselves—even if it's in a nonchalant manner. Nora, they may approach you or Elizabeth saying they are an insurance investigator or an attorney for your family. That's how I would approach it."

Danny J. replied firmly, "Declan, I am with you to the end. I know my da would want it that way."

Elizabeth felt a sense of relief that the family wasn't going to be tossed to the wolves now that their identities had been revealed.

Tallman began, "The men who robbed and cheated our families and friends managed to make a great deal of money while they garnered power. Over the years, they have washed the blood off their hands. I'm not talking about the Italian families. I'm talking about the two-faced bastards who acted like friends as they sabotaged all of us. My great-grandfather was a slave who came North as a free man and worked at any job he could find. There are those of you in this room who may not realize how hard it was for Blacks and the Irish to find work. They were in constant competition for the worst jobs. I cleaned stables, dug graves, and buried the diseased and the poor. I cleaned up vomit and emptied spittoons in Harlem. I was a hungry teenager looking for a big break.

"At one of the stables, I met a farmer who paid a truck owner to take his produce North. I recognized it was a perfect cover for running whiskey out of Canada. We could run vegetables, pigs, and cattle north into Canada and bring back whiskey. If we didn't run too much and kept our schedule erratic, it would keep us anonymous. All I needed was enough money to start the runs. During the same time, I did whatever was asked of me by a club owner, Sweet Tea. I became his driver and protector.

"One evening, he was attacked by a jackass with a straight razor as he left his club. I pushed in front of the blade and beat the jackass to the ground. Before that night, I was just another one of the Black kids from the neighborhood who he used as cheap labor. Sweet Tea thought he owed his life to me. He laughed—at first—but then he took me into his office, which overlooked his club. To his surprise, I proposed a deal. I told him my plan for running the whiskey out of Canada. If he would front the run, I could provide him with whiskey from Canada, and with my profits, I could get a club.

"'Kid, you got huge balls. I like how you think.' Sweet Tea chuckled as he pulled two cigars from the silver case on his desk. He passed one to me, then reached over his desk to light it. He liked my plan and made me an offer. 'You supply me with the whiskey, and I will let you manage one of my clubs. If you do well, we can make a deal for you to buy the club from me.'"

Marcus rubbed his temples, ran his hand through his curly hair as he let out a big sigh.

Tallman continued, "I was a very productive manager. Sweet Tea was happy with his whiskey supply. We were so successful that we had to double the Canada trips. It got harder to keep it on the down-low. Running the club made it impossible to make the trips myself. We began to lose our loads; they were being hijacked. Someone caught wind of my delivery service and decided it was easy pickings. I let it slip to a few of the guys at my club that we were picking up an extra big load to cut down on the trips North. I suspected it was someone in my trusted circle who had squealed. No one in Sweet Tea's crew knew where the booze came from. I was uncertain who to trust. I only took a couple of my top guys. We left the club without fanfare. We were ready for an attack, and we got one. They were all white bastards, dressed in business suits and armed to the teeth, but we were as well. We gave them hell and escaped with the whiskey and our lives. I got back to the club to find one of the guys— someone I had known for years—in my office with his feet on my desk. He was leisurely talking on the phone. He was more than surprised to see me. 'Tallman, I didn't know you were coming in tonight. I thought you were out for the evening.' He spoke directly into the phone before he hung up, letting whoever was on the other end know I was still among the living. Guilt radiated from his body, like steam, and sweat beads popped up on his forehead and temples. As he hung up the phone, he began blabbering about having no choice, that he was forced to give up the details of our run.

"Washington, one of the fellows who fought for his life and the whiskey, grabbed him by the throat and without a word being spoken, walked him backwards out of the office. I never found out who was involved—only that they had more money and power than any of us. If this traitor knew who it was, he took it to his grave. I nearly lost everything I had worked for. Our Canada trips had to be less frequent and more clandestine. I had Sweet Tea on my ass because his supply had slowed down. I finally made him realize our only option was fewer trips or lose it all. We agreed he would have to water down what he got, which I knew he was already doing."

Marcus squirmed in his seat and took a big swallow of Jameson.

The room was silent as the group digested Tallman's story.

Elizabeth's head throbbed as it all sank in. They were gangsters; without a doubt, and this was a vanilla version of their pasts. Nora was interested in how all these old guys were connected to one another, but more importantly, how did she fit into this bloody puzzle? While they were all in this room, it was quiz time.

Nora knew she had no time to waste. The demon that was stealing her memories was a constant threat. Declan was probably the only one in the room with firsthand information. Her green eyes shot a piercing glare. She watched as the old guys drank. She patiently listened as they reminisced. She needed her questions answered. She started with questions that at least had answers.

"Declan, how did I end up in an orphanage? Who decided that was a good place? How did the vanity manage to be salvaged and remain in our family? Who took care of it?"

Declan's lips tightened, his eyes got a faraway look as though he was searching for answers. "Ida Doyle was a good mother to all her children." He ran his hand through his hair and attempted a weak smile. "When she became ill, Michael and my ma, Mae, made arrangements to keep you safe. The best option for you and Keira was a boarding school run by the Sisters of Mercy. Ma promised to take care of the vanity. It stayed with my ma until you married Samuel. When you and Samuel moved to Brooklyn, Ma saw to it that the vanity went as well. For some reason, Samuel felt how special it was—even though you were indifferent. I often wondered if you had any memory of where it came from."

CHAPTER 34

Wearily, Ida pulled herself from her bed. She could hear Nora and Keira talking in low voices. "Ladies, what are you up to?" Ida was surprised by the sound of her own voice. It was a broken croak, barely a whisper. Her throat hurt when she spoke. Her chest was very heavy, and it was difficult to catch her breath. She slowly put on her housecoat and shuffled into the kitchen.

Keira was trying to comb Nora's red curls.

"What a sweet sister you are, Keira, to comb Nora's hair." Ida's voice was barely audible. She forced air into her lungs. Each breath crackled as she tried to inhale in short shallow bursts. She felt lightheaded. The girls were in their cotton slips, yet Ida was freezing.

Hannah came through the kitchen as the teapot began to sing. "The girls and I decided to let you sleep. You seemed very restless during the night."

Ida saw her daughter had grown into a lovely young woman. Ida spoke trying not to frighten her children, "Hannah, please stay with the girls today. I am a little under the weather and need some more rest."

Ida strained a weak smile as Hannah placed a cup of

tea in her hand. She caressed the warm cup as a chill went through her.

Hannah had never seen her mother this ill. She hoped that rest was all her mother needed, "Don't worry, Ma. Keira, Nora, and I will be very quiet while you rest. We'll finish getting dressed and go down to the candy store for a bit."

Ida walked cautiously to the dining room table and sluggishly dropped into a chair near the window. The sun warmed her back. Her chest was tight like corset ties pulled to the brink. Every breath was a painful task. She sipped the tea Hannah had poured. A plan had to be put into place. Hannah could not spend her youth raising her younger sisters, "Hannah, my pet, when you see Declan at the candy store, ask him to drop by." Ida wheezed out after gasping to get air into her lungs. She hoped Declan could get a message to Michael once Hannah told him how ill she was. Her ultimate goal was to set in motion a plan so Keira and Nora would be taken care of and remain together. She had considered walking to the candy store, but once she got out of bed, she realized that was not an option. Ida forced air in and out of her lungs. The shallow, crackling sound began to have a rhythm.

Her mind drifted to when she was a young woman. How much she loved Thomas. And although they struggled it was the happiest time of her life. Ida wanted Hannah to have the same love and innocent happiness without the extra burden of raising two little girls. She knew Hannah would sacrifice her own happiness for her younger siblings. Michael had been loyal to his promise to take care of the family, but would he be willing to take on her young daughters after she was gone?

Declan realized the seriousness of the message Hannah shared, although the young woman wasn't totally aware of its importance. "I'll bring your ma some soup from home." Declan told Hannah. He took it upon himself to call the doctor. He had to get the message to Michael.

Michael was checking stock and working on schedules in the back of the club.

Declan knew he was going through the motions to stay busy. Since the loss of Tara, Michael showed up daily, acting hard as nails, in case there was doubt in anyone's mind that he was in complete control. Declan wasn't keen on adding more grief to Michael's already full plate, "Michael, Ida Doyle sent word that she needs to see you. From Hannah's mood, I think Ida is ill. The doctor will meet you at the Doyle's apartment."

Of all the things Michael had swirling around in his head, this had never crossed his mind. Michael answered in a quiet, very matter of fact tone, "Declan, come along. I may need your help. I think I know Ida's concerns. I don't want her to worry. Stay on the stoop in case the girls come home. Distract them so they don't come up and get frightened." Michael climbed the stoop stairs, opened the entry door, and began the ascent to the apartment. It felt like his shoes were filled with cement. Each step was an arduous struggle. The muscles in his neck clenched and bulged as he tried to control his feelings. His throat tightened, and his emotions began to get the better of him. Each time he had made the trek up these stairs, it was after a bloodbath. As he reached the final landing, he closed his eyes, dug deep into the depths of his soul to regain some sense of composure. He had not felt this overwhelmed or sad since Tara's death. He hoped Ida was not as ill as she felt. Michael gently knocked. As he took another deep breath the door opened.

To his surprise Mae answered.

This woman has extraordinary senses. She always appears when needed.

Mae whispered, "The doctor is with Ida. We got her to rest in bed."

Michael felt very awkward until he heard a small gasping voice, "Michael, we must talk. I'm sorry to have to greet you from my bed, but Mae insisted. I fear I haven't much time. I need to ask, rather beg you to see that my girls are taken care of." Ida scratched out wheezing. She gasped for air every few words.

"Ida, there's no need to beg. The girls will always be my family. Your job is to get better. You will be up and around in no time. Please don't worry." Michael tried to sound reassuring as he spoke.

"Please, Michael ... no matter what ... we must come to an agreement ... now ... so I can rest peacefully." Her words became more strained as she struggled for every breath.

The doctor signaled for Ida to concentrate on breathing slowly and deeply.

Michael frantically searched his mind in an attempt to find something that would settle Ida's concerns. He looked toward Mae for help.

Mae softly suggested, "Ida, Hannah can stay with Maureen. That way, she will be close to all that she knows, and it will keep a family connection for Nora. Keira and Nora should continue to be raised together as sisters. If you agree to it, they can be placed in a boarding school. It will keep them both safe."

Michael felt fortunate to have such a trustworthy friend like Mae. It was apparent to him that Ida wasn't totally happy with the idea, but it was the best option for Hannah and the younger girls. This way, they would always have someone looking after them and a roof over their heads.

Ida considered Nora her child, but she knew there were other issues at stake. Ida nodded her approval as Michael reached for her hand, "I'm sorry it has come to this, Ida. Your family has lost so much. You have gone through hell." Michael kissed Ida's cold hand.

"Michael, I can say the same to you. My only regret is that I didn't see all the bastards who butchered my Tommy lying bloody in the street." Ida's voice was nothing more than a crackling whisper now.

Thoughts of No Nose flashed in Michael's mind as he spoke, "It will happen, Ida. We found the first, and it was as you wished."

No Nose was dead, but she didn't need the details. Michael continued, "There will be retribution for all of them. It will be bloody and loud. We will find those who paid the butchers. They will all go down, along with their henchmen, like a blood-soaked house of cards." Michael's whole being depended on knowing he would avenge the bastards responsible for the carnage.

He turned to follow the doctor into the other room as Ida's moist eyes slowly closed. It was as though she was envisioning it all.

The doctor shook his head as he patted Michael on the arm. His touch sent a chill down Michael's spine. His life had become one death after another. The loss of Ida was so sudden and unexpected.

Mae was busying herself in the kitchen. She stopped Michael as he headed to the door, "Michael, you can't control this. It's going to happen if God wishes. You can see that the Doyle girls, including Nora, are in a safe place. It has to be that way. Excuse my eavesdropping, but I could see you were at a loss. I would take Hannah in myself, but it would be inappropriate since Declan is still at home. Maureen is an excellent choice. They can watch out for one another, and Maureen will be able to see Nora without drawing any undue attention. The Sisters of Mercy in Tarrytown might be a place to consider. It's in the country, but it's close enough to visit."

"Mae, I'm way out of my league here with girls, let alone boarding schools. I must keep my distance. Please suggest it to Ida, and if she approves, would you please contact them? Let them know a benefactor has charged you with their care." Michael whispered.

Ida moved once again to the kitchen where she lovingly ran her hand over the table she and Tommy bought for their home. She slowly dropped into a chair. Mae tried not to disturb her as she could see she was deep in thought.

Mae went to make up Ida's bed. She had to squeeze by the vanity to tuck in the blankets. The tall oblong mirror made a creaking sound, wobbling as her body pressed against it.

Ida tried to breathe deep in an attempt to fill her lungs with air. She felt as though a pillow was stuck in her throat, blocking the air. Her chest ached with every breath. Ida loved to sit at the table where the sun came through the window warming her body. She closed her eyes. Her thoughts went to the day the couple moved into the apartment. It was just days before the older children arrived. She could hear her children's laughter. Tommy's voice called to her. A coughing fit brought her back to the present. Ida had to settle her girls' future.

The two women discussed Tarrytown as well as Hannah staying with Maureen. Ida had Mae write down her wishes; she requested Michael keep her boys out of harm's way, along with taking care of the girls. Mae assured her the vanity would remain safe; Nora would receive it once she settled somewhere permanent.

With the business of her children's future settled, Word was sent to let the girls return to the apartment.

Ida straightened her hair before she settled into her bed. Mae fluffed the sheets and blankets so Ida was comfortable, as much as she could be. The girls came in uncharacteristically quiet. Ida called them to her bedside. She quietly explained she wasn't going to be with them much longer. She told all three where and with whom they would stay. She made Tarrytown sound like a wonderful vacation. The two younger girls didn't understand the concept of death. Hannah attempted to be strong, once she left her mother's side, she stumbled to the davenport falling into it face first. The young woman broke down quietly sobbing into the cushions.

Ida's sons came in after the girls. They weren't easily convinced. Both boys took her illness and inevitable death very hard. They promised her they would make her proud and always watch out for their sisters.

Ida's children sat with her and talked about holidays and

family events. They all surrounded the bed embracing each other. Ida tried to keep it light, but with each breath she took it became more difficult for her to breathe.

As Ida turned toward the window she began to cough uncontrollably. Unable to regain her breath. She was gone.

The younger girls sobbed loudly. The boys tried to comfort them as they huddled around the bed.

CHAPTER 35

Declan drove Mae, Maureen, Nora, and Keira to Tarrytown. Hannah, Bradley, and Robert accompanied them. They wanted to see where their baby sisters were going to be living. The trip took close to an hour, the silence was deafening. Only once or twice did any of the children speak.

The sadness of the situation tore at Mae's heart. She wondered if Nora had any memory of the first time she was ripped from her family. She prayed the child didn't remember. Once was bad enough, but being torn from your family twice due to death would be unbearable for anyone—let alone a young child. The children perked up as they drove past Kykuit, the Rockefeller estate, and closer to the Sisters of Mercy compound.

In a time when most women were banned from owning property as men considered them inferior, the Sisters of Mercy were allowed to acquire wealth, earn wages, sign contracts, get loans, and incorporate institutions controlled solely by women. The Sisters of Mercy started with an orphanage in New York City during the mid-1800s. They also started a school where young women could learn skills such as sewing. At the Select School for Girls, the daughters of wealthier locals could get a "proper education."

The school looked more like a mansion than a boarding school, and it certainly looked nothing like an orphanage. They passed through the huge wrought iron gates and drove up a long gravel driveway. Huge trees shaded the car's path and blocked most of the sun from the driveway. Thick grass covered both sides of the drive for as far as they could see.

All the children, including the boys, were in awe. None of them had seen so much grass or so many trees except in a park. The side of the building, where Declan parked, was very old gray brick. A short set of stairs stretched out to a sidewalk. A porch ran the length of the building, and thick ivy crawled up several evenly spaced trellises. The other section of the building was more modern and several stories high. The newer section was constructed with crisp, clean red brick.

After helping Declan unload the girls' belongings, the family began tearful goodbyes. The older children promised to visit often. The boys reluctantly returned to the car. Mae, Maureen, and Hannah escorted Nora and Keira inside their new home. The vastness of the place scared the girls. It was not as inviting as the school Nora had visited with Elsa. There were hardwood floors, massive stairways, with too many doors to count.

Mother Superior appeared from behind one of the many doors. She was dressed in a stiffly starched, long black dress and veil, her black shoes snapped loudly with each step she took. She met the group in the entryway. She was polite but not overly emotional.

In the back of her mind, Mae envisioned herself grabbing both girls by the arms then charging out the door. She reined in her imagination and listened while Mother

Superior talked about how lovely the school was. Michael had given Mae a free hand at arranging for the girls' stay. Mae made sure these two, who had seen so much heartache and sadness, would not be treated like orphans who had to earn their way. They were special young ladies with a wealthy benefactor.

Nora looked around anxiously while Keira stood stiff as though stuck to a floor board. A loud bell jolted the group to attention. All at once, chattering voices and clapping footsteps echoed on the hardwood floors.

Mae was comforted by the way Mother Superior interacted with her young wards. Her voice was soft and pleasant as she greeted the stream of young girls who swept passed her.

Nora had looked forward to being able to attend school—but always with the thought of returning home to her ma in the afternoon. Keira was more apprehensive than Nora.

The two sisters slowly settled into their new home. Robert, Bradley, and Hannah visited often. It became a habit Mae and Maureen would pack a picnic lunch, and the day was spent in the shade of the huge trees on the compound.

Nora and Keira stayed in the same dormitory, so they saw each other every day. Nora was lonesome—she had never been without a family member within her reach—but she was excited about going to school. She was an enthusiastic student. Once she learned to read, she devoured books.

Early on, it was obvious the two sisters had very different interests. Nora preferred the company of books to people, spending a great deal of time in the library—even before she had mastered reading. She relished the solitude.

Keira enjoyed the company of the other girls and the outdoors. When their family visited and picnicked on the sprawling grounds of the convent, Nora would eventually slip away with a book. She would find a tree to read under, within a clear view of her family. Keira was very outgoing with a lot of friends. She tried to include Nora in the things they did. Nora would go along with Keira, but she rarely spoke unless spoken to.

Chapter 36

Michael felt as though he had been sucked into a deadly whirlpool that swirled violently around his life. With all the loss, pain, blood, and hate, he had lost nearly all he treasured. He felt a huge burden with the death of Tommy and Ida Doyle. Tara's death began his spiral downward into the darkness. He knew he had to conceal his feelings even from those he considered friends. There was too much at stake to allow his feelings to impact his judgment. He took responsibility for all who worked for him. He was well aware there were those who would turn on him if the price was right. Michael often thought of Conrad's da, William. He saw Michael as a survivor, but Conrad had always been at his side. Tara had been his rock. How could he make it out of this heart wrenching black pit, alone?

Stop feeling sorry for yourself. Snap out of it. You have to move forward for William's sake. Your son needs you more than ever and you need him.

Michael spoke very little—with the exception of getting things done at Cara Dílis, His grief encased him like a suffocating spider web. He showed no emotion to avoid being seen as weak. Declan could see how tortured Michael had become. He needed a place he could let go before he imploded. He needed a place where he wasn't known.

One evening after they finished at Cara Dílis, while William was at a movie with neighborhood friends, Declan drove Michael to Garnet's club.

"Where the hell are you taking me?" Michael growled.

"We are going to get a drink at a quiet place I know." Declan smiled.

Michael was surprised how quiet the club was. It was dark and nearly empty. Dockworkers at the bar spoke quietly among themselves.

Garnet came around the bar in her usual red feathers, cigarette holder clenched between her teeth. She snubbed out the tip then slid the holder between her full breasts. Garnet wasn't ashamed of who she had become; she was a strong woman who earned her own way at all costs. The club might have been merely a neighborhood watering hole, but she was in charge. She had the loyalty of those who worked with her and those she served. She was safe.

"Hello, Mr. Byrne. I am sorry for your recent loss. What brings you to my little piece of heaven?" Garnet spoke with compassion along with a bit of sarcasm.

"We are just looking for a quiet place to have a drink after a long day." Declan said as he gave Garnet a pleading gaze.

"Well, gentlemen, if you are looking for quiet, you have come to the right place. Let me show you to our best booth."

Garnet knew what Declan was up to. She could see the torment on Michael's face.

"I'll be right back with a bit of our finest. Do you mind if I sit with you for a bit?"

To Declan's surprise Michael responded,

"It would be nice to have a lovely lady with a smiling face join us."

As Garnet walked to the bar, Michael put his hand on Declan's shoulder,

"This is the first time in a very long time I feel as though I can relax without pretense. Declan, you have become a wise, caring young man, and I'm proud to have you as a friend."

Garnet came back to the table with the drinks and a loaf of soda bread. Michael was quiet for a while, as he listened to Declan and Garnet talk quietly.

Michael took a large sip from his cup and spoke, "Thank you both, I appreciate having a chance to catch my breath to think things through. My head feels like it wants to explode, so many thoughts, feelings that I can't escape."

He leaned back and closed his eyes. "I'm just resting my eyes and mulling things over in my head. I hope I'm not being rude."

"Rest your eyes, my friend. Declan and I can entertain each other for a few minutes." Garnet replied softly.

"Garnet, if you wouldn't mind, I would like to come down here on occasion to clear my head." Michael spoke with a soft heartbreaking voice.

He had no place other than his apartment to get lost in his thoughts. With William back at home, he felt like he had to present a strong face at home and at the club. At the Bad Penny, he could lose himself in his thoughts without interruption.

Michael was determined to see Conrad's plans for success fulfilled, but he had no idea what Conrad's big deal was. He tried to put it out of his mind for the time being. Right now, he was more concerned with keeping everyone safe. He searched for any clues into his friend's death. On Sundays, he visited Tara's grave to talk things over with her. His heart ached for her. He found solace as he watched his son begin to spread his wings.

William was a smart young man, able to resolve difficult situations with common sense and reasoning. Ironically, Michael saw Conrad in his own son. He insisted that William continue his schooling. He wanted him to be able to outfox anyone who confronted him. He hoped that when the time came and Prohibition ended, William would be ready to manage the legitimate businesses that he was sure he would have. Michael saw Cara Dílis as a start. He would save enough to get another club. Someday he would have a fine hotel—just as Conrad had planned. There would be no bankers or partners involved; he wouldn't make that mistake. Too many of his associates had trusted the wrong people and lost everything—or worse lost their lives. He would be the aggressors, there would be no question that Michael Byrne was a man to be reckoned with.

He found comfort in Garnet's club. The grieving man was able to sit in a booth, near the fireplace, and drink without any distractions. Declan was at his side on most occasions since they were still traveling in pairs for safety's sake. Although things were quiet in the neighborhood Michael was concerned it might be the quiet before the storm. He relished the quiet even if it was temporary. It gave him a chance to regain his bearings. The Italians were in a major power struggle within their families, but it stayed in their neighborhoods. Declan and Michael spent time at

Garnet's discussing plans for the future and who they could really trust.

Garnet looked forward to seeing Michael. She knew he was devastated by the loss of his wife, but he had begun to open up to her about his life and friendship with Conrad. She enjoyed listening to him. They became close friends. He was the only person she had ever told about how she came to the city and how she ended up at the club.

The trips to Garnet's left Michael with a sense of strength. Being able to let down his guard helped him have no qualms about his ability to keep the family safe. He would recognize an enemy. He was ready for whatever came after this quiet period. It didn't take long for the quiet to shatter.

CHAPTER 37

One evening, not long after Michael felt more like his old self, a disheveled old drunk stumbled into Cara Dílis. His hands were covered in blood. His shoes left bloody prints as he staggered to the bar.

"He's dead, he's been punished. I'm here to tell you I did it." The old man spat. His hair looked like it hadn't seen a brush in months. He reeked of alcohol, urine, and just plain filth.

Declan was behind the bar, and Michael was sitting on the other side of the bar. They looked at one another as the other patrons noticed the old man. Michael gave Declan a nod, and the two of them walked in the old man's direction. They each put a hand under one of his arms and backed him out into the street.

Eddie came from behind the bar and wiped the blood off the floor and the door handle. Eddie signaled one of the porters to fetch Flannery.

"I did it … no one told me to. He needed to die. I did it."

Michael asked quietly, "Old friend, who did you punish?"

"Uh, Duke Lansing. I punished him." The old man slurred every word.

Michael looked at Declan they both knew he meant No Nose.

"Where is Mr. Lansing now?" Declan quizzed.

"In the alley … I wanted him to end his life where he ended your friends' lives." The old man staggered toward the alley.

Declan spat, "Bullshit, Michael! This is bullshit. Someone is fucking with us. This ass didn't kill anyone. We both know that."

It was as though someone was picking at a painful scab, evaluating Michael, trying to get him to explode. Michael leaned over the body; obviously, it wasn't Lansing. Whoever it was, he was barely alive, "So, are you one of Lansing's friends? Did your buddies decide you should die in my presence? Very considerate of them. You feel like freeing yourself of their names before you meet your maker?"

The man was in no condition to say anything; his tongue had been cut out. He was gasping for air. Blood splattered and gurgled from his mouth as he gasped. He was breathing his last breath.

Michael looked down and watched him die and spoke under his breath, "Ida, another one is dead. It wasn't loud, but it was bloody. He was only one of the weapons; the rest of the murderers are still out there." He placed his hand on Declan's shoulder. "It is definitely bullshit. Things have been too quiet. The sewer rats who dropped this garbage at our front door are more dramatic than they are smart. The old drunk isn't from around here. They found him close to home, and we are going to take him back there."

Flannery came around the corner.

Michael snarled, "Flannery, someone dropped this piece of shit on our doorstep."

"I'll take care of him. Did he say anything before he croaked?" Flannery asked.

Declan snapped, "Not a word … they took his tongue."

Neither Michael nor Declan went into detail about their possible connection to the dead man, but Flannery wasn't oblivious to what went on in the neighborhood.

Declan was all for taking the old drunk home to find who hired him, but he wasn't so eager to ride in the same car as the smelly old coot. "Michael how about we put this pile of shit on the trolley—and not in our car? The car will have his stench for weeks."

"Point taken, Declan. I'm with you. Let's take a nice trolley ride with our smelly buddy to see where we land. We'll have Sullivan and his partner follow us in their car."

"What's your name, old man?" Declan asked.

The old guy wiped his bloody hands on his shabby jacket. "Peter is my given name, but I mostly go by Gofer." Spittle splashed from between his lips.

Declan and Michael sat across from Peter as the trolley bounced and creaked over the cobblestone streets. The old guy was three sheets to the wind, but he knew where he lived.

It was obvious to Michael that whoever was behind dropping the body at the club was about as bright as a coal mine. They were testing the waters and taunting Michael to get a reaction. They had to be wondering if Michael had any clue about who was behind the attempted hijacking of the New Year's load and the bloody slaughter of Tommy

Doyle and the rest of Michael's friends. This was unfinished business for Michael. He wanted to respond. He had to respond to keep his hard stance in place. These morons had led Michael and the rest of his friends right to them.

Peter was oblivious to what was going on. He had been paid in hooch and was happy as a drunken clam.

Michael remembered what he had told Ida: "It will be bloody and loud."

Declan and Michael held Peter up as they got off the trolley. They looked around for any signs of trouble. They were in a run-down and dank neighborhood of old tenements. Fire escapes looked down on the narrow street.

Michael signaled to Sullivan and his partner to park at the end of the block. "Move to the alley. I don't want to be a sitting duck if someone looks out a window."

Declan walked the old drunk to the end of the block and sat him down.

Peter immediately rolled over onto his side and passed out.

Declan continued on to the car Sullivan drove. He and Michael had handguns under their jackets, but more firepower was needed to light up these gutter rats. He returned with a shotgun for Michael and a Thompson for himself. "Loud!"

"Bloody … for Tommy, Andrew, and Flynn." Michael's eyes narrowed as he spoke.

There was one apartment on the second floor that glowed bright like a Christmas tree. The voices that came from the apartment were loud and amplified in the alley. Silhouettes passed by the window.

"Four … five at the maximum," Declan whispered.

Michael held out four and then five fingers to the other men, they nodded in acknowledgment. He waved them to the front of the building.

Michael and Declan entered the building. The stairwell was dark and reeked of vomit and urine. The stairs creaked with each step.

At the second-floor landing, Michael and Declan stood on either side of the apartment door. Sullivan and his partner stationed themselves behind Michael and Declan.

The voices in the apartment continued to ramble on. It sounded as though they were in the rear of the apartment. There was to be no discussion. Michael wanted them dead. He tried the door, the knob turned with a clunking sound. The door creaked as he slowly opened it.

The voices within remained at the same level.

Michael and Declan entered the apartment and moved along the wall The other two men followed them. There was a short hallway then a windowed wall with faded curtains that divided the sleeping area from the small kitchen.

Michael watched for a moment as the men in the apartment played cards at a worn-out table. In an instant, once they were aware of the armed men in the room, the fireworks began.

Michael emptied the shotgun into the room. The pellet spray filled the air, and blood splattered the walls. The curtains flew in all directions as the bullets peppered the room. The men at the table never got their weapons out any farther than their laps.

Declan sprayed the room with the Thompson. The other two men stayed near the front of the apartment. Michael and Declan needed no help in making sure it was a loud and bloody display. It was over in a flash.

Michael walked gingerly through the carnage and weapons. He wanted to see the faces of the bastards who thought they could get away with robbing and killing his family. He looked at each of their faces. They were all strangers. Michael calmly took off his jacket and washed his hands in the sink. He looked at the bodies as he dried his hands and put his jacket back on. As he and Declan left, he spat on each of the corpses. This bold response to the robbery and killings would leave no doubt that Michael was in charge of an organization that could be as ruthless as it needed to be.

Michael and Declan rode back to Cara Dílis with Sullivan. Michael felt guilty that he was energized by the events of the evening. He left Declan at Cara Dílis and walked to his apartment to bathe and change clothes. He returned to Cara Dílis and pulled Declan aside. "I'm going down to Garnet's place. You don't have to come with me."

"Sweet Jesus, Michael. You can't be waltzing around alone, especially after today. I'll go with you. I'm ready for some quiet drinking."

CHAPTER 38

When Michael and Declan entered the club, Garnet was deep in conversation with an older man in a suit. The old guy looked out of place, but Garnet seemed to be in control. She nodded at them as they headed to a booth in the back. The man glanced at Michael as he walked by.

The bartender brought two teacups to Michael's table, just as Garnet and the man finished their conversation. She and the old guy both stood up, shook hands, and he left the club.

Garnet stood at the bar for a moment. She took her cigarette holder from between her breasts, lit a cigarette, and took a long drag. The bartender brought her a cup. Garnet took a quick swig and signaled for another. She walked toward the table where Michael and Declan were seated.

Michael didn't say anything about the old suit. Her business was no concern of his.

Garnet sat down and took another slow drag from her cigarette. "I know we are just getting to know one another, but the man who just left owns this hovel. He's looking to sell it. I know it's a shithole, but with a little loving care, it could become a great neighborhood club. Michael, I'm not asking for a handout, but I could use a partner. I don't have enough to buy it outright, and even if a bank would give a loan to a woman, I refuse to line the pockets of bankers." Garnet took another drag from her cigarette and slowly spoke. "Would you consider fronting me the money to buy him out? I have most of it. I would pay you back with interest. Like I said, I'm not asking for a handout, but I wouldn't mind having a partner."

Michael smiled as he spoke, "How much do you need?"

"Oh, Michael, you won't regret this." Garnet threw her arms around his neck.

The three of them toasted to the new owners of the Bad Penny. Michael put the violent events of the day out of his mind and drank with his friends to their new enterprise.

Garnet would need help with the paperwork. She had managed to get the customers in and keep things open, but she gave all the paperwork to the owner. The next morning, she put on her most businesslike outfit then headed out to see Mae. She had no doubt that Mae knew how to manage the paperwork. She could show her the ins and outs.

As she walked up the stairs to Mae's apartment, she began to feel uneasy. She had only been there once, and that was a much different situation. She hoped she hadn't misinterpreted Mae's kindness. Garnet softly tapped at Mae's door.

"Well, hello, my friend. I understand you are now part owner of a club. Congratulations." Mae smiled as she dried her hands with a dish towel.

Garnet's doubts disappeared with Mae's welcoming hug. "Oh, Mae, I am so happy to see you. You have no idea how worried I've been."

Mae gently held Garnet's hands and whispered, "Slow

down, Garnet. This isn't like you at all. Take a breath, tell me how I can help you?"

"Mae, I know how to run a club. I've planned and hosted parties. I can get men to drink and show them a good time, but I've never actually handled the business end of it. I know you are savvy. Can you teach me? I don't want to disappoint Michael. He has put his faith in me."

"Garnet, no worries. You can do this. I'll see to it that you know everything you need to know and more." Mae giggled. "Garnet, there is no doubt in my mind that you can do this. It's merely being given the chance by someone to prove you can handle it. You gave me that opportunity once, and now it is my turn."

They agreed that Garnet would do exactly what she had done for the previous owner, but instead of just handing off the paperwork, she would bring it to Mae. They would go over it together. It only took a few weeks for Garnet to realize she was already doing most of the paperwork. It was just a matter of recording what money came in and what went out. Garnet had forgotten that she had managed a household years ago. The club was similar to running a household; it just included drunken men instead of children.

Mae and Garnet made a great team. They both were extremely efficient businesswomen. Garnet was concerned about making enough money to survive Prohibition, but with Michael's help, she always had a bountiful supply of liquor and protection, which the former owner didn't have.

Garnet never let on to any of the patrons that she was an owner. She put enough money aside to spruce up the club. She concentrated on cleaning up the club. Once she settled into being part owner, her thoughts moved past

Prohibition. She planned for a future when having a drink and sharing time with friends didn't have to be done in secrecy. Although the club was a speakeasy, it never drew the attention of the cops. They had more to worry about than neighborhood dives where the beat cop had a regular spot at the bar. If trouble arrived at the front door, the patrons left out the rear.

CHAPTER 39

As soon as Michael passed through the heavy door, the change in the club was undeniable. Garnet had complete control of the club, but he didn't expect such a rapid improvement. The place shined, candles flickered on the tables, and a piano was squeezed in a corner near the fireplace, playing upbeat tunes. It felt warm and comforting.

"Hello, partner," Garnet said with a gushing smile.

Michael couldn't remember seeing Garnet smile with the exception of the day they became business partners. "Hello, Garnet. You are looking well." He sheepishly replied.

They headed to his usual booth, and Garnet gave the bartender a wave as she passed him.

Michael said, "You have been a busy woman. The place looks great—and the piano."

"Oh, Michael, I'm so glad you approve. After I brought in the piano, I thought it might bother you since you come here for quiet time."

"Garnet, it's a perfect touch."

The bartender brought two teacups and a loaf of bread to the table.

Garnet spoke confidently, "Michael, the way I see it, all we have to do is offer the neighborhood a place to relax and take the load off. Neighbors need a place to visit with one another and have a drink. I'm going to save as much money as possible and once this ridiculous law is repealed, we will have an established club."

"Garnet, I think I have found a smart business partner in you. I am also looking to spread my business wings once things are set straight with the law. Between you and Mae, I think I have a strong start." He laughed and took her hand in his. He felt like he had known her all his life.

Declan slid into the booth next to Michael. He'd been making sure the liquor made it to the downstairs storage room without any problems. When he realized Garnet and Michael were holding hands, he felt embarrassed, as though he should have said something before he plopped down in the booth. "Sorry, boss, I was just going to let you know the liquor is safely stored."

"You are fine, Declan. There is nothing in my life that is a secret to you. I am comfortable in saying I trust you both with my life. Business is looking up, and we can do great things together." Michael felt a twinge in his neck as he spoke. Fear haunted him. Maybe he shouldn't speculate about the future. "Declan, take the rest of the night off. I'll call you later."

Declan nodded and left.

Michael squeezed Garnet's hand and pulled it to his lips.

"Not here, Michael. I … it just isn't the right place for me. Please come over to my place for tea." Garnet gently pulled her hand away.

Michael understood what Garnet meant. The club had been her place of carnal business up to a short time ago.

Her apartment was a short trolley ride from the club.

They hopped off the trolley and talked about the future. Michael buried his fears and felt the happiness of the moment. They climbed the stairs to her apartment as though they were the only two people on the planet.

When Garnet opened her door, Michael was surprised that the place was so welcoming. There were bookshelves full of books, fresh paint, and curtains. Her kitchen already had a tea service on the counter.

"I don't entertain here. This is my sanctuary. Books have always been my escape. I love a good book with a cup of hot tea." Garnet giggled.

As Michael looked at her he realized she had been through a great deal for such a young woman—or anyone for that matter. Her past was never mentioned; it was a wound better left untouched. He took her hands and pulled her close. He kissed her palms, her neck, and then her lips.

"Michael, I've never been with a man I cared about. I don't know what to expect." Garnet choked back her tears.

Michael gently kissed her lips again. "We care about one another. It will just happen. There are no expectations, *mo mhilse*" (my sweet).

The two slowly moved to her bedroom, fell on the bed, and curled into each other's bodies. Their passion was deep and loving. Both had been alone for too long.

CHAPTER 40

The more time Michael spent planning the future, the less time he spent dwelling on the tragedies of the past. When he went home at night, he was able to spend time with William and truly enjoy it.

He listened to what his son was studying in school and on occasion, William would hint about a girl he was interested in. Michael talked to William about the future without mentioning the dark side of his business.

The apartment didn't seem so cold or sad anymore. Tara's presence was always felt. Now he was able to remember how happy they all were, and he was able to leave his grief in the past. Michael's top priority was, as always, William. He became less obsessed with finding Conrad's killer. Someone would slip and drop the bastard into his hands. This allowed him to concentrate on making his business successful.

He sought Mae's aid to assist with his personal accounting. Since she was already in charge of Noinin and Keira's expenses, it made sense.

Michael absolutely didn't want his money entrusted to a bank, and Mae made sure any outstanding expenditures were taken care of. Michael took care of the club side of things, which Mae didn't need to be concerned with.

One afternoon Michael and Declan were elbow deep in paperwork, trying to figure out how to get more product. The task of keeping two clubs supplied was becoming increasingly difficult. They had considered going to Canada to check out the lay of the land. They knew Tallman Fletcher had figured out a way to use delivery trucks to get hooch into New York, but even he was having problems. The two men were totally taken by surprise by a loud knock on the club door.

Thinking it was Robert, Declan took a minute to answer the door. When he swung it open, his jaw dropped as he saw Dan Malone standing in the doorway.

Dan had walked into the candy store and headed straight to the back. He passed right by Robert who was working behind the bar.

Michael jumped up, and papers flew as he pulled himself away from the table. "Mr. Malone, how are you? Please come in. What can we do for you?" Michael said as he tried to remain calm. He signaled for Dan to sit at the table where he and Declan were working.

Dan spoke in a very matter of fact tone. "Well, Michael, actually it is I, who can help you. I have an offer from Nick Leary."

Shit, Michael thought. *He's heard we are having problems and wants to take over.*

Dan must have read Michael's expression. "Hold on, my friend. There's no need to panic. I'm here with an advantageous offer. I would never steer you in the wrong direction or hang you out to dry. I know the last few years have been hard on you. As you know, Atlantic City is wide-open, and they have no intention of ever abiding by the

Volstead Act. Shit, you can buy hooch anywhere on the boardwalk. The city has become an entry point for foreign booze with little confrontation. The resorts are booming while the politicians are getting rich and drunk. Nick and his partners have speedboats offloading huge amounts of whiskey and rum from ships sailing under Newfoundland's flag. The ships don't come into US waters. The speedboats have to bring the hooch to shore and unload it without fanfare. They even have firemen and other city employees, near the boardwalk, helping unload the boats once they reach shore. The resorts are flowing with good hooch—not the watered-down spit we are forced to serve."

"What does Atlantic City's bounty have to do with us?" Michael asked.

"Well, one of Nick's Republican political partners is looking to head to Washington. He needs to separate himself from the fray between local law enforcement and the Prohis (Prohibition agents), especially after the recent shootout between the rumrunners and the Coast Guard. The Atlantic City prosecutor arrested three Coast Guard crewmen for abuse of authority for using their guns. It's a real shitstorm. Nick is looking for some men who are willing to take on the boat running. He doesn't want to draw any more attention to himself or his dealings in the city. In return, he will furnish a decent wage for the runners, the speedboats, and as much whiskey and rum as you need. What do you think? Is this something that would attract your attention?"

Michael's head swirled. *Mae will have a list of guys I can depend on. I don't want to leave everyday operations short by using too many of my guys. I'll have to meet with the guys and see how many are interested.* Then he spoke, "I would need full control over who is on the speedboats and who takes part in the deliveries. Is that a problem?"

Dan replied without hesitation, "My friend, you will have total control. I am only in it for the whiskey and rum. I have men to offer; but like Nick, I can't draw attention to my business. You are on the fringes, are honest, loyal, and have access to a fine group of trustworthy Irishmen."

Malone was well aware of Mae's ledgers; he had been using her referred individuals for years.

Declan was in awe; a silent prayer was answered. There were issues with moving the booze from New Jersey to New York, but that was nothing compared to trying to transport it from Canada.

Michael spoke politely, but sternly, "Dan, I don't want to become part of Nick's Jersey organization. We are in this for the booze, that's it. Nearly everyone in Atlantic City who is on the public payroll—city and county—is owned by Nucky Johnson or Nick Leary. And none of my men—or me—will be paying a kickback to any damn politicians. I don't want any part of that bullshit. We need to remain anonymous and independent. That is our deal. We load and unload the speedboats, and Nick will pay my men and supply us with the booze we need for our clubs. He isn't to have any control over us—or there is no deal." Michael was somewhat surprised to hear his own voice making demands of Dan Malone.

Dan said, "I understand. He is looking for someone he can trust who can do the job without a lot of bullshit. That's easily solved. You and those you choose will work for me, in name only. He has no reason to know who you or your men are. Does that work for you?"

Michael answered, "Dan, I don't trust many men. That circle has gotten much smaller over the past few years, but I trust you on this. We will make this work for us as much as it works for Mr. Leary—even if it's in Atlantic City and he has politicians at his beckon call. We are merely moving booze for you—no more."

Dan's eyes narrowed as he spoke, "Michael, I don't expect you to be on one of the speedboats. This is a job for those you trust within your family. I know Declan's ma has a huge list of trustworthy men."

Shit, Declan, thought. *I didn't think Dan had any idea I even existed—let alone who my ma is.*

Michael replied without hesitation, "Dan, I'll be on a couple of runs—just to be sure everything is on the up-and-up. I don't want to have any issues. I certainly don't want to get into a shootout with the Coast Guard. I want Nick Leary to understand there are those of us who can do a job and remain anonymous. Seems to me someone got very cocky. I can just see a speedboat being chased through the water by the Coast Guard and some goon thinking it was a good idea to open fire on them. Dan, I want us to be invisible. We may not be able to totally accomplish it, but there has to be a happy medium."

Dan spoke with confidence, "Michael, this can make or break us. I have no intention of being broken. A lot of men in Atlantic City are getting rich selling booze. No reason why we can't get in on the action. I may be able to get ahold of the Coast Guard patrol schedules."

There was excitement in Michael's voice as he spoke,

"I see it this way. As you said, the ships are sailing under foreign flags and aren't going to chance entering US waters. They will stay outside the three-mile limit. We need to be able to get to the ship, load its cargo onto the speedboats, get to shore, and unload without being seen. No problem. Shit, if we know when and where the Coast Guard is patrolling, that's one problem down. I say we make sure to unload when there is little to no moon. Unloading once we're in Atlantic City is nothing. The city is wide-open."

Michael continued, "We just have to get our share to New York. Since we're landing near a fishing port, how about we use fish as a cover for the delivery trucks?"

Dan Malone nodded. "Fish? Sounds delicious to me."

"Sweet Jesus, Michael. How long do you think we can pull this off?" Declan asked.

"Kid, as long as we need to. We have been pushing booze up and down the state, trying to keep our heads above water, now we have a chance to stock up and make a killing at the same time. It will be tricky, but it beats getting hijacked and slaughtered on a lonely road somewhere. None of this leaves this room. The smaller the number involved, the safer we are."

"We can get this done," Dan said with a slight smile.

Michael and Dan Malone shook hands, and Malone was gone.

CHAPTER 41

Keira counted the days between her family's visits. She would tell Nora every morning as they dressed for Mass how many days until they saw their family again.

Nora would smile and say nothing. It was as though Nora didn't think of them at all.

Each spring, Maureen, Hannah, and Mae—accompanied by either Robert or Bradley—would pick up the girls and take them home to the city for a short visit. New dresses and family dinners were all a part of these trips.

Nora always seemed to keep her distance from the family. Mae couldn't help but think the child had lost so much that she was unable to get close to anyone. She was always polite and only spoke when spoken to. This was taught by the nuns, but Nora took it to an extreme. She didn't even talk to her siblings. Keira and Hannah rattled on for hours about nothing, but Nora remained silent.

During one of the spring visits, she and Keira went to the candy store to visit Hannah. While Keira and Hannah were chattering about something, Nora wandered to the back of the store. She stood in front of the back entrance and took a deep breath. She could smell the cigar smoke, her head began to swim. Smells, voices, and memories jumbled together and swirled in her mind.

"Papa, Momma, where are you?" she screamed then fell to the floor.

Hannah and Kiera were at her side in a flash.

The door to the club flew open, and Michael and Declan bolted through it. The child's cry shot through Michael's heart like a bullet. He knew it was Noinin. *Which Momma is this poor child shouting for?* He scooped her up, pulled her close, able to hug her for the first time since Conrad and Eveleen were murdered. His chest tightened. "Girls, get your sister some water." Michael placed the child on a chair near the counter.

Nora shook her head as she came to. Her red hair tossed wildly, as though she was shaking the jumbled mess from her mind. She whispered, "I'm sorry … what happened?"

Michael said softly, "It's all right, child. You fainted, but you will be fine."

A warm sense of comfort flowed over the child. She didn't know what it was, but she felt a connection to this stranger. He seemed familiar, but she didn't recognize him.

Michael tried desperately to contain his emotions. He saw to it that Nora and Keira each had a bag of candy before he walked them back to Maureen's apartment.

Maureen met them at the door, her jaw dropped when she saw Michael.

He spoke before Maureen could even take a breath, "Seems this little one needs to rest a bit. She fainted at the candy store. I didn't want her to walk home alone, so I escorted both young ladies."

Maureen replied politely, "Thank you, Mr. Byrne. That was very kind of you."

Nora wanted to go to the candy store on a daily basis in hopes of seeing Mr. Byrne. His presence left her with a great sense of comfort. Nora's fainting became a perfect way to reintroduce himself into her life. It gave him a chance to see how she was doing firsthand. It was not too personal; he was just a family friend who helped her out.

Nora asked him to come to the convent with Maureen to visit her and Keira.

"I'll try my best, but work keeps me very busy," Michael said. It was as though he had a window that linked him to Conrad and Eveleen. The child who had lost so much had reached out to him. He was elated to have the chance to be a part of her life again.

But his focus had to remain on getting the hooch safely off the ships and delivered. Tarrytown was over a hundred miles from Atlantic City. He couldn't use the pretense that he had business in the area. The relationship would remain in the neighborhood—for safety's sake.

Nora began to count the days between visits to the city. She longed to see Mr. Byrne again. She was unable to put a name to it, but she felt close to him.

Mother Superior was sure Nora would stay at the convent and become a nun.

Nora enjoyed the library and books, and she enjoyed the tranquility of convent life. She lived in her own little world, surrounded by books. She had no thoughts of the hardship that existed outside the gates of the convent. The convent was her cocoon.

Shortly after she returned from her spring visit to the

city, Nora's nightmares began. She would awaken in a sweat, inconsolably sad. Keira would hold her and try to calm her fears, but her sobbing only got louder. Her sobbing was so loud during the night, that the dorm monitor would have to call Mother Superior to soothe her.

The child was unable describe her dreams, but an overwhelming sadness engulfed her. Without any warning, the cocoon that protected her from the sadness of her tragic past had exploded. Nora buried herself in schoolwork, ran errands for Mother Superior, and read at every chance. She escaped into the stories. Books that piled up in the dormitory were read until she fell asleep.

CHAPTER 42

Michael plunged headfirst into his new venture with Dan Malone. Daily operations at Cara Dílis and Garnet's place continued without interruption. Mae had gathered a group of trustworthy, work-ready single young men to meet with Michael. Michael got everyone together at Cara Dílis. The men were told where to report and what their jobs were. They were told the clubs needed extra people. After looking over the group, Michael turned to Declan who casually asked a select few men to stay and excused the rest.

Michael spoke to those who remained, "Friends, we have an opportunity to make some real money—all of us— but it comes with great risks. If you feel you aren't up to it, leave now. Only those who can truly place their lives in my hands need to stay. I won't go any further until I know who is with me."

All the men Declan selected knew and trusted Michael and his reputation, They stood firmly with him.

"Together we have been through hell. We have a chance for a payday equal to the risk. It is totally on a volunteer basis. You must be absolutely sure of your decision. If you have any doubts, leave now. There will be no bad blood if any of you choose to stay at the clubs to cover the daily business."

No one left.

Once he felt comfortable the men would stand by his side, Michael explained what had to be done.

There was a rumor that Dan Malone was in control. Only those close to the family knew the truth. Michael let the other families believe he was now part of Malone's family. It brought safety to the neighborhood. Dan protected them all. Michael was able to take a breath and concentrate on building a future rather than constantly looking over his shoulder.

Dan came through with the Coast Guard schedules. Michael didn't want to know how he managed it. Dan just commented, "You get more bees with honey." It was left at that.

Nick Leary, with all his connections, couldn't get that done. He didn't have Dan's convincing charm. Nick was brazen and used threats to accomplish tasks. He was forced to step back to keep his politician friends happy. They still wanted the booze, but they didn't want the violence associated with Leary.

Michael, Dan, and Declan coordinated the Coast Guard's schedule along with the nights with no moon, thanks to the *Farmer's Almanac.* They also calculated the number of men and trucks needed.

Feeling the protection of Dan Malone's name, Michael took a trip to Atlantic City. As he walked on the boardwalk, his thoughts drifted to the last time he was there. The crowds and the commotion that surrounded him were muted. It had only been a few years, but it felt like a lifetime ago. He and Conrad had taken Tara and Eveleen to see the sights. He twisted his cigar between his lips, desperately trying to remember Tara's voice, her laugh, and her smell. He was finally able to think of Tara without getting a constricting knot in his throat. He wished Tara and his friends could share in the successful future he planned. He finished his cigar. It was time to concentrate on the business at hand. Thoughts of Tara and Conrad swam in his mind. It was as though he was able to talk to Conrad, but he wasn't ready to talk to Tara outside of the cemetery.

Conrad, I think I finally found a way to survive Volstead and accomplish our dreams. Sweet Jesus, I wish you were here.

After walking the boardwalk, Michael headed to the New Gretna area near Great Bay, New Jersey. He found an inlet off the Mullica River located between New York City and Atlantic City. This was the site selected to offload the booze. The moon lit up the sky as Michael took short puffs from his cigar to keep it lit.

The water was calm. The moon's reflection lit up the water and the shoreline. The shoreline wasn't visible from the waterway, and it was deep enough for a skiff to slide onto it and remain unseen as its contents were offloaded into trucks. A skiff was a much better description of the boat than a speedboat. They were merely wooden hulls with powerful engines. The skiffs offered no protection as that added weight. The lighter the skiff, the faster—and the faster, the better.

Michael's plan was to offload the ship and get the skiff to the cover of the shoreline as fast as possible.

Thick woods surrounded the area. It was good cover for the men and trucks. The Crab Island Fish Factory was a perfect cover for why Michael had trucks and men in the area. The area was known as a rum-running spot. The Coast Guard kept a vigilant eye on the inlet. Those unloading the skiffs would wait in the woods until the skiff landed, and then they would move the liquor from the skiff to the waiting trucks. False lids packed with iced fish were placed on the barrels, and then the barrels were resealed. The skiffs could hold seventy barrels of a wide variety of booze. Michael's men would deliver the booze to Atlantic City. There was no reason to let Nick know how the booze was being handled plus there would be no confusion about how much was offloaded.

Once a schedule was reached, it was balls-out. Everyone met at Cara Dílis, and no one left. Michael wanted to be sure the least number of people knew what was going on. After a routine was set, Michael allowed Declan to take charge. "Never on a skiff!" That was one of Michael's prime rules for the young man. He managed the offloading, delivery, and payments.

Declan saw that the booze was distributed—along with the fish—and brought the money back to be dispersed at Cara Dílis. Simplicity was the key. "No unwanted attention." If the men expected to continue being part of the deliveries, they could not be flashy with the money. They all understood, and no one had a problem with it. The money was too good to mess it up.

CHAPTER 43

Declan saw how tightly wound his mentor was, "Michael, how about we head to Garnet's for a couple of drinks?" He said nudgingly.

It didn't take long for Michael's reply, "Sure, we have some time to get away."

Garnet was behind the bar, and she looked stunning. Her black dress clung to her like a shiny second skin. The front plunged and hugged her breasts. The back was bare to her waist. Her blonde hair framed her face. She looked out of place. The club looked great, but she looked better. She smiled and waved Michael and Declan to a booth as she threw a red boa over her shoulder. "Well, look what the wind blew in. I've missed you. I must tell you I am thrilled with our new business arrangement. We've been really busy lately." She slid into their booth, pulled her cigarette holder from between her plentiful breasts, and lit a cigarette.

"Yes, hopefully we will all see the end of the tunnel soon." Michael said softly as he reached for her hand.

With a swift wave of her free hand, Garnet signaled the bartender to bring all three of them drinks. She took a long drag from her cigarette before she said, "I'm glad you came in, Michael. I have something on my mind."

"Oh, sweet Lord, last time you had something on your mind, I became a part owner of this place." Michael laughed.

They saw each other whenever they could grab a moment, but the new booze delivery kept them both busy. They were very quiet about the fact that they were a couple.

"And that has been a good deal for both of us. Someone has offered me a generous sum to buy the Bad Penny. I would like to use that money to buy a larger club. I could buy you out, or if you trust me, we can continue to be partners. Once Prohibition is repealed, the golden goose will stop laying those lovely golden eggs. We need to be ready."

Michael loved watching Garnet talk. Her smile was like a bright light. "I agree. Selling this place is a great idea. I'm all for a larger, nicer club—one that will really stand out. I can't use any of the extra money I'm making right now. It would throw up a huge red flag. If you can make enough selling this place, I'm with you. I am interested in getting a larger place myself, but I won't give up Cara Dílis. It's part of my family. We are doing well right now. I don't see things dropping off for us."

Michael had plans of his own, but he wasn't ready to share them. He had to be sure he had enough money and that what he wanted was available. He was planning for his future—and for the futures of William and Noinin. Noinin had been on his mind lately. Now that the child was back in his life, he had to remember to call her Nora rather than the pet name Conrad had given her.

William was continuing his education at business school. Michael was confident his son, despite what he had been through including the resulting scar, would be happy and successful. However, the sad little creature, who had lost everything she loved, was cloistered from the world and surrounded by a dark, cloudy past. Unless he interceded, her future would be equally cloudy. He wanted Garnet to be a part of his future, but he wasn't sure how to explain all the gears that spun constantly in his mind.

Garnet said, "Mae and I have already spotted a really nice place. We can look at it together whenever you have time."

"That sounds like a date." Michael laughed. He had no doubt that Garnet would be very successful—with or without him.

Garnet was right. The two women found the perfect spot. The two had become very close friends and fed off each other's strengths, which made them no match for Michael.

New speakeasies had popped up all over the city. Garnet was counting on her skills as a welcoming hostess, her access to good booze, and her loyal friends to get her place on the right path. Over the years, Mae and Garnet had befriended many people who needed a hand, and they were more than eager to get the club up and running.

It took several weeks for Michael to clear time to see the new club. When he finally was able to meet Garnet and Mae at the new club, he was surprised to see how much the two had accomplished. The new place was larger than Cara Dílis. The exterior had a pale pink awning that stretched all the way to the curb. A matching thick pale pink rug, with a large gold G and M embroidered into it, reached from the door to the awning's edge. The interior was much more elegant than Cara Dílis. Light colors and bright lights set off the entryway. The silver floors were polished to a mirror shine, and crystal seemed to be everywhere. It gave the impression of being inside a champagne glass. A dance floor and a bandstand were already in place.

Garnet said, "I want to attract crowds similar to those who go to the Cotton Club in Harlem. Customers are looking for something not quite as wild—not to say white only—but I want a more intimate, reserved atmosphere. I want my place to be the place you take someone special for an evening out." Garnet turned her head to catch Michael's eye.

The Cotton Club, previously called the Club Deluxe, had been owned by the first African American heavyweight champion, Jack Johnson. He sold it to Owney "The Killer" Madden after Owney was released from Sing-Sing. Madden had redesigned the Cotton Club to look like a plantation with an exotic jungle/plantation theme for a white-only crowd.

The new club was nowhere near the size of the Cotton Club, which could seat seven hundred guests, and there was no direct competition between the two places. Garnet had no restriction on who was welcome. She just wanted to entertain a different crowd than she was used to: no more back rooms with sweaty drunks or assholes who vomited or passed out at the bar. It was finally her chance to be treated like a lady.

Michael couldn't hold back a grin. "So, this is what the two of you have been up to? I thought you were just looking for a place."

"Michael, this place has been in my head for years. You made it a reality. You and my friends." Garnet giggled and put her arms around Mae and Michael.

Mae pulled Michael aside and whispered, "Michael,

Garnet has been scrimping and saving for years to get this done."

Michael didn't know what to say. He would have never—in his wildest dreams—have thought it was possible. "Ladies, in the future, any ideas you may have about clubs, please seek me out." Michael laughed. "So, what is the name of our new club?"

"I wanted something new that would draw the right crowd. I decided on GeM. It's simple and it has both our initials."

He was a little concerned that the club was right on the agreed-upon border he had made with the Italians. The club didn't compete with anything the Italians had, so he felt it wasn't an issue, but he wanted to make sure. He contacted one of his associates, Gino Noninni, to let him know it wasn't a push to enter their territory.

There was no issue. Gino laughed and said, "If you get tired of the place, let me know. I've already checked it out, and your lady has done a great job."

Michael didn't realize anyone had noticed that Garnet was his lady. He thanked Gino for the compliment and headed out the door.

CHAPTER 44

The new club was a lot for one person. Mae did the weekly bookkeeping and the staff schedules, leaving Garnet free to make sure all the inventory was on track, the kitchen was humming at the right speed, and the club guests were having a good time.

The office was large enough for both women to have their own work areas. The office was the only area that the two hadn't refurbished. It was obvious the prior occupant was a man as the furnishings were dark and masculine. The furniture included a monstrous mahogany desk that ran the length of an entire wall. Matching wooden privacy shutters covered a large oval window that overlooked the club.

As Mae walked by the gold chaise opposite the huge desk, she noticed a fluffy yellow pillow with a lightweight quilt on it. "Garnet don't tell me you are sleeping here. It's a club—not an infant you have to hover over. Please promise me you will go home tonight. Get a real night's sleep in a bed. The club has been open for a good while. You need to relax. You are doing a great job."

Mae no longer dressed in widow's black. She wasn't as flamboyant as Garnet, but she enjoyed a variety of colors and designs. She was in daytime attire: a light blue lace dress with a solid blue lining that hit just below her knees. Her hair was no longer pulled tightly in a bun; she had it up with curls at the crown of her head, which bounced with each step.

Garnet moved from behind the desk, and her light green dress flowed around her feet. Its capped sleeves of white marabou feathers swayed, like grass in a breeze, when she moved. The dress clung to her waist, but it flowed loosely as it reached the floor. This made it easy for her to move around the room. A shimmering hairband held back her short blonde hair, creating a puff of curls at the back of her head. She looked elegant. Her ever-present cigarette holder was snuggly tucked between her breasts. "Don't make me sound like a crazy person who can't let go for a minute. I promise to go home at the end of the evening."

A red light started to flash next to the desk. Another leftover from the prior owner, it notified anyone in the office that there might be trouble in the club.

"Crap! What the hell is this?" Garnet whispered.

"I promise, Mae, I will head home right after work. You have my word on it." Garnet headed to the door.

Mae finished her paperwork before she headed home.

When Garnet got downstairs, she heard a very crude drunk arguing with the bartender. She signaled for the bartender to back away as she moved toward him. Behind the drunk stood a few men ready to toss him out the door. Removing an unruly person without the rest of the customers noticing was an art.

Garnet sat down next to him.

He looked up when he sensed her presence. "What the hell do you want, bitch?"

Garnet smiled. "Just want to make sure you are having a nice evening."

"I want a drink ... not conversation with some whore who thinks I'm beneath her ... telling me what to do."

"I don't want to tell you what to do, but I can't let you ruin the evening for my other guests." Garnet was trying her best to keep the situation under control, but she had a bad feeling about this drunk. He was a mean drunk, which was a really explosive combination. She turned and signaled for the hat check girl to get his overcoat ready. Most of the staff was alerted to what was going on. They were just waiting for Garnet's signal.

He was getting louder and ruder. "I could own this place in a heartbeat. You're nothing but a cheap whore who screwed her way into a cushy job. You are nothing. I'll show you who is in control." He slapped Garnet across the face, nearly knocking himself out of his chair and onto the floor.

Before he could regain complete control of his body, a cracking slap rang out in reply. Garnet responded without even thinking. It was a response she didn't have any control over. She thought she had left her anger from her past treatment behind her, but this mook had brought it to the surface. She was embarrassed and surprised that she had lost her composure and let a worm get the best of her.

The men behind the drunk swept him up and took him outside. She felt relieved that she had seen the last of him. He would sober up and not even remember where he had been.

"You piece of shit ... don't you ever come near this club again or I, personally, will destroy you." The doorman snapped, as the men tossed him out the door and to the ground.

The rest of the evening was uneventful, and the club was busy right up to closing.

Garnet made her final rounds, checked the kitchen, verified the liquor was safely secured in its hiding place, and made sure all the tables were set up for the next day. Finally, she checked all the doors.

"Garnet, do you want me to wait for you and see you home?" One of the men who worked security asked.

"No, honey. I'm good. I only live a couple of blocks away. Go on home. It's been a long evening. I'll be out of here soon."

Garnet learned the hard way not to appear helpless. If you look like a victim or are too dependent or trusting, you become a target. She went up to the office, got her cloak and bag, and headed out the front door. She felt strange as she began her walk home. The street was quiet, and the streetlamps were putting off less light than usual. The air was fresh. She took a deep breath to release all the uneasiness she felt. She had come a long way over the years. It was a tough ride, but she had held on and prevailed. The fresh air gave her a sense of relief, like the first breath she took after she left the captivity of the shelter. She thought of Victor, the man who helped her escape that horrible place, and wondered what he was doing. Her mind drifted as she walked. As she passed a narrow alley, she heard a familiar snarl. Her body stiffened, and her stomach churned at the disgusting smell and noise coming from the darkness.

"Hey, whore, you don't have anyone to protect you now." It was the drunk. His voice held a note of surprise. He didn't expect Garnet to be walking down the street.

"You too drunk to find your ride home?" Garnet snapped.

He sat on a pile of wooden crates, pulling at his eyebrow, as though he was trying to translate what Garnet had said. As it sunk in, he lunged at Garnet. He wadded up his fist and took a huge swing, and Garnet fell to the ground. She could taste the blood inside her mouth, and one of her teeth was submerged in the blood. She pushed the tooth to the side of her mouth. The blood started to ooze from between her lips. She pulled herself up and stood right in front of the drunk. "You feel like a big man hitting a woman? You piece of shit." Garnet's mouth was filled with blood, but she wanted to be sure he knew she wasn't afraid of him. She would never know what a truly evil creature he was.

The drunk took another swing, and his fist landed square on Garnet's jaw. It swung her body around and sent her flying. She smashed, headfirst, against the corner of the building. Her skull made a horrid crunch, which left a jagged, bloody wound. Her blonde hair dripped sticky red, and her body folded like a twisted accordion. As she dropped to the ground, a hollow thud echoed through the alley. The blood oozed from her head in a puddle around her, as her life seeped out. As her body contorted, her cigarette holder slipped from her breasts.

The drunk crushed it with a twist of his shoe. He slipped in Garnet's blood and fell. The drunken beast used the wall to drag himself to his feet, smashing loudly against the garbage pails. He staggered out of the alley, sliding along the brick building and down the street. He kept himself upright by leaning his blood-covered body against buildings and windows as he stumbled away from the carnage he created. Garnet's blood left a bloody trail that followed the animal down the street.

CHAPTER 45

Mae woke with a jolt to loud pounding at her door. She pulled on her robe and slippers as she shuffled to answer it. "Who is it?"

"It's me, Ma. Open up." Declan croaked.

Mae pulled her hair out of her face and tightened her robe. Declan's voice had an unfamiliar sound of urgency. She opened the door to find her son distraught and crying. "My God, Declan. Son, what is it?"

"It's Garnet … she's been killed."

"That's not possible. She was going straight home after she closed the club." Mae's tears gushed forth, as she grabbed a chair to balance herself. "No, no, no, no … you're wrong. She was going home right after work. She promised."

"Ma, I'm sorry, but I need your help. Come with me to tell Michael. You know how very close they are … were. I fear this may send him over the edge." Declan tried to remain strong for his ma and Michael.

Mae sobbed while she dressed as fast as she could. She had to control her grief for Michael's sake. *How can I do this? I have to be strong for Michael. So much tragedy … how much more can this man take?*

They walked in silence to Michael's place, the only

sound was Mae's sobs. It was as though the neighborhood knew they were bringing bad news. The normally noisy sidewalk was oddly hushed as they moved closer to Michael's apartment. William was just getting up when they knocked on the door. They spoke in low voices until Michael entered the room.

"A pleasure to see you both on this fine morning. Shit, why are you here?" It struck him like a rock, this wasn't a social visit.

Michael sat rigid at the kitchen table, without making a sound as Declan explained that Garnet had been found in an alley, beaten to death. The bastard left her purse with all her belongings next to her and slithered away. No one in the neighborhood had heard anything.

Michael was only half listening. He looked at his son.

William was at his da's side in an instant, holding him steady.

Michael was unable to speak.

Mae held her breath and then exploded with tears. "I'm sorry, Michael. I caused this … it's my fault. I made her promise not to sleep at the club. It's my fault. Oh, dear God, I've killed my best friend."

Michael pulled her hands to his lips and gently kissed them. He and Declan were able to calm her down a bit. They both assured her it wasn't her fault.

When Declan took Mae home her tears had dried up, and all that remained were sobs. The young man stayed, his hope was she would be able to grieve without blaming herself.

William stayed by his da's side. Later he went out to get dinner.

Michael sat alone in the apartment; the deafening silence rang in his ears. Deep in thought, the city outside was silent. His mind was on Tara, Conrad, Eveleen, and now Garnet. He wished he had let Garnet know how much he loved her. They should have had more time together. His body was heavy with the pain of his losses. He ran his fingers through his hair as he sat on the edge of the couch. *How do I go on? What have I done to be cursed this way?*

Michael promised himself from that day forward, he wouldn't let anyone get too close. His heart couldn't endure another loss. He wasn't sure he had a heart left. It was too painful to acknowledge Garnet was gone.

Mae understood his anguish. Every inch of her body ached with grief. Her tears flowed without notice. The sadness poured over her in waves, seared her blood, and surged from her head to her toes. She began to bite her lip to regain control of her emotions. Garnet was the closest thing she had to a sister. From the time they met, when Mae scrubbed drunk's vomit off the floor and Garnet serviced men at the Bad Penny, they had never judged one another. They realized they were very much alike. She thought of how hard Garnet's life had been and how she had overcome so much. She never complained; she just worked to move beyond the ugliness and pain. Mae would use the memory of Garnet's constant quiet strength to battle her own grief and find the strength she needed to help Michael. Garnet's strength was now hers. She took care of whatever Michael needed done.

Garnet was put to rest quietly and lovingly. Michael went to her service, but he stood away from everyone. He left before anyone could console him for the loss of his business associate. Garnet had been much more than a business partner—even though neither of them had acknowledged it publicly. Their close friends knew what they had and what Michael had lost.

He couldn't stomach being anywhere near GeM. It reflected Garnet at every turn.

Mae spoke to Michael daily to see how he was doing. Shortly after Garnet's funeral, she bit her lip and swallowed deeply before she asked him if GeM should remain closed. It was all he had left of Garnet, and closing the club seemed too final. She had put her blood and soul into the club, and her memory had to remain alive in it.

After a few days, Michael met with Mae in her apartment. He hadn't slept. Without saying a word, she poured him tea and waved him to sit down. He took a long sip of the tea and reached across the table for her hand as he spoke in a hoarse grief filled voice, "Mae, I can't express how broken I am. I never got a chance to tell Garnet how much I loved her. She brought me out of the darkness, but her death sent me plummeting back. I can't imagine I will ever be happy again. I can't go back to GeM, yet I can't give it up. I know how much you loved Garnet and how much you two put into the club. I want you to run the club for me … please. It is all I have left of Garnet."

Mae was stunned by his request. She held her breath and tried not to break down. Since GeM had opened, Mae had worked behind the scenes—doing the paperwork and managing the payroll—but Garnet was the star that lit up the club. "Michael, I understand your pain. Garnet knew how much you loved her by how you treated her. I know she loved you deeply. I didn't want to step foot in the club again, but if you think we can keep her memory alive with the club, I'll do my best." Mae tried to sound confident, but she still wasn't sure she could bear being in the club with only the memory of her best friend as comfort.

Michael accepted Mae's answer. His heart was broken into a million pieces, but he refused to let Garnet's dream of a grand club die with her.

CHAPTER 46

Cara Dílis and the shipping schedules kept Michael and Declan busy. Michael concentrated all his attention on the shipping schedules. They kept him hopping. With Dan Malone in the picture, things moved smoothly. His name alone meant greater protection for everything Michael worked on.

There were only a couple of times when one of the trucks ran into trouble, but the drivers and crew managed it. There was a shootout, but the hijackers were not prepared for Michael's men. A couple of mooks thought the fish trucks were an easy mark. They had no idea what was on the truck— let alone who. The shootout was loud and fast. A lot of bullets were spent, but Michael's men and the load were unscathed. Another time, a truck got stuck in mud. A cop actually helped them. He was given free fish in return for his help.

Michael didn't let the smoothness of the trucking go to his head. He kept a close watch on everything.

Dan was happy, and Nick Leary was thrilled. He had all the booze he needed with no apparent connection to the illegal booze running. Michael hoped he could keep this deal running smoothly until Prohibition was over. Then he'd be free to see Conrad's dream of clubs and hotels become a reality.

Chapter 47

Elizabeth spoke with as much confidence as she could muster, "For all those years, Michael looked for the murderers of his friends, and William kept his secret, both protecting the family. They shared a great responsibility, but what if we tried a different approach? Instead of looking for a shooter, who is long gone, we look for who benefited the most from all the hardship. The common denominator among all of you in this room was a money-hungry power grabber. Each of you spoke of an event in your lives that pitted yourselves— or your fathers—against a common evil. The person either stole from your family, stole an idea, or threatened you to prevent your family from competing with him.

"Here is what we know for sure. On the afternoon Conrad was murdered, he had an appointment downtown. We know he was looking into land in Nevada. We know he talked about leaving the city, but who else was involved in his great deal? If it was a land deal, there had to be records of a purchase. We must merely obtain records from the 1930s." Elizabeth felt positive the group could find out who was behind the murders. It seemed cut and dried to the young woman. A quick trip to the hall of records was the solution.

Declan interjected, "Elizabeth, it is a sound idea, but

there were many bastards scrambling to make a quick fortune during that time. It wasn't just a single person involved in our individual troubles. These bastards … forgive my vulgarity … were very slick operators. They would be smooth as silk in front of you, and then the minute you let your guard down, they would steal the teeth out of your head. They all worked from the same playbook. Given the time that has passed, anyone involved in Conrad's slaughter and the butchering of the rest of our friends could have easily covered their tracks. We are talking about very powerful and deceitful people."

Elizabeth squealed like a child, "I agree, Declan, but if they were able to cover all their tracks and had what they wanted, they would no longer have any interest in our family. So, why, after all these years, would they still be tracking our family and searching our belongings?"

William shouted in excitement, nearly lifting himself from his chair, "The child is correct. There must be something we have missed. After my da finally told me what he had been carrying on his shoulders for so long, I thought for sure I could find who was behind it all. Elizabeth is right; someone still knows the truth. We must force them to come out from under their rock."

Declan was less than happy with this epiphany, "This leads us nowhere. We are right back where we started—years ago. We don't even know if Conrad's murder had anything to do with his big deal."

The room became awkwardly silent as they realized they had learned a lot about the past and everyone in the room, but they hadn't gotten any closer to finding out who was shadowing the family.

William spoke again, "But we have each other now. We can search our memories and see if something we previously thought was nothing, might mean something."

Nora spoke in an attempt to convince the others in the room, as well as herself, "William is right. There is something … something that may be right in front of us … something so obvious we overlooked it. A record of some sort, paperwork, documents." Her entire life had been altered forever. Like a head slap, the vanity shot into her head. It had been in her possession for as long as she could remember. *The mirror and its newspapers!* She had assumed the old newspapers had cushioned the mirror. The women were so involved in cleaning up the broken glass and planning for their trip that the papers were placed on the top shelf of the closet. *The glued document drawer, the wedding rings, and Conrad's stickpin.* Her mind was rushing with excitement. Her past was in the papers that they stored in the closet. "The vanity … oh my God … the vanity was the answer before I ever knew the question."

Declan spoke softly, "I think Michael put the jewelry in the document drawer before he asked me to move it."

William spoke, "My heart is jumping out of my chest. This may be what they have been looking for all these years. We must move very cautiously; this information must not leave this room."

If the family was to finally see justice, this information had to be kept among this small group, especially since it was unknown what secrets the vanity held. A slight sense of satisfaction hovered over the room. The conversation turned to reminiscing about their adventures.

After a few minutes of talking about old times, Declan

stood up and said, "It has been a long day. Let's all get some rest."

Danny J. slowly stood up and headed to the door. As he got to the stairs, he turned and said, "Please be sure to let me know what you find out. I am as eager as you all to finally put an end to this chaos."

Once Danny J. was out of earshot, Tallman tapped Declan on the shoulder and whispered, "I will be in touch with you soon."

Declan nodded and said. "Agreed. We should spend some time together." He asked Nora's family, William, and Luke to stay. "I have something I need to talk to you about." He poured another drink. "I must explain something to all of you. Nora's whole childhood was filled with secrets and heartache. I decided it would be better for all involved if I waited for a good time to approach your family about other family business. Well, obviously, there was never a good time. I'm truly sorry William, that I left you out of the loop. When things started to look bright for all of us toward the end of Prohibition, your da decided he needed to secure a future for you and Nora. He fashioned investments for you both. I have been waiting for a time when I could share this with you." He hung his head.

William quietly spoke, "Declan, as I got older, I knew there was something different about Nora. Whenever she visited, Maureen made a point of bringing her by. Da told me who she was after she left the convent to live on her own. When he told me, I thought he might have put something aside for her."

William directed his conversation to Nora, "He was heartbroken that you lived the life of an orphan. He felt you were the daughter he could never have. Although he never said it, I think he felt responsible for Conrad's murder … like he could have done something to stop it. He never got over the fact that you had such a tormented upbringing." I suspected several properties had been set aside for you, like GeM. Da never let anyone touch the interior—even after Mae passed away. It remained as Garnet had dreamed it."

Nora choked out, "I don't understand. What are you saying?"

Elizabeth placed her hand on her mother's knee while they waited for Declan to finish his explanation.

"Over the years, because Michael didn't trust banks or bankers, he bought real estate. It was always on his mind that Conrad wanted to own hotels and clubs. The Didean would have made Michael and Conrad very proud. William, you have done well. Michael would have been thrilled to see GeM still open. As William said, my ma managed it until her death. It is one of the properties Michael wanted you to have. There are other places that have been open and operating for many years … properties that were left to William when Michael died … and joint properties that were held for both of you. You share ownership in them. And now that our secrets are out in the open, I am free to release the accounts to you. If I thought you needed the income, I would have found a way to get the funds to you, but I was terrified you would be exposed. I kept track of you and your family, and you have done well."

Nora was unable to make a sound, Elizabeth was dumbfounded, and Brendan was only able to squeeze his wife's leg.

Nora found a voice and scratched out, "You're saying we are partners in a hotel?"

Declan turned to her and answered, "There are three properties, all are as elegant and profitable as the Didean. They are well-managed properties, and you are free to do what you like with them. Now that your identity is in the open, there is no reason for you and William not to control the properties. Please forgive me."

Nora cleared her throat. "Declan, there is no need for forgiveness. You all have looked out for me since I was a child. I just wish I had been able to be closer to Michael. Many unclear memories make sense now." Suddenly, she felt drained. Her brain was shutting down, and her body needed to refuel.

Declan saw her predicament, "There's no need for you to do a single thing. I will see that you get reports on the properties and the profit checks. If you choose to, you can become active in the daily operations. It's up to you and your family. We don't have to go over it at this moment. If you like, we can visit the properties before you head home— whenever you are ready."

William wasn't surprised. "Declan, your shoulders have carried a heavy burden for a very long time. We are grateful to you for your loyalty." He took a deep breath. "As my da got older he was prepared to die. He had outlived, by many years, most of those who meant so much to him. He would lean over me and say, 'You are my angel on earth. You make my life worth living.' He lived to see that the lives lost were not in vain. He had fulfilled the dreams he shared with those he held dear."

Nora was still digesting her new family history and a

New York property ownership. *Shit, I can't even balance my checkbook and now this?* "This is an amazing surprise among a week of surprises. I don't know about the rest of my family, but I need to get some rest to digest all of this."

The group rode in silence all the way back to the Didean. As they exited the town car, Nora realized their lives were forever changed. The doorman was a bit confused as the group silently stood, in awe, at the entrance of the hotel.

Once in the room, Nora's head swirled with all the new information. She headed toward the shower. A nice hot shower always helped clear her thoughts. She hoped it would prepare her for what was yet to come. As the hot water flowed over her, a dark heaviness sank deep into her chest. Why didn't someone let her know her background sooner? They thought they were protecting her, but she had lived her whole life thinking she was someone else. How would her life have been different? She stood in the corner of the huge shower and cried for the family and the life she never knew. For a second, she caught a whiff of light perfume and a faint smell of a sweet cigar. In an instant, the aromas were gone. Their familiarity comforted her. The heaviness was lifted. It was unclear to her how or why she knew the smells.

Corazon called into her, "You need help?"

"No, I'm OK. All of this just hit me like a pile of bricks." Finished with her shower, Nora sought out her daughter.

Elizabeth hugged her mother tightly. "Momma, I have no words. This has been mind-boggling for me. I can't imagine how you feel."

The family gathered in the living room of the suite and discussed their new windfall and how it would impact their lives.

Elizabeth quietly spoke, "Sure, it's all well and good that we have property, but what about the people who wanted Momma's family dead? All of us are knee-deep in whatever this is. Will they follow us home and attack us?"

They had no answers.

The hot shower and her medication had strengthened Nora for the moment. There was a new urgency. She needed to find out all she could about her father, Michael, and their business. She was terrified the sludge would overcome her before she was able to get all the answers she needed. "We are exposed. We don't even know to whom or why. Once we get home and go through the papers from the vanity, I pray we will have our answers. Hopefully, whatever information the vanity documents reveal will bring an end to this nightmare." Nora tried to sound confident and unafraid, and she managed a weak smile.

Elizabeth reached for her mother's hand. "OK … for the time being, let's look on the bright side. We are part-owners of several exclusive New York properties. Let's extend our time in the city by a few days, take a grand tour, and enjoy the hospitality of the Big Apple. Now how about we have some champagne to celebrate Momma, Nora Eveleen Quinn?" Elizabeth rubbed her mother's shoulders.

Brendan poured the champagne, then they toasted Nora, her newly discovered fortune, and her new family. Thoughts of an unknown assassin lingered in the back of their minds. The little man who entered the room was never found. He had somehow managed to use his hat to cover his face when he went by cameras. He must have slipped in and out through the kitchen unnoticed. He never entered or exited the front of the hotel.

CHAPTER 48

They accepted Declan's offer to show them the properties. They sat silently in the town car while Declan presented the history of each place. The properties were all older, but each had been thoughtfully renovated. Cara Dílis was the club Conrad and Michael opened together. Declan explained that Michael had a female partner, Garnet, in one of his first purchases after Conrad's death. Michael and Garnet were very close friends. They were partners in two clubs during Prohibition. GeM was special to both of them. She died before the end of Prohibition. He didn't specify how she died. Garnet was also very close with Declan's mother, Mae. After Garnet's death, Mae took over GeM for Michael.

The manner in which Declan spoke of Michael's partner, made it obvious they were more than close friends. After Prohibition, Michael started buying additional properties. Declan didn't go into detail about Michael's profits or his businesses, other than the clubs opened during Prohibition.

Each property was as elegant as the Didean, and the group didn't see such luxury in the Southwest architecture. They had lead crystal chandeliers, thick carpets, rich wallpaper and furnishings, along with staff begging to please. All were modern with an air of the era Michael and

Conrad had lived in. That was probably Declan's doing. He was continuing their legacy.

The group stayed at each of the properties for at least one night. Nora's favorite was a club, not a hotel. It was decorated in shades of pink and silver. It had just the right amount of pink. It didn't look tacky or cheap. The carpet was gray, deep wool pile, and the white wallpaper had touches of pale lavender, and pink. White columns led to a dining area and a huge bandstand.

Declan saw her reaction, "This club is one of the clubs Michael owned with Garnet. Garnet and my ma ran the club. Garnet was a good friend to all of us, and she died too young. Ma took charge after Garnet's death. After my ma passed, William took over. He has managed it for years."

Nora enjoyed being pampered, but was ready to get home. She was eager to go through all the papers in the closet. They had to hold the answer to the mystery that had hung over her life for as long as she could remember. It had to be resolved before the fog and sludge took everything from her.

It felt like they had been in the city forever. The West coast family met the East Coast family one last time at Cara Dílis the night before they headed home. William sat with both families in the front of Cara Dílis for drinks. They all moved to the back to have a speakeasy experience. They ate, drank, and listened to a band.

Nora celebrated her newfound family and friends, who were now like family. She wondered what the future held. She promised to stay connected with Angela and her family. Poor Angela had no idea what had been going on. She just thought she had reconnected with an elderly aunt and her family from the West.

It wasn't hard to imagine Michael, Tara, Conrad, and Eveleen sitting at a table in the back room. William, Declan, and the rest of the "family" had dedicated their lives to the generations that came after them—just as Michael and Conrad had envisioned.

CHAPTER 49

Conrad stood in front of Eveleen's new vanity mirror, adjusted his tie, and gently placed his stickpin in the center. Rainbows reflected vibrantly off the walls of the apartment as he fastened the pin. He felt guilty not including Michael in this meeting, but Michael's hot temper could get the best of him. Conrad couldn't risk losing this opportunity. A calm head was needed to conclude this plan.

Everything was falling into place. All that was left was pinpointing the property on the map, and they would be on their way to paradise. Once the deal was sealed, he would share it all with Michael and their wives. They would all be thrilled. A generous smile flowed across his face. Michael would be as pleased with him as he was with himself. Conrad descended the stairs and passed Declan on the stoop.

"Conrad, can I drop you somewhere?" Declan asked.

"No, son. I have a quick meeting downtown. Let Michael know I'll meet him at his place later." He spoke as he disappeared around the corner.

Conrad rode in silence as the cab slowly chugged through the bustling city. The sun danced in and out of the shadows of the buildings. His stickpin sent a rainbow through the cab each time the sun caught it. He was oblivious to it all. He was lost in thought about the future.

As the cab rounded the last corner then slowed to a stop, he became aware of his surroundings. The building's huge white columns summoned him. His stomach recoiled as he walked up the stairs. His anxious hands opened the huge double doors, but his confidence grew as he walked into the building. His shoes echoed loudly on the polished floor. Sunlight poured into the building from high windows, leaving square patches along the floor like a lighted quilt.

Today was the day he would find out the exact location of the property. The desert property had been purchased at a previous appointment. It was a cash deal with no bank loan. The man who handled the sale told Conrad to keep the documents safe. An appointment had been made with one of the deed registrars, Mathew Wilson. "A snap to pinpoint the property and we're finished." It was Wilson's job to research the parcel's latitude and longitude and pinpoint the physical address of the property on a map. Once the property was located the deed could be finalized.

Conrad walked passed the workers in their wooden stalls.

"Good day, Mr. Quinn. How are you on this fine morning?" The man's voice was sickeningly sweet.

Conrad didn't recognize him from his previous visit. He looked suspiciously out of place. He came out of nowhere and stood directly in front of Conrad. A chill went up Conrad's spine, and alarm bells rang in his head.

"I'm well … thank you. I'm here to meet Mr. Wilson. Is he available?" Conrad didn't want to give the mook too much information. The hair on the back of his neck stood up, sending another chill down his back. Wilson was who he was to meet—the only person he was to meet. Conrad wished Michael was by his side. This was wrong; it was going sideways. His business meeting had taken an ugly turn, and he was without his trusted partner. *Shit.* He had to control the situation—no matter what.

"I can help you with whatever you need." He snapped to attention as he spoke which caused a blob of greasy black hair to slap onto his face. The man's attire was totally wrong for an everyday businessman. He was dressed well, but he didn't fit in. Conrad couldn't put his finger on it, but he noticed the guy's gray eyes as they darted side to side when he spoke. His large red nose was running, and he wiped it with his sleeve. He was anxious, which made Conrad anxious. He didn't look much like a businessman—more like a bouncer or a wise guy. The man's hands were calloused and dry, like he worked in a factory or in the street and definitely not in an office. He was in constant motion, swaying back and forth and rubbing his hands together. The rubbing was like sandpaper scraping across a piece of wood. No one in the bank seemed aware of him. Conrad needed to get away from this slob as quickly as possible.

"Mr. Wilson is not in the office today. I'd be more than happy to help you. I'm Stan Bennett."

Conrad wanted as few people as possible to be aware of his business. The more the man talked, the more apprehensive Conrad became. "Thank you for the offer, Mr. Bennett, but I can wait for Mr. Wilson's return. I'm in no hurry." Conrad tried to sound nonchalant, but his stomach began to churn—and a lump grew at the back of his throat.

Bennett chirped back, "It may be a while before he returns. He had an accident last evening."

The hair on Conrad's neck danced and sent electric shock waves throughout his body. The tips of his ears burned. This guy was bad news. Conrad smiled and said, "Not an issue … it can wait." His pulse pounded in his temples. He had been so careful to keep his plans to himself. He hadn't even shared them with Michael. There was no reason to keep his best friend in the dark. He wished he had included him. It would just be such a great surprise. The fewer people involved, the better. Not including Michael was a very bad idea. He knew he wouldn't get any argument from Michael on that point. If the deal went sideways, no one would ever be aware of his purchase. He thought about how he could get out of there without looking like he was panicking. He gave Bennett a big smile and said, "Well, give Mr. Wilson my best. Have him give me a call on his return. As I said, I am in no hurry."

Conrad shook Bennett's hand, turned, and walked away as though he was taking a leisurely stroll in the park. He concentrated on his footsteps to keep his stride in check. It took all he had to walk slowly out the door and down the stairs. He stood out front, trying to remain calm, while he waited for a cab.

Once in the cab, Conrad pulled his pocket scarf from his breast pocket and wiped Bennett's sweat from his hands. The drive back to the apartment was a blur. He was certain Wilson was dead—and Bennett was either responsible or was aware of who was responsible. He mulled it over in his head. Of all the hoods he had come across, he had never seen this guy. He was obviously a piece of slime. Why was he so eager to aid him? Wilson must have told someone about his purchase. He certainly hadn't told anyone about the deal. He had asked Dan Malone for advice about who could pinpoint a property's location. As far as he was concerned Malone was the only other person aware of the purchase. Who employed this slob?

As he rode back to the apartment, he knew he had to tell Michael what he was up to. It was settled. When the two of them were alone before dinner, he would tell Michael about the purchase. It wouldn't be the celebration he had planned, but he wouldn't have to continue to keep his purchase from his partner and best friend.

Conrad was relieved that Declan wasn't waiting on the stoop when he returned. He ran up the stairs to his apartment, thrilled no one was around to slow him down. Eveleen had left a note. She was with Tara. He wandered around the apartment. He had to find a safe place to hide the documents—somewhere no one would bother to search. He glanced around the apartment, Eveleen's vanity caught his eye. It was clear he wasn't going to be able to pinpoint the property for a while, but he was confident that he and Michael could complete whatever was needed to find their property. If the documents were in a safe place, there was no need to worry. They could go out West and check things out. The area sounded rough to Conrad.

Not in the document drawer, too obvious. Behind the mirror. His mind raced. It would be easy for him to get to, and no one was going to take the time to remove the mirror to search for papers. It took only a couple of minutes to remove the tabs that held the mirror in place. Conrad removed the mirror and put it on the bed. He placed the documents between two pieces of newspaper, replaced the mirror, then began to tighten the tabs. He could have secured it better, but he was interrupted by Eveleen's voice and Noinin's red curls bouncing through the door. He was always amazed at the energy his daughter displayed. He acted as though he was straightening his tie as he finished the last tab on the mirror. His daughter jumped into his arms. This little beauty could put sunshine into the darkest day. He gave her a big hug and nuzzled her neck, which made her giggle loudly.

"Hello, ladies. How's your afternoon been?" He had to get the events of his afternoon out of his mind.

"We've had a lovely day, my sweet." Eveleen gave him a peck on the cheek along with a long hug.

"Remember, we are all going to dinner this evening. I must go down to the club for a bit. Eveleen, *Mo ghrá* (my love), change for dinner and come with me. We'll drop Noinin with Maureen until we are ready to leave for dinner."

The couple changed and went off to the club. Conrad hoped to talk to Michael before dinner. He was confident he had hidden the papers where they couldn't be found, and there was nothing to fear. He would hang onto the documents until he and Michael traveled West. They could pinpoint the property from the deed away from prying eyes and register it in Nevada. *It will be much easier for the two of us to locate the parcel ourselves than to have someone else take care of it.*

CHAPTER 50

Nora said her goodbyes to Declan and William at the hotel. If someone was watching, there was no need to draw any more attention. Although it was painful, a part of her that had been absent since her childhood had been found. She was determined not to allow her old body to give up before she had gotten all the answers.

A town car drove them to the airport, and it looked like a scene from a *Keystone Cops* movie as they arrived. Tickets had to be verified, and boarding passes were needed. Everyone was chattering like a bunch of honking geese. There was more luggage headed home than was brought.

A redcap, a slender young man with a quiet manner and quick smile, took charge of the bags. "All right, family. Let's get you to where you need to be." He led them along with the piles of luggage to check in and then to the proper gate.

In the chaos of the busy airport, Nora realized how quickly her life and her sense of self had changed. The family she had known—who they were, how they lived, and how they died—had all changed in a finger snap of time. Maureen's death had finally allowed the woman to announce to all involved that Nora was her niece and she had survived the slaughter that had stolen her parents along with all who loved her. As a result, all the family members' lives were forever changed. The perpetrator of the carnage had to be alive; otherwise, the family wouldn't have been shadowed.

Declan had upgraded the tickets to first class, the first step toward a changed life. When Nora dropped into her seat, relief flowed over her. Finally, she was headed home. There was also dread. Would the family remain safe? They were thousands of miles away from protection. Whoever was looking for them knew exactly who they were and how to find them. She felt an electric charge of urgency. She had to stay out of the fog and sludge long enough to find the truth. The documents stuffed in the closet had to hold the answer that everyone had searched for since the murder of Conrad and Eveleen.

Elizabeth ordered drinks to toast Nora's new life and the family's exciting future.

Poor Corazon had been at Nora's side during all this turmoil. Nora gripped her friend and caregiver's hand to assure her she was part of the new life. As the plane's engine moaned in the background, Nora finished her drink, lost in thought, she fell into a deep sleep. She slept for the majority of the flight. It was a peaceful sleep, no nightmares or quicksand.

It was good to be home. The house no longer felt like the place where Nora would melt into the walls. She had a new energy, a quest to solve the mystery of her parents' murder. Why was her family being tracked?

Elizabeth was eager to get to her mother's home. Brendan came with her to help. It seemed like he wanted to be sure nothing else was broken.

There was a round of hugs and tears before they started going through the papers in the closet. The four of them headed to Nora's room, it seemed brighter than usual. A comfortable warmth filled the room.

A light perfume scent and a familiar cigar met Nora as she entered the room. *Ha! Michael, guide me to the answer. Papa, Momma, show me. It must be here.* Nora held back tears as she headed to the closet.

Brendan said, "This time, I'll move things for you."

The vacuum tracks were still fresh from before their trip. No one had been in the room in their absence.

Brendan opened the double doors of the closet and gently brought down the pile of papers. Where would they begin? No one had paid any attention to where the papers had come from. The papers from behind the mirror, the papers that lined the sealed bottom drawer, and those that lined the other large drawer were all in one pile. Brendan placed the pile on the bed. On top of the pile was the jewelry. Brendan asked, "Shall we go through all this stuff right here—or do you want to move to the dining room table?"

"We can sort through the papers more easily at the table." Nora picked up the velvet bag and held it tightly as though she was waiting for it to talk. Her twisted fingers slowly rubbed the monogram: CQ. She opened the bag and gently poured out the contents. The rings came out first, then the stickpin.

They were mesmerized by its beauty. The women had forgotten how impressive it was. It lit up the room with rainbows that bounced from one side of the room to the other. It was as if Conrad had heard her and was trying to guide her. Each one caressed the pin, in amazement of the rainbow it created, as it was passed around the room. Enough time was spent admiring the pin. The Job at hand had to move forward. Answers had to be found—no matter how painful they were.

The pile of papers made its way to the dining room in Brendan's grip.

Corazon made a fresh pot of coffee, and Nora poured a large mug, took a gulp, and set it on the granite countertop. Her mug was not going to be the one to spill something on the papers that covered the table.

The other three followed her lead.

Nora said, "Make four piles. It will be easier that way."

There were all sorts of newspaper pages, just things someone would line a drawer with. The piles covered the table. The papers crunched as they read in silence.

Brendan groaned in horror, "Holy shit! Here is an article about Conrad and Eveleen's slaughter. It has photos. Oh, dear God, this is gruesome."

They gathered around him. It was truly gruesome. The worn photos showed the car riddled with bullets, thick blood like liquid darkened the gutter. The photographer hadn't gotten near the family. According to the article the young family in the car had been wiped out at the hands of an unknown assailant, and a young man who survived was thought to be in a city hospital. There was no mention of Michael. The police had no leads about why the family was slaughtered or any idea who might want to do such a horrendous thing.

This was followed by another long silence as they read about store sales and movie times.

Elizabeth said, "I think we can get through this a bit faster if we sort the papers by date and then go through them."

They sorted the piles, by date. Some of the papers were folded tightly. Brendan found an article about an employee from the Register of Deeds office who had gone missing. Mathew Wilson had disappeared after work one afternoon. The police suspected foul play but had no leads. That was one day before Conrad and Eveleen's murder. He put it to the side and went through more papers. It stood out from the other papers. If the man didn't have any connection to the family, why would it be folded and saved? His name had been underlined to draw attention to it. It was not something random.

The search seemed to be going nowhere until they found another article about the murder of several men outside Cara Dílis. The men had been savagely beaten to death. One of the men was Tommy Doyle, again no leads to who was responsible for the slaughter.

Nora spoke quietly like she might disturb the papers, "My father. I'm sorry I didn't sort the papers when I took them out of the drawers. I had no idea that they held any importance. We know that Michael had Declan bring the vanity to Tommy and Ida's apartment. It appears as though more than one person collected articles, and some are just random papers. Who saved the article about Conrad and Eveleen's murder? I think my mother, Ida, may have put the article about Tommy's murder in a drawer. Sweet Jesus. They have been gone so long. They are the only parents I remember."

There was no way of knowing what was random lining

and what was saved deliberately without going through all of the papers.

Brendan said, "Let's take a break. We need to eat something. My eyes are getting blurry." He was always ready to eat.

The house had been closed while they were away, so take-out was the best choice. Since the dinner table was covered with papers, they ate in silence on the patio. They tried to visualize what they were looking for. What was the key to all of this? Were any of the papers connected? The articles included murders of family members, both biological and adoptive, random ads, and an article about a missing employee of the Registrar of Deeds in New York City.

Nora shouted, "Shit, we are looking for a deed ... I'm almost positive! I think Michael thought there was a connection between the missing guy and the murder of Conrad and Eveleen." Nora jumped up. She was ready to get at it again. Her time was at a premium. There was no time to waste.

Brendan said quietly and sympathetically, "The papers aren't going anywhere. They've been in that vanity for years. If there is a deed among them, we'll find it. A couple more minutes to refuel will pay off later."

A deed to what? Nora's mind swirled. She sat down again.

Elizabeth said, "Let's finish our meal first, Momma. I'm still seeing newspaper print every time I close my eyes."

They finished eating without another word.

Nora was eager to get back to the papers. Corazon rubbed her friend's shoulders, then she cleared the take-out containers. The rest of them followed Nora back to the papers.

There were articles about Conrad, Eveleen, and their young daughter's funeral. The writer paid special attention to the child who had been savagely murdered with her parents in a hail of gunfire. It was bizarre for the old woman to read about herself dying as a child. The special attention that the child got in the article made it clear that Michael had spoken to the writer to confirm her death. There was also an article about Tommy's funeral. It all made sense if Ida had saved the articles, but then they found Ida's funeral notice.

Who the hell clipped that article? It struck Nora, "Declan and Michael must have taken the vanity to Mae's apartment after Ida died. It's crazy. This damn vanity has been in our family's possession since I was a small child—and no one ever bothered to look in it."

Sadness swelled in her chest. The vanity reeked of sorrow. She couldn't stand to be near it. It held all the death and sadness that engulfed her life.

Elizabeth spoke calmly, "Momma we had no way of knowing that this old piece of furniture that everyone ignored held so much information. For that matter, it wouldn't have meant a damn thing to any of us if we hadn't talked to William and Declan and the rest of the old guys in New York."

It was getting dark, and they had been reading and sorting for hours.

Corazon turned on the light above the table. They were at the bottom of their piles. Elizabeth let out a sigh and rubbed her eyes. "What have we missed? We have gone through every stinking paper."

Brendan suggested, "OK, let's change chairs and go through the papers again. There's no need to read them all again. The piles are smaller now, and the unrelated articles have been sorted out. Look for anything that might be stuck between the papers." He put his hand on Corazon's shoulder. "Corazon, would you go through the ads to see if there is anything pressed between them? Look for legal documents or anything related to the family. We won't know what's important until we find it."

Corazon said, "Of course. I would be happy to."

They shifted seats. It was like musical chairs without the music. The second search was for something stuck or pressed between the pages or written on the pages.

Nora took Brendan's spot. His papers were all neatly stacked. Her stiff fingers moved one paper at a time, as she tried to keep his piles neat. The pages were beginning to crack from being disturbed after so many years.

After finding nothing in several papers, Nora came across some papers that had been pressed together tightly. Terrified of tearing them apart, she gently opened each page. Brendan had already done this, but she went through every page just in case, until they were completely opened and flat on the table. In the middle of the pile, after the pages were slowly pulled away from both sides, a thick paper appeared. Something was attached to the back of the paper. Unable to control herself, she ripped the paper apart. Brendan had been very careful to keep all his papers intact.

Everyone at the table jumped.

"Sorry, but there is something stuck to this paper. It's

pissed me off." Nora gave the stiff paper a strong pull, and a brown envelope fell onto the floor. She jumped out of her seat to pick it up, but before she could manage to get out of her seat, Elizabeth grabbed the envelope.

"Shit, shit, shit. Open it!" She shouted, as her daughter picked up the envelope.

Elizabeth looked at the envelope and turned it in every direction.

Brendan snapped, "Come on, Lizzy. We've gotten this far. Open the damn envelope."

Slowly, making sure nothing inside was damaged, Elizabeth slid her index finger into the envelope and gently pulled out a document. It was folded in thirds. She placed it on the table and pulled back the folds. There was an eagle imprinted on the top, and it had green scalloped borders. It looked like a child's school merit award. It held the description of property, a plot of land, identified by parcel numbers, with latitude and longitude, somewhere in the Nevada desert, near Las Vegas, with railroad access.

Elizabeth squealed, "Sweet Jesus. Oh, shit! Oh, dear God."

"What the hell?" Brendan came around the table and looked at the paper. "Shit, what do we do now? We are messing with the big boys. I couldn't have imagined this in my wildest dreams."

"Blessed Mother, protect us. We have to contact William and Declan. Conrad must have made the purchase. This may be why my family was destroyed." Nora wheezed without taking a breath.

Elizabeth called Declan and shared the discovery, he was as dumbfounded as the rest of the family. "I'll give

William a call. The papers from the other three properties need to be finalized. When you return, we can go over all the documents. I'm going to contact the real estate attorney we use here. She has been very helpful in the transfer of properties that we are currently involved in. More importantly, she can be trusted to keep her mouth shut. She works for an exceptionally large firm. I think they will jump at the opportunity to represent our families."

Nora's mind spun. *Conrad purchased property in the desert near Las Vegas in his and Michael's name. Do we now share ownership? It sure looked like it. How do we even approach this? The deed only has a parcel number: 020-230-011 with latitude 36.172 and longitude -115.14. An attorney was the best choice—a very good attorney.*

They stared at the deed for what seemed like an hour.

Brendan broke the silence, "Well, this is an unexpected turn of events."

The entire table erupted in laughter.

"Ya, think?" Elizabeth shouted.

Brendan said, "I need a drink. What do you all say to a large shot of Jameson to toast Conrad Quinn?"

They drank their Irish whiskey, and talked about the past as they continued reading, but it was no longer a challenge to find something important. It was a journey into Nora's past. One that was buried in a dark corner of her brain.

Nora found peace in the stories of her lost past, however tragic. She found a new energy that could hold the fog and sludge at bay.

Elizabeth found it difficult to sleep. "Brendan, do you think we are in danger?"

"No more danger than we were in a week ago, in New York. We just know what's at stake. It explains why that little old man was so bold about going through our room and why our belongings were searched. We do need to be cautious. Let's keep this quiet."

Elizabeth thought, *The deed was assigned to Conrad and Michael. What good would it do for someone to steal it? They wouldn't have any claim to the property. Murdering Conrad wouldn't get them the property either.* A body-shaking chill rose from her toes to the top of her skull. *What if Conrad's murder had nothing to do with his big plans and his desert purchase?*

It felt like an eternity for Declan to call back, but it was only a day.

Elizabeth was more anxious than ever. "Is there a legal claim? Who could possibly care if we have the deed? Surely, the property has been sold several times. Is there even a rail station on the property anymore."

Declan replied in an apprehensive voice, "I'm not sure of the legalities. The attorney is checking on all of it and will contact us. William and I agree it's definitely a huge deal. This may be the reason for the murders, but I'm not entirely convinced." His voice became tense, "I had a visit from Tallman Fletcher yesterday, and he let me know that Dan Malone's son was not being truthful when he said he didn't have any connection to his father's business during Prohibition. We'll discuss it when you get back to the city. You all need to hear what Tallman has to say face-to-face. I don't want you to get it secondhand."

Nora's skin crawled. Everything about Danny J.

disgusted her. He was so arrogant and had absolutely no class. Bringing the old guys together was a good idea.

After the phone call, Brendan spoke in a soft, but firm tone, "Lizzy, I know our life is going to change because of the properties and the money you all have gotten, but, shit, baby, we need to live our life. We can't jump on any and every clue those old guys produce. They have spent their lives chasing these ghosts. They don't know anything else."

"I know it has been a crazy ride, Brendan, but maybe putting them all in the same room loosened some cobwebs or made connections that no one saw previously. Momma deserves this. We must get as much information as possible." Elizabeth shivered as she felt the dark cloud surrounding them. She was compelled to help her mother see this through.

CHAPTER 51

Once again, the luggage was packed. They took a first class early-morning flight, with no worries about hotel rooms.

A driver picked them up at the airport. He headed straight to the Didean.

Declan called shortly after their arrival and said, "The driver will bring you to meet with us later. We'll see you for dinner along with some very interesting conversation." He hung up so fast there wasn't a chance to agree or to say goodbye.

Being so preoccupied on the first trip, the city lights had gone unnoticed. The city was an amazing sight at night. The glow of all the lights were a welcome distraction from all that was going on. Their destination was another mystery. They rode in silence.

Brendan held his wife's hand and tapped it as the car stopped.

Elizabeth reached for her mother's hand.

The driver held the car door patiently, as the family exited in front of a brownstone in a quiet residential area. The driver led them toward the stairs. A porch light met them with a warm yellow glow. Thick ivy grew along the doorway and around a wrought iron fence that encircled the building.

Before they started up the stairs, the door opened suddenly. Declan stood in the doorway and motioned them inside. He looked in both directions before he shut the door.

"More cloak and dagger," Brendan whispered in his wife's ear.

Elizabeth smacked him as Declan led them to a library.

An orange glow rose from a large lamp on a corner table, and a radiant fire gave the room a comforting warmth. The spring weather had turned wet and cold during their short absence. Bookshelves were filled from the floor to ceiling with books of every genre. The walls were rich cherrywood. An antique roll top desk sat on one side of the room, and a bar was on the other. Both were the same shade of cherrywood as the walls. The windows were draped with puffy white curtains. It was not what Nora expected from a man like Declan. It hadn't occurred to her that he was married with a family. She surveyed the room for photos of his family. Maybe there would be someone she recognized. She made eye contact with Tallman. She was embarrassed like she had been caught intruding on Declan's privacy.

Tallman sat by the fireplace swirling a large glass of brandy.

Declan went to the bar and lifted an empty glass. "I suggest a drink while Tallman explains what he knows."

Elizabeth said softly, "Coffee for me. I need to keep a clear head."

Nora nodded. "Clear heads all around." She gave Brendan a smile of approval as he walked over to the bar and took a glass of brandy.

"Please have a seat." Declan poured coffee from a carafe.

The room was soothing with the warm fire and wooden shelves and paneling. It was easy to see why Declan had chosen the library over one of the pubs. Nora sank into one of the huge chairs as Declan brought over the coffee. The warmth of the room contrasted with the blood and slaughter that was about to be discussed.

Tallman looked at Nora and said, "Young lady, I'm not going to make any excuses for my past. Everyone you met when you were here last had a rough background, but for the most part, we were honest with one another—at least that was what I thought. Dan Malone's son lied through his damn teeth. Please excuse my language. I didn't say anything at the time because I wanted to have a chance to talk to Declan before I called him out on his bullshit. Again, my apologies. I hate liars, and Danny J. is full of lies."

The doorbell rang just as Tallman completed his sentence. There was a commotion at the door, finally William entered the room. His lips were tight. He looked angry. He was accompanied by a large man in a dark suit.

Nora felt a chill, and her stomach began to twist and roll.

"Sorry we are late." William swung his arm in the direction of the large man, "This is my—well, for lack of a better word—this is my driver, Richard. He makes sure I can get to all the places I need to, including upstairs." He laughed.

Luke came in a second later with William's wheelchair.

Tallman explained, "Good evening, fellows. I was just getting started. As I was saying, I've come to believe Dan's son is nothing like his dad. Dan Malone was a loyal friend to many. He didn't mince words, you knew what was on his mind, and he was as sincere as they came."

Declan said, "There's no need to sugar-coat it. Tell them, damn it."

"Although Danny J. was young he was engaged in some of the Malone ventures. I crossed paths with him on several occasions. I asked some of the old guys who are left what they knew about him. They all had the same impression. He was an entitled, spoiled, selfish, and jealous shit. He thought he was a tough guy because of his pop's reputation. I was told he was extremely jealous of Dan's relationship with Conrad and Michael. He thought his father showed them too much attention. He had spouted off once in a bar that he would see to it the two of them were destroyed if he had a chance. He was always a conniving piece of shit."

Luke spoke up, "But being a piece of shit doesn't make you a murderer."

"I agree with you, Luke," Tallman replied. "As I started to put dates together, I realized I visited Dan Malone the week Conrad was murdered. Danny J. was rushing out the door of Dan's original pub as I entered to meet with Dan. He was ranting and raving about his pop, not trusting him or his decisions. Dan told him to shut his yap, and when he had some good ideas, he might trust his decisions. Danny J. slammed the door. He was just a kid, so I didn't think much of his tantrum. Dan turned to me and said the kid was going to end up dead in the gutter if he wasn't careful. He said he had no self-control, and for some unexplained reason, he had a chip on his shoulder. The kid thought he could horn in on someone's business without any consequences. I didn't connect that conversation to Conrad's murder until we met with all of you. Danny J. lied about knowing anything. I know it isn't much, but why would he lie if he wasn't involved? You had to see his rage to understand why I feel so strongly about this."

"How do we prove any of this?" William spat.

Elizabeth growled, "We must know who destroyed Momma's family, and we must know our family is safe." Her mother gave her arm a squeeze.

Declan put down his glass and walked from one side of the library to the other. "Danny J. has always been wound as tight as a Swiss pocket watch. After the murders, he disappeared for a while. I always thought Dan had sent him away for his safety since we had no idea who the murderers were or who they wanted dead. I think Dan fronted him money to start a club, which went belly-up within a year, and he never took over any part of his father's business. He was never as successful as his da. He always looked for a shortcut. No one trusted him, especially after his da cut him loose. Shit, why didn't that ever dawn on any of us?" Declan glanced at his desk. "I think, with a bit of pressure, even at this late date, he may pop off without realizing he is revealing himself. I say we invite him back to the pub and set him up. I don't think it will be hard. He is an arrogant shit, and if we give him an opportunity to brag, he'll bite. I say we find a document among my ma's papers that says Conrad and Michael owned Dan Malone, and Michael had kept him and his business afloat for years. That should get the fireworks going."

Nora and Elizabeth were ready for a drink, and Brendan filled their glasses and refilled the glasses of the others. They toasted to the plan.

Declan smiled, went to his desk, and pulled out a ledger. "One of Ma's ledgers should do the trick. Everyone knew Ma had names and addresses and the goods on all sorts of folks. She also oversaw a lot of Michael's accounting. Once again, it will be put to good use. No doubt my ma would be proud to be a part of ending this." He looked at Nora. "Sorry, child. Ma helped Dan Malone sponsor Irish immigrants. She found trustworthy, hardworking Irishmen, and Dan gave them jobs. That's the brief version."

William lifted his hand to the scar that ran down his face. "I want this piece of shit to suffer. How do we make that happen?"

Declan replied with a wink, and with an air of sarcasm, "It would have been easy in the old days since everyone was horrified by the slaughter of an entire family. Now, William, I'm afraid we will have to let the law handle it."

Nora and her family ignored the wink. She wanted her family to return to some sense of normalcy—at least as normal as her body allowed. Revenge was left to the experts, but she had no problem with Declan doling out justice in any manner he saw fit.

A time was set for the old guys to gather. Everyone was included, and Declan was to use the pretense that he had discovered something new during a recent search of his ma's ledgers.

Nora and her family were driven back to their hotel. They didn't want to know the details of how they planned to deal with Danny J. She was comfortable with the thought that he would be dealt with appropriately.

CHAPTER 52

Dan Malone wished he could get his son, Danny J, to grasp the idea of loyalty and hard work. His son had been raised wanting for nothing and never had to struggle. It made him someone who wanted to benefit from the work of others, but never get his hands dirty.

Dan pleaded with his son, "This is not how I raised you. You aren't even finished with your schooling, and you think you know better than me. Why do you think I took you to dinner the other night? I wanted you to realize that those people, along with myself, worked our asses off while you went to private schools. You are just a fucking pup. You have no life experiences."

"You are living in the past, Da. If you see something you want, you take it."

Dan growled, "Not if that something isn't yours to take. Bastards who think that way are men my da and I—and all the people I came up with—hated. They thought they were better than us and could walk in and take what we poured our blood and sweat into. It has nothing to do with living in the past. It is being able to look at yourself in the mirror every day, being a loyal friend, and earning what you have. It's not expecting to benefit from someone else's sweat and hard work. You would think otherwise if you ever worked a damn day in your life. Conrad and Michael came here with nothing. They worked hard for me and for themselves, and they are finally coming into their own. You stay the fuck away from them. Son, I won't allow you to interfere with them." Dan slammed his fist on his desk.

Danny J. snapped back, "Da, you have no respect for me or my ideas. You have always put Conrad and Michael above me."

"What ideas? You don't have any ideas. You are acting like a leech, trying to suck the lifeblood out of others." The veins in his neck bulged. "That's bullshit. Don't be ridiculous. I helped them out when they were starting out. It's the same way I helped you, but you had the benefit of my name, my money, and an education. They worked and saved to get where they are. Yes, they come to me for advice when needed. You have worked for nothing. I have given you every opportunity and advice. You always take the easy way out, and you have nothing to show for it. At this moment, I can't stand the sight of you. I will make sure my friends all know you don't represent me. My loyalty to my friends remains unmoved, and they have been loyal to me at every turn."

Danny J. grabbed his hat off the chair and dashed towards the door. He slammed into Tallman in the doorway. "Move aside." Danny J. tried to shove Tallman.

Tallman stood his ground, and Danny J. bounced off his tall frame and hit the doorway with a loud smack.

"You'll see. I'm not going to walk away from a great opportunity just because you don't like it." With that, he disappeared into the darkness of the pub.

Tallman felt embarrassed that he had walked into a

family argument. "Shit, I'm sorry Dan. Is this a bad time? The bartender said you were free."

Dan pulled his sleeves above his elbows. "I am disgusted by my own son. He's turned out like the slime I spent most of my life dodging. He has no loyalty to family or friends. It's all about how he can make the great deal—without any concern that it's not his deal to make. He thinks he can walk in and take control of a business, and no one is going to say a fucking word because they are loyal to me." Dan took a deep breath and signaled Tallman to take a seat. "I'm sorry, Tallman. What's going on?"

"I feel pretty silly coming to you now. I just need to buy some extra product for the next couple of weeks. I've had to limit my trips up north. Someone try to hijack a load recently. If you have product to spare, I would be in your debt. Business has been pretty good lately." Tallman said trying not to sound like a mooch.

They completed their business, and Tallman loaded his product into the back of a truck. A few years ago, he wouldn't even have spoken to Dan Malone, but dangerous times and the business they were both in brought about new partnerships. Dan Malone was considered a friend. They both respected and trusted one another. Having someone to trust was how they survived.

Tallman shook Dan Malone's hand and tried to assure him that Danny J. was mouthing off like all kids do—and it would blow over.

Over the years, Tallman and Dan never mentioned what went on that night.

CHAPTER 53

Danny J. stormed passed Tallman and into the street in front of Dan Malone's pub. He stumbled angrily to a car that awaited him. He jumped in and bellowed at the driver, "Get me out of this fucking place!"

"Where do you want to go, boss?"

Danny J. snapped, "Go, damn it. Just drive. Head toward Midtown. I'll tell you when to stop."

Duncan had been Danny J.'s driver for a year, but he had never called the driver by his name.

My name is Duncan you spoiled prick. The driver wanted to shout. Duncan overlooked Danny J.'s uncouth behavior as he treated everyone like mud on his shoes.

After a short time, Danny J. said, "I need a drink. Take me to the nearest club."

Duncan stopped the car in front of a club, and his rude passenger bolted out. "Wait here for me. I need to blow off some steam." Danny J. pushed his way passed the man at the door and went inside. "Out of my way."

In the darkness of the club, Danny J. spat his venom at anyone who got close. He ordered a bottle of whiskey and slid into a corner table. The bottle banged with his clumsy movements. He shouted vulgarities at anyone who happened to be near his table. He hurled a drink at a stranger he thought got too close. The stranger was ready to give him a shellacking, but another customer pulled him back and clarified that the asshole was Dan Malone's boy. No further explanation was needed. The offended fellow wiped the drink off his shirt as he backed away until he was out of the scope of wrath.

Only when the whiskey bottle was close to empty and walking near to impossible was Danny J. ready to leave the bar. No one in the bar spoke as he left, but the tension and anger followed him like steam exiting a broken pipe. He bounced off the walls and knocked most of the photos off them as he stumbled to the entryway. At the doorway, he staggered into the gutter.

"Shit." Duncan flicked his cigarette out the window and lifted the drunken blob out of the gutter.

"Don't touch me, you gimpy bastard. I'll show them … they'll pay … all of them." Puke oozed from the corners of his mouth.

Duncan lifted the drunken blob out of the gutter, used his boss's pocket scarf to wipe him down before he plopped him in the back of the car.

Danny J. remained sprawled out on the back seat all the way to his apartment.

Duncan was forced to carry the limp drunk up the stairs, he came around in time to lift his key out and open the door. He staggered inside, slamming the door on his companion's face. It took all he could muster to maneuver an uncooperative tanked-up body the distance to the couch. He dropped into it like an overfilled sack of potatoes.

Duncan breathed heavily during the two flights down

the stairs to his sparsely furnished apartment. Once inside he inhaled deeply to calm his mind and lungs. He shared the space with a mook named Duke Lansing. Lansing was rarely at the apartment. He spent his off hours drunk in the local whorehouses. Times like these gave Duncan cause to rethink living in the same building as his boss. He tolerated Danny J.'s constant insults and erratic behavior because being a driver was the best job he could ever manage. His stumped leg, a gift from the Kaiser, slowed him down, but he could manage driving a car. He couldn't hold a job at the docks or anywhere that required him to be agile. He hoped Danny J. was down for the night and that he wasn't going to attempt going out again. He didn't want to get too comfy—just in case his boss came to. He pulled off his overcoat. The old springs of the bed made a loud squeak as he dropped into it. He left his shoes on as it took extra time to manipulate his shoe and artificial leg. He lifted his legs onto the creaky bed and drifted off to sleep.

Danny J. woke up at about two in the afternoon. He was still half drunk. The sun blazed through the dirty windows that overlooked the alley. Cigarette butts, dirty glasses, and clothes were strewn across the room. It smelled of stale smoke, sweat of an unwashed body, and vomit. He wandered around the apartment like a child mid-tantrum. He knocked over furniture, smacked glasses, and kicked at the floor. He lit a cigarette, grabbed a bottle, and plopped into an overstuffed chair. He drank for a couple of hours. The more he drank, the madder he got. He was mad at the world, but his da was the brunt of his anger.

It seemed like Duncan had just closed his eyes when he was jolted awake, as though he was shot from a cannon, by the pounding at his door. He pulled himself up from the creaking bed, wiped the sleep from his eyes, and shuffled to the door.

"Get up, you lazy shit. I need a ride," Danny J. slurred and spat.

Still half asleep, he shouted, "My name is Duncan … damn it." As soon as the words flew out of his mouth, he regretted it. He saw a large bulge under the spitter's overcoat.

"Don't you worry, asshole. Drive me one last time, and you won't have to worry about what I call you ever again."

As he drove, he didn't show his fear. It wasn't fear of Danny J. because he would gladly knock him flat, but he was no contest for what was awkwardly hidden under his overcoat. The drunk struggled to maneuver himself, along with the large object bulging beneath his coat, into the front seat. Duncan was sure his days were numbered. His passenger never rode in the front.

A slur that reeked of whiskey and vomit burned Duncan's nostrils. "Just drive. I'll tell you where to go when I recognize the neighborhood."

Duncan wished the rotten mess was in the back, beyond his burning nostrils. The two rode in silence. Duncan's blood pulsated throughout his body. He was sure this was his last ride.

Danny J. knew exactly where he was going. He directed every turn. Duncan did as ordered. On the last turn, young boys stood talking under the glow of the streetlight. A lone car sat near where the boys stood.

In a drunken move, Danny J. clumsily pulled out the weapon hidden under his coat. The gun slammed against the dash of the car and then the window. *How could I be so lucky to find both bastards sitting like ducks in a pond? I don't even have to leave the car.*

With the huge gun draped across his lap, he rolled down the window. The gun barrel slammed against the car's interior with every crank of the window. He growled, "Go around the bastards."

Duncan continued slowly down the street, unaware of his passenger's exact plan. He had no choice but to go along or die. As the hate-filled car rolled through the neighborhood gunfire ripped into a parked Chevrolet. Through the ear-crushing blasts of bullets, the shocked driver saw silhouettes being violently tossed around with each burst. The drunken shooter spat his vomit-filled venom into his face. "Go, go, get the fuck out of here."

Duncan's stomach rolled, and his ears rang loudly as he sped to the corner. He saw the commotion in the street through the rearview mirror. In the middle of the street, one of the young boys was motionless on the ground. After driving a short distance, Duncan was unable to control his mind or body. Before he was able to get the car to a complete stop, he started puking. He puked and silently cried. If he died, it wouldn't matter. He'd been involved in a horrendous taking of lives, and he would never be able to forget or forgive his involvement.

CHAPTER 54

Nora and her family rode in silence all the way back to the Didean. As they entered the glistening lobby, she grabbed her daughter's arm and guided her and the others to the bar. Drinks were ordered as they sat in a dark corner booth.

Elizabeth looked at her mother and whispered, "OK, what is it?"

Her voice was a mere whisper as thoughts became words, "Am I a horrible person for having a lingering thought? Am I horrible if I hope the old guys give Danny J. everything he deserves? He ruined so many lives with his greed and selfishness. I want to see him punished while I'm aware." She hoped verbalizing her thoughts might make her feel differently. There was no need to carry the dark thoughts to her room. A lifetime of dark places already filled her mind. She wanted to leave it at the bar. There was rage rather than relief. Rage that had been building since the letter about Maureen arrived. She had been bounced around after her family was murdered. She and her sister—shit, the child she thought was her sister—ended up in the convent. The horrendous murders had altered everything about her life. The dark places in her mind held all the violent ugliness that she buried as a toddler. Events too painful to remember. The rage swelled to the surface, tears started to well up. She only had so much time before the fog and sludge overtook her. There was no time to waste. The usually quiet woman lost it, "No! This piece of shit destroyed my family and many others. This scum managed to obliterate all the family I knew—and the one I never had a chance to know. I am heartsick, but mostly I am angry, angrier than I have ever been. My family, all my family, needs and deserves justice. They need to finally rest in the peace of knowing this animal has met the justice he earned."

Elizabeth replied quietly to her mother, the others at the table nodded in agreement, "It sounds very dark, but I feel the same way. How the old guys choose to handle this is their decision. I am positive they hold as much anger as you do. They are the ones who have lived with targets on their backs all these years. I say put an end to him however they see fit. With all they have lived through, I'm sure they will handle him with the same consideration that he extended throughout the years."

The dark thoughts were left at the table with the empty glasses as they headed up to their rooms.

Nora kissed her daughter good night and got ready for bed without saying anything. She said good night to Corazon and climbed into the huge bed. Her thoughts were clear. A cleansing breeze flowed through her mind and cleared a section of fog.

CHAPTER 55

Nora was pleased to awaken to the smell of coffee. Her old body had made it successfully through the night without carrying any of the previous day's baggage.

Brendan said to someone on the phone, "Yes, we can meet downstairs in an hour. That will give us time to get ready. OK. Breakfast downstairs in an hour."

"What was that all about?" Elizabeth spoke as she pulled her hair back into a clip.

"Declan is coming to pick us up and wants to have breakfast with us. He wants to talk to us about Mae's ledgers." Brendan answered as he poured them coffee.

The group drank their coffee and talked of little things. They avoided any mention of Danny J. His name set their blood to boil. How he met his end wasn't their concern. On one hand, Nora didn't want to know anything about his final justice. On the other hand, she wanted to hold the gun and pull the trigger until it was empty. He needed to suffer for all the pain he had caused.

They showered, dressed, and had one last cup of coffee before they headed downstairs.

Declan was already seated at a table. A worn black leather ledger was open on the seat next to him. The dining room was fresh and bright. Tall windows let in a muted glow of the morning sun as it peeked between the buildings. All the tables had white tablecloths with centerpieces of blue candles surrounded by fresh flowers. The floor shined like a mirror. The shoes Corazon had set out for Nora made a loud snapping noise as she walked, which drew Declan's attention.

Declan smiled as the group approached. "Good morning. I hope you were able to get some sleep." He stood to greet them.

"I am surprised to say that I did sleep well." Nora gave him a hug.

Brendan and Elizabeth both nodded and shook his hand.

As soon as breakfast was ordered and the waitress was out of ear shot Declan began, "I never really looked at Ma's ledgers. There is so much information in them. I thought you might be interested in reading about the Doyle family. She wrote a couple of pages about them over the years. There is even a page of how she was involved in sending you and Kiera to the sisters of Mercy.

"Danny J. has no idea what these pages hold. That is our ace in the hole. Everyone knew how my ma carefully selected people for Dan Malone to sponsor. That's where he is going to trip himself up. He's so damn arrogant that he won't be able to control himself. I will get great pleasure in watching him squirm and squeal like the pig he is. All you need to do is simply follow my lead. Nora, you won't have to do much. He's going to do it all for us. William, Luke, and Tallman are going to meet us at the safe haven."

While they finished their meals, Nora read as many

pages as possible in Mae Moore's ledger. It was full of information about the Doyle family and many others who Mae had helped. The ledger explained why she was placed with the Doyle's. Mae was an incredible soul. Reading about how the people who came to the city struggled to make a better life for themselves made her even angrier at Danny J. He had an easy good life, but it wasn't enough for him.

Tallman, William, and Luke were awaiting the group's arrival at the safe haven. The air was thick with anticipation as they followed Declan to the table. The table settings were exactly the same as the first meeting. Nora's worn face was red-hot, and her blood was reaching a boiling point. She held both Corazon and her daughter's hand in an effort to quiet her fury before Danny J. arrived. They all tried to keep the mood calm as they waited for him.

Elizabeth worried he had grown suspicious and wasn't going to show up.

Nora felt a lump in the back of her throat. She cleared her throat as the door flew open, and Danny J. stood there in all his arrogant glory. His suit hung strangely on his body. It looked like he was trying to camouflage his bulk by wearing a long, loose jacket. His tie was longer and wider than it should have been in an attempt to cover his belly. She took in all the flaws of this wretched person. She couldn't bring herself to shake his hand. Instead, she reached for a coffee cup and took a long composing drink.

The others were better at shielding their feelings.

Declan signaled the bulky frame to a place at the table to sit, "Danny, come get yourself a cup of coffee. We wanted to include you in an interesting find in my ma's ledgers."

Danny J. waddled to the table. "Ledgers? What are you talking about?"

Declan gave a very slight glance toward William and then toward Elizabeth and her mother. He had no idea the ledgers even existed. All the people who had worked for his father throughout the years and helped build his father's business were in the ledgers. Good, hardworking, loyal Irish men and women, and this disgusting ass was clueless.

"Danny, I'm surprised you are not aware of the ledgers Ma kept. I thought your da would surely have told you about them. They were a huge part of his business." Declan was unrolling the rope for Danny J. to hang himself with. "She had notes on everyone your father employed and their backgrounds. She referred only the most loyal, dependable workers, but I wasn't aware until just a few days ago how much other information she kept. I was going through the ledgers before I showed them to Nora, and I found some very interesting entries."

William leaned forward in his chair, "Please continue, Declan. We are all interested in anything that will answer our questions."

The entire room seemed tense. Nora thought, *Can he feel it in the air? Can everyone hear my heart beating?*

"Well, Danny, from what I can see in the ledgers, Ma also kept track of debts. You know, small loans that the folks she referred had. Also, larger loans. Conrad and Michael didn't believe in banks—nor did your da."

Declan was cut short by Danny, "Yeah, yeah. I know my da lent them money. That's not news. He was always doing something for those two bastards."

William whacked the table.

Declan gently patted the back of William's hand. "Watch yourself, Danny. You are talking about our family, and your da didn't loan them money. It was Conrad and Michael who loaned your da money after they bought their first pub. There are several different entries in the ledgers. It lists when your da was in a hard spot how Conrad and Michael bailed him out. Not just once. Even after Conrad's murder, Michael kept your da afloat."

Danny's face was beet red. He squirmed in his seat, lifted his hand and started to pull at his eyebrow. Then he jumped to his feet and slammed his fists on the table. "That's bullshit! My da never needed money from them. He should have squashed them like the vermin they were. I tried to tell him. He was a damn fool. I had to take things into my own hands. He still didn't get it. You are full of shit! My da never borrowed from those two …"

The air in the room was suddenly as thick as cheese.

Tallman sank back in his seat. "Shit, I am so sorry."

Declan's hands shook with anger as he closed the ledger. "What the fuck are you saying, you piece of shit?"

"I only wish I had killed them all. They were in my way. You had to move fast to get what you wanted. Michael should have gone down with his smart-ass partner."

"Oh my God. Oh my God." Nora's entire body shook, and her stomach revolted. For all these years, this piece of shit felt no remorse.

Elizabeth grabbed her mother, and Corazon held her hand.

Brendan wrapped his arm around his wife's shoulder. It was as though they were trying to shield each other from the horror Danny J. was spouting so easily.

William snapped to his feet, and he was around the end of the table in one step.

Declan nudged Luke to grab his da. Declan was in front of Danny J. in a flash. There had to be more to this than his greed. He needed answers.

"Why in the name of God would you slaughter an entire family? What were you after?" Declan wanted to beat the life out of this repulsive slug, but he had to have the answers to his questions. Questions, they all had carried for so many anguish-filled years.

"Shit, I just wanted what they had. They had my da's respect and the respect of their entire neighborhood. Their guys were loyal to the death. If they were all gone, I could have it all and take over their business. Michael, the dumb mook, wouldn't give up. Every time I thought I had him, he somehow managed to survive." Danny J. smiled, twisted his eyebrow, and gazed into space like he was reliving it all.

Declan rolled his hand into a tight fist and slugged Danny J. across his jaw with a cracking blow that brought him back to reality. "There are no words to describe what kind of scum you are. I will get great pleasure in destroying you. I'm not too old to remember how to make someone like you suffer."

Danny J. stood silently. His mouth oozed blood. He licked the blood off his lips, missing a large glob that dripped onto his shirt. He casually sat down and took a sip of his coffee. "Michael's whore punched me, and she didn't live to tell anyone."

"You worthless piece of shit. You are beyond words."

"Loud and bloody. You can count on it. That was Michael's promise to Ida Doyle." Declan whispered into his ear. He turned to Nora. "I'm sorry, but it is time for you all to leave. I hope you don't mind."

Nora's blood was ablaze in her tired veins. The heat from her anger rose from her toes to the top of her head. She tried to compose herself. "Declan, William, I understand you have business to deal with, and we certainly will not stand in your way. My family needs total, biblical justice … loud, biblical justice."

Danny J. was oblivious to the conversation going on around him. A twisted hand was raised and slapped him with all the strength it had left. Her worn palm was still stinging when she reached for her daughter's hand. Danny J. made no attempt to respond. He sat frozen, oozing blood. He never tried to wipe his mouth.

As Nora's family headed to the door, Tallman reached out to her. "Child, I wish I could have connected the dots a long time ago. Things were different then. We would have never gotten together like we have in the past few days. I am so sorry."

She gave him a hug. "Sir, you have nothing to be sorry for. That pathetic excuse for a human caused all this pain. May God forgive me, but I hope he pays loudly and profoundly."

Tallman choked out his words, "I can't believe Dan Malone knew about any of this. He wrote off Danny J. I know he would be crushed and ashamed if he knew his son was responsible for this nightmare. Shame is something his son has no concept of."

The car was waiting for them outside. Nora pushed herself into the comfy seat, rubbed the soft upholstery, and caught a familiar whiff of cigar. She dug deep into her brain for anything that reminded her of her parents—Conrad and Eveleen—but there was nothing. She promised herself she would continue to search for reminders. She glanced at her daughter and Corazon. She took a long look at Brendan. He was always by their side, protecting them. She thought of all the twists and turns her life had taken. Uncontrollable tears poured out—tears for the life she lost and the darkness it left her with. Her tears were mostly tears of anger that Danny J. still felt no shame or remorse after all these years. She gasped for breath in between her tears. "I have no pity for that man. He needs to suffer. Am I an awful person to think that?"

"Momma, he is not our concern. We have a family that we love, and they love us. The past few weeks have been agony. William, Declan, and their families have been tortured for decades. It ended tonight."

CHAPTER 56

Nora's daily routine didn't change much after they returned home. She felt free from the sludge and darkness. She was eager to hear from Declan, and it seemed like weeks awaiting his call. In reality, it was only a week before he contacted the family. The attorney had tracked down the property's location. He was very brief and adamant. He, William, and Luke were flying out. The property's ownership was too complicated to discuss on the phone.

The men arrived with no fanfare, rented a car, and got a room at a nearby resort. William was aided by his 'driver.' The older man was determined to call him a driver rather than his caregiver. William traveled with a walker and a smaller wheelchair than the one he used in the city. He had new energy, probably because a huge rock had been lifted from him. He was free to show his affection, and share memories without fear of bringing evil to those close to him.

The obvious bond between Declan and William was renewed by the realization that they were finally free of the dark secret they had held for so long.

The men were excited when they all met at the resort. It shot through the room like static electricity. They sat in a quiet dining room that was styled like an old adobe mission, adorned with shiny colorful Mexican tiles and paintings of vineyards bursting with grapes and brightly dressed *caballeros* on horseback.

The dread of an unknown assassin was replaced by a nervous energy surrounding the possibilities of what Conrad's big deal held.

As a young Hispanic woman in a flowing skirt served margaritas, Declan took charge of the discussion of the property, "Parcel number 020-230-011 with latitude 36.172 and longitude -115.14 was where the search for the property began. An initial transfer that removed the property from Conrad and Michael's name was recorded on the same date Wilson disappeared and one day prior to Conrad's murder. Was Wilson killed because he forged the deed, was he a loose end, or was he paid to disappear? The forged deed was transferred and recorded in the name of a corporation and not an individual. No one ever contested the transfer— until now. The attorney was unable to pinpoint a 'person' connected to the now-defunct corporation. Signatures were scrawled—unable to be read—and more than likely deliberately."

"So, are you all owners of a piece of Nevada desert or perhaps a silver mine?" Brendan took a large gulp of his margarita.

Declan took a long deep breath. "Family, this is one more incredible story to add to our list. The property's physical address is 1 North Main Street, Las Vegas Nevada."

Elizabeth squealed. "What? That's downtown Las Vegas. How is that possible?"

Nora sipped her margarita and absorbed what was being said. *It has to be a mistake.*

"It's more than possible. It's a damn fact." Declan couldn't hold in his excitement any longer. "The Plaza Hotel and Casino sits directly on Conrad and Michael's property. When Conrad bought the property, it was part of a land auction. Around the same time as the auction, Union Pacific built a rail station adjacent to Conrad's piece of land. The current owners of the Plaza were aware of old gossip that the original property was mysteriously acquired in an unscrupulous manner. No one ever contested the ownership, so sales came and went without argument. The Plaza was built around 1970, and no one was interested in who owned the land thirty-five years before them. Now that our attorney has contested ownership with the original legitimate deed, they are extremely concerned. The property owners and those who lease and operate the hotel and the casino met and discussed the possibility of legal action. Someone in the group—the attorney was not privy to the specifics—did not want to chance a light being shined on their operation by the gaming commission. They don't want to be a part of any investigation. A very substantial offer has been submitted to our attorney for pain and hardship and to silence any talk of legal action. They are offering a partnership in the property and the operation of both the casino and the hotel or a huge buyout. The attorney suggests the buyout as there may be some shady dealings going on. Conrad and Michael worked hard to get on the right side of things."

"Sweet Jesus." Elizabeth grabbed Brendan's arm.

Nora nearly shouted, "So, with a couple of swift motions, we have brought our family to its rightful place and come up with a hotel and casino while we were at it. Oh, my dear God. I am dumbfounded."

Another round of margaritas arrived in time to toast the family's ownership of a downtown Las Vegas hotel and casino along with its subsequent sale. They ordered a huge Mexican meal to share with the New York family. They talked for hours, and William shared things he remembered about Nora as a toddler. He and Declan spoke about how she was always in motion. The red-headed tornado, who captivated Conrad and Michael.

William reminisced how his father dreamed of a large hotel to honor his best friend, Conrad. Las Vegas was a boomtown, but William and Declan saw to it that Michael had several elegant hotels in New York and continued the Irish legacy of lifting others and giving back to the neighborhood. Conrad would have been proud of all of them.

The group went their separate ways after an evening of family discoveries and sharing.

Nora was comforted by a fresh understanding of where many of her fears, dreams, and feelings originated. The sludge was weaker now that the dark corners were cleared away. So much information about her early childhood had been tossed about, and it was impossible not to be saddened by so much loss. The overwhelming sadness had always been there, but she had managed to block the memory of that horrific night in order to survive.

She made her way to bed. There was no fog or sludge, but she was swept away by sadness. She only had a slight memory of her ma and pa. Tears rolled down her face.

As she caught the tears with her sleeve, a sweet scent surrounded her. A voice whispered, "Noinin, Mama and Papa love you." A new warmth enveloped her frail frame. Nora felt secure in herself and relaxed for the first time in her life.